**"Guess I need to get to bed soon. I require more sleep these days, for some reason."**

That caused Patrick to smile. He liked Kyra's sense of humor, even under trying circumstances.

"I wouldn't mind getting some sleep too," he told her. "Especially since tomorrow might be a busy day."

"Hope so." Then, as they both rose, she looked at him. "I think it's a good idea if you get a good night's sleep too. And hanging out on the sofa—well, I doubt you can sleep as well as if you were in bed." She took a deep breath and, hands on her baby bump, said, "In fact, I'd like it if you hung out in my bed with me. You should be able to hear if anything goes wrong from there too."

His eyes widened. "Is that an invitation?" He kept his tone light. He knew that, even if it was, she wasn't requesting a night of hot sex.

Still—

"Yes, it is," she said. "The bed is big enough for both of us to sleep without touching."

And that was the answer he'd figured.

Dear Reader,

This is my fifth book in the wonderful long-running Colton series.

*CSI Colton and the Witness* is book number eleven in the twelve-book Coltons of New York miniseries, which features a family of twelve siblings who mostly go into law enforcement, often to hunt serial killers, including the Black Widow, the Landmark Killer and the Jewelry Slayer.

In *CSI Colton and the Witness*, CSI Patrick Colton works for the FBI but is assigned to assist the police in the 130th Precinct of New York City to find the Jewelry Slayer, a serial killer who murders women to steal their valuable jewelry. He leads that CSI unit with CSI Kyra Patel—who happens to be pregnant, although her baby's father is out of the picture. When Kyra is attacked by the Jewelry Slayer at a crime scene while collecting evidence and sees his face, her coworker Patrick will do all he can to protect her. He moves in with her—and stays even after her baby is born. The attraction between these coworkers may be inappropriate, but they'll do anything necessary to protect each other. And that attraction continues growing...

I hope you enjoy *CSI Colton and the Witness*. Please come visit me at my website, lindaojohnston.com, and at my weekly blog, killerhobbies.blogspot.com. And, yes, I'm on Facebook and Writerspace too.

*Linda O. Johnston*

# CSI COLTON AND THE WITNESS

Linda O. Johnston

HARLEQUIN

ROMANTIC SUSPENSE

Special thanks and acknowledgment are given to
Linda O. Johnston for her contribution to
The Coltons of New York miniseries.

Recycling programs
for this product may
not exist in your area.

ISBN-13: 978-1-335-59382-5

CSI Colton and the Witness

Copyright © 2023 by Harlequin Enterprises ULC

For questions and comments about the quality of this book,
please contact us at CustomerService@Harlequin.com.

Harlequin Enterprises ULC
22 Adelaide St. West, 41st Floor
Toronto, Ontario M5H 4E3, Canada
www.Harlequin.com

Printed in U.S.A.

**Linda O. Johnston** loves to write. While honing her writing skills, she worked in advertising and public relations, then became a lawyer...and enjoyed writing contracts. Linda's first published fiction appeared in *Ellery Queen's Mystery Magazine* and won a Robert L. Fish Memorial Award for Best First Mystery Short Story of the Year. Linda now spends most of her time creating memorable tales of romance, romantic suspense and mystery. Visit her on the web at lindaojohnston.com.

## Books by Linda O. Johnston

### Harlequin Romantic Suspense

#### K-9 Ranch Rescue

*Second Chance Soldier*
*Trained to Protect*

#### The Coltons of Colorado

*Shielding Colton's Witness*

#### Shelter of Secrets

*Her Undercover Refuge*
*Guardian K-9 on Call*
*Undercover Cowboy Defender*

#### The Coltons of New York

*CSI Colton and the Witness*

Visit the Author Profile page at Harlequin.com for more titles.

Once more, and as always, this story is dedicated to my dear husband, Fred. I also again want to thank all the other authors in this enjoyable series, as well as all the wonderful editors for the Colton books.

# Chapter 1

Nighttime wasn't always the best time for Kyra Patel to perform her job, especially now, but she always did what she had to, whenever and wherever it was.

Looking around under a streetlight on the chilly November evening, she smiled grimly as she picked up a small, torn piece of cloth from the pavement at the side of the curb of the area where she was working along with the other person in charge of her crime scene investigation team.

She loved her job as a CSI. Never mind that even in daylight it was more difficult these days to kneel and—carefully, in her gloved hands—pick up items from the street to examine and determine whether any or all might be evidence that could help identify and convict the perpetrator of the crime they were currently investigating.

But Kyra was more than six months pregnant, so

bending and kneeling were becoming more of a challenge.

One she still met well. Like now, as she attempted to locate evidence near small St. Edwina's Park along First Avenue in Manhattan, in the 130th Precinct where she currently worked as part of a special FBI team brought in by the local police to pursue serial killers.

And where a murder and robbery had occurred only a short while ago, at the edge of the park and not far from one of the large nearby buildings with a convenience store on the ground floor that was open all night.

The body of the deceased victim, a young woman named Susanne Shermore, had been taken away for further examination by the medical examiner. But Kyra had seen the body on the ground there, stabbed repeatedly, although the murder weapon hadn't been found.

"You doing okay?"

Kyra glanced up to see that Patrick Colton, her fellow FBI agent with whom she ran that CSI team, had rejoined her.

Not surprising.

They worked together often. And this was a major crime they were now investigating together.

Kyra started to rise slowly from her kneel and saw Patrick hold his hand out to help her. She took it, using his firm grip to help her stand easier and more quickly.

Nice guy.

More than a nice guy. Even in the dim light, she could see, as always, that he was one handsome hunk in his long, zipped-up jacket, with a great-looking angular face, light brown hair in a thick mop on top of his head, and hazel eyes that appeared caring and concerned as they looked at her.

But his appearance was irrelevant. They worked together.

There was nothing between them but their jobs.

A shame, maybe…but the way it was. Even though she would like to find the right man to be the father to her child.

"I'm doing fine," she said, pulling the edges of her jacket closer together, although they didn't completely cover her baby bump. "And I've found a lot of potential evidence here." She showed him the items she had placed into protective plastic bags now lying on the curb beside her, including the swatch of fabric that the victim had apparently ripped from the perpetrator's clothing—probably a shirt since it was light blue and plaid. Then there were a couple other items she had found lying in the dirt on the pavement—including a pen and a metal pointed nail file the victim had apparently pulled from her bag and attempted to use as a defense weapon—which might have fingerprints on them, although she saw no blood. They'd have to be checked at the precinct anyway.

Also there was a pair of sunglasses. They appeared more masculine than feminine, so maybe they belonged to the killer.

Another piece of evidence that could be helpful was a credit card with Susanne's name on it. She might have been holding it, but if the killer had somehow gotten that out of her bag and dropped it, it might also have his prints on it.

Was anything else lying in the surprising amount of dirt along the street? Kyra thought she'd gotten everything important there, although she'd be happy to have Patrick double-check.

In any case, what had happened seemed fairly clear. Susanne had apparently fought back, to no avail, although she'd struggled hard enough to cause those evidence items to drop to the ground.

Her boyfriend who had joined them now watched from a short distance away, talking to one of the officers who'd arrived to secure the site. He'd said she had been wearing a Rolex watch and two gold rings. Plus she'd had other valuables with her in a Birkin bag.

They'd all, including the bag, apparently been stolen by the perpetrator. None of them were there now.

"If only she'd come inside with me," the boyfriend had wailed. "We had just left the theater and were walking home by way of the park, but I stopped to buy a bottle of water." He'd pointed to the convenience store. "Oh, I wish I hadn't. And I didn't see what was going on or I'd have run out here too."

With those kinds of valuables visible, Kyra wasn't surprised the woman was targeted. And it wouldn't have ended differently even if the boyfriend had been outside, she figured.

Because Kyra believed she knew who the perpetrator was: the criminal referred to as the Jewelry Slayer. He hadn't yet been identified, but that was one of the things she was attempting to help with.

She'd discuss it further later with Patrick and others on their CSI team.

Right now, Patrick was looking at the evidence Kyra had collected in those clear plastic bags. While she'd started going over things here, he had worked farther down the street questioning a few people who'd apparently been in the area when the crime had been committed. Kyra didn't know if he'd learned anything useful but doubted it, considering his presence with her now, looking over the evidence.

At the moment, the area was cordoned off with crime scene tape the officers had attached, though she didn't see any people hanging out behind it at this hour, and the cops weren't nearby either. Often at these kinds of sites, curious onlookers who wanted to know more of what was happening would hang around, but the few people she'd noticed before must have left already.

Had any of them seen anything? If so, had they revealed it to one of the cops, or to Patrick? She'd have to find out soon but doubted it, since anyone who had witnessed something would probably have been told to remain there for further questioning.

"I hope there are lots of prints on these but doubt they'll be much help," Patrick said, now kneeling near Kyra beside where she had placed the limited evidence she'd found so far—and she doubted there was much more around here. He helped her insert each of the small bags into a larger one she would use to bring it all in for further evaluation.

What was here might actually help them catch the Jewelry Slayer this time. Who knew?

Or was this yet another murder by the Jewelry Slayer that might not be solved? Judging by the past lack of success, she was concerned that was the case.

If only—

"Help! Please!" screamed a woman's voice from the direction of the convenience store but somewhere in the park.

"Stay here," Patrick said immediately. "I'll go see what's going on. Maybe someone else is being attacked."

"Please be careful," Kyra said as he stood and headed

off in the sparse light in the direction of the cry. She had no doubt the Jewelry Slayer would be fine with killing an FBI agent, and since they wore professional clothes but not uniforms, despite being in law enforcement, the killer wouldn't necessarily know who they were—not that it was likely to make a difference to him.

But she hoped that if whoever had screamed was under attack, Patrick would be able to help her. She knew Patrick well enough to recognize he would do all he could.

Glancing often in the direction he'd gone, Kyra continued scanning the ground in case she had missed something, although she felt fairly sure she'd found all that was there.

Would it be enough to—

Someone darted out from the other side of some trees near her, a guy in a black hoodie pulled forward to cover his face.

"Hey!" she called as he quickly approached. What was going on?

Before she could react, he grabbed the bag and pushed her hard, starting to run his foot over the area where she'd been collecting evidence, clearly attempting to erase anything that might be left.

"No!" she shouted while struggling to maintain her balance. She reached toward him, unable to grab the bag but yanking the hoodie so his face was uncovered.

She got a good look at his face—young, with a furious scowl and a bit of dark facial hair.

"You stupid, interfering cop," he growled, advancing toward her.

She screamed and covered her belly protectively, but he didn't stop.

Not till Patrick appeared again, running from the direction where he'd headed before.

The guy didn't wait. Still holding the evidence bag, he fled before Patrick could reach them.

Kyra felt relieved that her baby was okay. That she was okay.

But she also felt furious with herself.

Sure, she had seen him, but she didn't recognize him. And if that had been the Jewelry Slayer, she had missed an opportunity to take him into custody—and prevent him from killing again. Plus, he had stolen the evidence she had so carefully collected.

"Kyra, are you okay?" Patrick finally reached her, too late to catch up with the guy who had attacked her—and apparently run off with the evidence bag.

Patrick definitely wasn't happy, and he was worried.

"I'm okay," Kyra responded, but her voice cracked and he didn't believe what she said. She still stood there, on the sidewalk now, holding her stomach.

What if something had happened to her baby?

What if the guy who'd come after her had managed to somehow harm both Kyra and her unborn child?

Damn. He liked his coworker. A lot. If only he'd been right here, beside her—

"I'm calling 911," he said. "Getting an ambulance here. We're taking you to the hospital to get checked out."

"That isn't necessary," she said, although her tone still wasn't convincing. Plus, her dark eyes appeared strained, and she was bent over a bit so she appeared shorter than her usual slender, tall height.

She still looked lovely, with her long dark hair pulled

back behind her head in a clip. Her lips were pink and smooth, though drawn into a stressed frown.

Without saying anything else, Patrick called 911, then explained to the operator who he was, where he was and the situation with his coworker who was pregnant and required immediate medical assistance and a ride to the nearest hospital to get checked out.

When he hung up, he looked at Kyra. She was staring at him, her expression suggesting she wasn't exactly happy, but she accepted what he'd done—was maybe even okay with it.

Though she was standing, she still seemed slumped a bit. He wanted to hold her, for support. To hug her— but of course he didn't.

Although he would have grabbed her if there was any indication she couldn't remain standing by herself.

"You could just have gone after the suspect," Kyra said. Was she accusing him of ineptitude? But then she added, "I appreciate your joining me though, and I doubt you could have caught up with him. I'm probably fine, and so is my baby. But… Well, to be sure there aren't any internal problems, I'll be glad to get an examination. So, thanks. I just hope we find a way—"

"To catch the SOB who did this to you," he finished, aiming his scowl in the direction the guy had fled.

"And stole the evidence that would undoubtedly have his fingerprints and more, and would have pointed to him as the killer." She seemed to hesitate. "I'm not sure you were close enough to see what happened, but—"

"I saw that you pulled off his face covering. Right?"

As glad as he was that his fellow crime scene investigator now might know what their target looked like, he'd been alarmed that the guy would hurt her even more after she viewed him that way.

But Patrick had stepped up his run, and the guy must have seen him then since he took off as Patrick drew closer.

"Yes," she responded. "I got a good look at him. Would I recognize him again? I certainly hope so. But what happened to that woman who screamed? Did he somehow harm her too?"

"I was definitely played," Patrick growled, clasping both hands into fists. "She disappeared into one of those buildings before I reached her, and I couldn't locate her inside. Didn't look like anything was wrong. She must have been a collaborator of our perp, trying to draw my attention from you so he could steal the evidence back. And it worked, damn it."

"It's okay," Kyra said, clearly trying to soothe him when she was the one needing soothing. Protection.

And he had failed her.

"We'll find her too, hopefully," Kyra continued. "And we'll definitely find our perp and get back the evidence."

Patrick certainly hoped so. He would do all in his power to make that come true.

But what if the guy who'd attacked Kyra had been another collaborator of the killer?

Well, for the moment, what was most important was to take care of Kyra.

Where was the damned medical—

A siren sounded nearby. Good. Help was finally arriving.

At least some of his frustration eased a little.

But his CSI duties were kicking at his mind. He needed more information from Kyra about her attacker, but this wasn't the time to ask her those kinds of questions. Most important right now was to make sure she, and her baby, were okay.

Plus… Well, it would help if they could verify her alertness and health if she actually did point out their perp. It wouldn't do them any good if he hired a lawyer who claimed their eyewitness was too out of it to have gotten a good look.

An ambulance rolled up to the curb beside them, the usual kind from the Fire Department of New York that resembled a pickup truck with a red stripe along the side and a white enclosure at the rear where patients could be examined and transported.

A couple of EMTs exited from the front, both in beige jackets with yellow and gray stripes, again what Patrick was familiar with.

One EMT was a woman, the other a man. They both hurried toward where Patrick stood beside Kyra, who remained standing beside him but appeared exhausted. He wished he'd helped her sit down on the curb.

But the EMTs took over now, seating her on a gurney they removed from the ambulance, looking her over, asking questions including the length so far of her pregnancy—nearing seven months, she told them. Since they worked together, Patrick was aware of that, even though he wasn't exactly familiar with how large the pregnancy bump should look by now.

Nope, he wasn't married. Didn't have kids. Wasn't sure he ever wanted any, although with the right woman in his life… Nope.

Still, his mind started to wonder what it would be like to be close in that way to Kyra, this woman who was almost as high-ranking as him on their crime scene investigation team.

Yes, he liked her. Admired her. And—well, found her much too attractive, although he'd never let her, or anyone else, know that.

"Okay," the male EMT said, turning to look at Patrick. "She doesn't seem in bad shape, but we'll take her to the hospital for further examination, just to be sure."

"Good idea," Patrick said. "I'll come along."

He knew there'd be room in the ambulance, even with his large equipment bag. And since they knew he was in law enforcement he figured they'd let him join them.

No one said otherwise, at least.

And under the circumstances, when the attacker knew she had seen his face, there was no way Patrick would let Kyra out of his sight.

## Chapter 2

Kyra was in a small, private room in the emergency area of the nearest hospital to the crime scene, one of New York City's best. She appreciated that.

She also appreciated the care with which she had been treated by the EMTs who had come when Patrick called for help—even though she hoped she didn't really need medical attention.

She'd be fine. The guy had pushed her, but he hadn't struck her or harmed her physically in any other way.

But she couldn't be sure about her baby—and that was what was important.

"How are you feeling?" Patrick had stayed with her through all of this and now sat on a chair near the narrow bed where she lay, still in her loose white blouse and black pants, but she'd taken her jacket off since it was warm in here.

Same with Patrick. And he looked good in the outfit the CSIs on their team always wore, like her a white shirt and black pants—although hers had been modified somewhat because of her pregnancy.

"I'm okay," she responded. And she thought she was. She had already been checked by an emergency room physician and now waited for an ob-gyn, with more expertise in prenatal care, to conduct a follow-up— and make sure her baby was doing as well as possible.

It didn't sound as if they would admit her into the hospital, and she was glad.

Although if she needed to stay to ensure her baby's health, of course she would.

Patrick seemed a bit antsy as he sat there, which wasn't surprising. He checked his phone a lot, although she hadn't heard any sounds suggesting he'd received calls or texts. But he could be getting emails.

He could also be checking to see if there were any official reports, or even media reports, on the murder of Susanne Shermore and what had happened in the area afterward. All things she would want to know too.

She figured Patrick really wanted to be out there attempting to find the person who'd attacked her—the Jewelry Slayer or one of his cohorts—rather than sitting around in a hospital. But sweet boss that he was—well, sort of boss, since they both were in charge of their CSI team—here he still was.

Protecting her by hanging around.

She'd already suggested that he leave. She'd stay on alert, and she figured no one should be able to attack her in the hospital.

Not even the man whose face she'd seen…

But it had been so fast. Could she actually identify him?

She'd certainly give it her best try when given the opportunity.

Was he actually the Jewelry Slayer or a crony, like that screaming woman must have been? Under the circumstances, she had to believe the former.

And could he somehow have been watching afterward? Did he know where she was now?

Was he finding a way to sneak into the hospital to get her?

Well, she'd remain alert. And she'd again suggest that Patrick leave so he hopefully could help find the guy and the evidence he stole. But before she did another doctor came in—the ob-gyn she'd been waiting for.

That exam went quickly, as the other one had. She felt a little uncomfortable raising her shirt so the middle-aged woman in a long white jacket, Dr. McGrath, could check her stomach area and listen for the baby's heartbeat with a stethoscope. Patrick was her coworker. He didn't need to see her partially nude.

Although somehow the idea of being nude around him—and his being nude around her—sounded inviting…

Ridiculous. Her hormones must really be off-kilter with the baby inside her.

Maybe it was a good thing that she no longer had a man in her life.

"All seems fine to me," the doctor soon said. "I'd suggest you get an appointment with your regular physician for a follow-up. Someone will be in here soon to finalize your exam, and after that you should be free to leave."

Then, after aiming a curious glance at Patrick as if she thought he might be the baby's father—or wondering, if he wasn't, what he was doing here—the doctor left the room.

"One more visit," Kyra said. "Then I can get out of here."

"So I heard."

"You know, you can leave anytime," she told Patrick, ignoring the intense look in his eyes, as if he wanted to see what she was thinking. Well, she wanted to know what he was thinking too, though she guessed it was that he wanted to go after their suspect. "I'm not sure how long it'll take before I'm released, and as you know, I called my parents a little while ago. They're on their way here now."

Oh, yes, she'd called her wonderful but overprotective parents to let them know what was going on, since she knew she'd have to eventually. And since she fortunately was being released, they could drive her home.

"That's a good thing," Patrick said. "But in any case I—"

Before he finished a man in a suit entered the room. He was tall and carried some paperwork as well as an electronic tablet. His name tag identified him as Dr. Allen. He asked some repetitious questions of Kyra, including what had happened to bring her here, and she figured he was an administrator since he made notes on the tablet and handed papers to her. "Do you have any pains now or anything else we should know about?"

She took the paperwork. "I think I'm okay, and, as I was told, I'll check with my regular doctor as a follow-up."

"You should stay at home for the next few days to recuperate, or at least to be certain there are no further issues."

Really? Well, she couldn't exactly argue with this professional. And although she didn't hurt or anything, she did feel tired.

But staying home for a while?

Well, she'd think about it. But she wished Patrick hadn't heard that.

The paperwork turned out to be discharge papers, including further instructions and a requirement of a signature by Kyra saying she did not require further care at this time and had no issues with the care she'd received.

And she didn't. Not now, at least.

As she finished signing the papers, which also referenced her insurance—supplied by the FBI—a knock sounded on the closed door, and it was opened.

Despite Patrick's look of concern and steps in that direction, Kyra couldn't help smiling as two people entered. "Mom! Dad! Thanks for coming."

Her mother was immediately at her bedside. Kyra knew she resembled Riya Patel. Her mom's hair was long too, though not as long as hers, and almost the same shade of brown although there was a bit of dye involved. They both were tall and had longish faces with dark eyes, and her mom had a few wrinkles at the corners of her mouth and eyes. Riya was proud of her Indian heritage, although she was born in the US, unlike Kyra's father, Sanam—Sam—who was born in the Indian state of Gujarat.

"How are you, honey?" Her mom immediately embraced her, then stepped back beside the bed and looked Kyra over. She wore an attractive long beige blouse over brown slacks. "Are you okay? You said someone attacked you, though you indicated you weren't hurt, and—"

"And we came as soon as we could." Her dad also stood beside her, grabbing her hand. He was tall too, his hair short and black, and he wore glasses with black frames over his dark eyes. He had a slight Indian accent. Like her mother, he was dressed casually, in a black shirt and matching trousers.

Both had very concerned expressions on their faces, and Kyra was quick to reassure them—or attempt to. "I'm fine. I've been seen by a couple doctors, including one who concentrated on the baby, and everything is okay. I didn't want to worry you by calling, but since I thought at first they might keep me here in the hospital I wanted to let you know. But, fortunately, they've released me. I'm able to go home."

"Really?" her dad asked. "But someone attacked you. Who was it? Someone related to your job? Are you still in danger?" The expression on his face suggested he wanted to go after whoever it was, and that wasn't going to happen.

Kyra hesitated just an instant. She couldn't tell them she was perfectly fine that way—not without perhaps lying to them. She decided to admit that yes, it was job related, but she'd be really careful and—

Before she could say anything though, she saw Patrick approach the opposite side of her bed from her parents. "Hello, Mr. and Mrs. Patel. I'm Patrick Colton, and I'm Kyra's fellow crime scene investigator, in charge of our team with her. I'm really sorry this happened. I was with her in the area where she was attacked, though not close enough, and I came with her to this hospital. And—" He looked away from her parents and straight into Kyra's eyes. "I think she's safe now, but I want to make sure of it. No way will I let her out of my sight once she's out of here."

What! Kyra opened her mouth to protest, but her parents were talking now, thanking Patrick, introducing themselves, expressing their concerns even more.

She felt confused. She appreciated Patrick's protectiveness, but it didn't make sense. They were coworkers. He had no obligation to protect her.

But she still felt a warmth inside that he'd made the suggestion.

Well, when things quieted down, she'd let them all know her opinion—that she didn't need his help.

Or did she? Maybe if she wasn't pregnant, but even though she was an FBI agent, she wasn't as able right now to take on all the duties she could have before she was expecting a baby. And she might even do what had been suggested and stay home for a day or two.

Still—

"Oh, Kyra." Her mother grasped her hands and looked into her eyes. "You definitely have a wonderful colleague. I'm so glad he'll be taking care of you."

But was she glad? And how could he possibly take care of her?


Stay with Kyra? Oh, yeah.

Patrick stood there smiling slightly as her parents remained close, thanking him.

They seemed like nice people, these two folks who resembled the woman who ran his crime scene team with him.

But listening to them wasn't why he was doing this.

Hey, it was part of his job. Assuming the attacker was the Jewelry Slayer and not a minion, he knew he'd been seen by Kyra and would undoubtedly come after her. Despite all security efforts, it might not be difficult for someone as determined as the thief who murdered people to steal their jewelry to find the home of someone who currently worked with the police department. And he'd definitely know how to find her if she returned to work, as she wasn't supposed to yet.

Never mind that Patrick suspected he had feelings for Kyra that shouldn't be there. He absolutely didn't want any harm to come to her and would hang out with her to fulfill his law enforcement obligations.

"Okay," he finally said after listening to Mrs. Patel's thanks and shaking Mr. Patel's hand. He pulled away and approached Kyra, who still sat on the bed. "What I want you to do is hang out at the hospital now, Kyra, till I go home and get some clothes and other stuff to bring as I stay with you for the next few days at your home. It'll be better for you to be in an environment like this hospital with a lot of people around till I return—and of course I've already called to get some of the local police department's officers to patrol the area."

"It's very kind of you, Patrick," she said. "But unnecessary. I can be observant and take care of myself when I go home now. I can even come into the office tomorrow." She kept talking before he could mention she'd been told to stay home. "I'll be fine. And I want to help identify—"

"But, honey," her mother began, grabbing Kyra's hand. "I know things are set up nicely at your apartment for the baby's arrival. The nursery is adorable. But for you to be there alone at all right now would be just too dangerous. I'd be terrified that whoever attacked you would show up there. And this nice Patrick's offer to stay with you? Absolutely! And I'm sure he'd be there when you go to your office too, although I don't think tomorrow is a good idea or maybe for a while. But Patrick seems like such a nice man. One you can rely on. That's so wonderful." She looked toward Patrick and smiled widely.

Her husband took her hand and also regarded Patrick in a way that suggested he liked the idea of his taking care of Kyra too.

Patrick had an urge to tell them how things really were between their daughter and him: strictly professional. But he left it to Kyra.

Kyra seemed to sigh as she looked first at her parents and then at Patrick, her expression grim—but at least she appeared resigned, even if she hadn't said yes yet.

But she would. He would make sure of it.

Patrick couldn't help admiring his coworker's bravery. But it was irrelevant.

He had to make sure she remained okay. The only way he could do that was to stay with her tonight and for as long as it took to capture her attacker. And let her go to the office? Well, he'd have to determine the wisdom of that as the investigation continued, possibly with only her remote assistance.

"Okay, then," he said. "I'll be back as soon as I can. I'll let the people in charge here know you'll remain till I return. And I'll make sure the patrols stay around the area as well."

He looked Kyra straight into her dark eyes briefly, as if punctuating what he'd said with a strong glance. He half expected her to protest again, but she regarded him with a wry look that seemed resigned.

Good.

He hurried out of the room, making sure the door was closed securely behind him. Too bad he couldn't lock it.

Fortunately, there were several other doors in the hallway, so even if their suspect knew Kyra's general location, it would be difficult for him to find her here.

And Patrick spoke to Dr. Allen, the guy who'd last come in to get Kyra to sign papers, who fortunately stood at a desk at the end of the hallway. "I'm leaving Ms. Patel here for a while, but I'll be back for her." He handed the guy a card that had his name and phone number on it. "Everything should be fine, but if someone besides her parents, who are with her now, asks for her, please don't let them in, and give me a call."

He figured the Patels had identified themselves on their arrival and asked where their daughter was. And had been given the information.

Well, fortunately that had been okay, but the Jewelry Slayer could do something similar.

"Is whoever hurt Ms. Patel looking for her?" Dr. Allen asked. He appeared concerned.

"We don't know, but it's a possibility. We want to make sure she remains okay."

"Of course," the doctor said. "I'll notify our security to keep on the watch around here too, just in case."

"Perfect," Patrick said, although he suspected that hospital security wasn't always perfect. But it would be better than nothing.

He finally left, calling a rideshare company to pick him up as he'd done earlier to get to the crime scene. Fortunately, it didn't take long. And Patrick was still carrying the equipment bag he had brought along.

As he waited near the street outside the emergency

area, he called Captain Colleen Reeves, head of the 130th Precinct's police department. She answered right away.

"Everything okay with Kyra, Patrick?"

"She's doing well," he said as he watched some cars pass on the road nearby that curved around the outside of the several-story building. None stopped, so his ride hadn't arrived. And several of the vehicles were police cars. "I'm leaving her at the hospital for the moment to get some of my belongings, but I intend to stay with her at her home for the next few days and work from there. No sign of the suspect that I've seen, but I don't want to take any chances."

"Good idea. And considering her condition, it'll probably be good if she takes a break for a few days. Although knowing Kyra—"

"Yeah, I'm sure she'll at least be in contact by phone. Any indication of where her attacker is yet?"

"Unfortunately, no. We've got a number of detectives and others combing the area where she was attacked—both because of what happened to her and the homicide that occurred there. We're hopeful, but nothing yet."

"Got it. Well, I'll stay in touch too, but consider both Kyra and me unavailable physically for the time being."

"Sounds good." A pause, then, "Take care of both of you, Patrick."

"Count on it," he said. And he figured she would.

The Uber finally arrived, a red sedan driven by a guy in his fifties. Patrick took a moment before entering, but there was no indication he was being picked up by the suspect they were after.

He gave the guy his address and they drove off. The driver seemed friendly but other than commenting he was familiar with the neighborhood they headed for he didn't say anything else.

His silence was a good thing. Watching the buildings they drove by, Patrick found himself thinking about his current situation. Really thinking about it.

There was definitely a lot going on in his life. Yes, he and Kyra, crime scene investigators, were after the Jewelry Slayer—for an additionally good reason now, and not just because the guy had stolen the evidence Kyra had been collecting regarding the murder committed there.

He'd attacked Kyra. He needed to be caught. Soon. Very soon.

But in addition to that, Kyra and Patrick had already been working with others in the FBI and local police department to find the Landmark Killer. Like the Jewelry Slayer, only different, the guy had been murdering people in New York City. He didn't steal anything though, and he committed his murders at New York landmarks.

And after all the investigating that had been going on in that case for many weeks, they now knew he was the FBI director's former assistant, Xander Washer.

Patrick was furious with that guy and his murderous nature—and their inability so far to catch him. Even more, a couple of weeks ago, Patrick, who'd been on the case for a while, had received a taunting text message from the Landmark Killer.

It had said: Remember how you missed collecting DNA evidence a few years ago from that Upper East Side hotel and the killer struck again because of you? Sort of like now. You'll never get me.

Oh, yes he would. Or if he didn't, someone else in the FBI or local police department would.

The missed evidence? That made him even angrier. At the time he was working on that case, his former colleague Ursula Andrews had been his girlfriend. She'd been at that crime scene, though he hadn't—and she'd been the one to miss that evidence.

That had led to their breakup.

And now? Well, despite what he was up to now—intending to stay with Kyra to protect her and her baby—and also despite the fact they'd been working together now for several months and he found her highly appealing, and not just as a coinvestigator, he was determined never to date a colleague again.

Plus, he wasn't interested in ever becoming a father, and Kyra was definitely very pregnant.

Okay, he cared for her, but the strange feelings he'd been having about her must be because he'd already felt particularly protective of her despite their being colleagues, thanks to her vulnerable condition. That was now magnified because of the current situation.

So, sure, he would stay with her for a few days to protect her even more.

Damn, he was overthinking this. But he couldn't help thinking about her parents then. The attitude the Patels had showed to him when they visited Kyra in the hospital while he was there? Drat it all. They'd seem thrilled he was going to join her at her home and protect her.

Maybe they even believed a relationship could develop between them. After all, their daughter was not married, and she was expecting a baby.

But there was no way that could happen.

Sure, he wanted to protect her. But in case Kyra had a thought like her parents seemed to, Patrick would make it very clear to her that he would never get married or have kids.

He considered himself a lone wolf. One she could continue to work with, of course.

But nothing more.

## Chapter 3

Kyra awaited Patrick's return with misgivings.

Oh, she loved being with her caring parents. But they were reading more into Patrick's promise to take care of her than it really was.

"He's such a nice man," her mom said, continuing to smile as she sat beside Kyra on the bed. "And so handsome. Tall, and strong looking. I'll bet he'll do a wonderful job of protecting you. And maybe the two of you can develop a relationship. Your baby needs a daddy, after all."

"Oh, Mom," Kyra sighed. "Like I've been saying, yes, he's nice, but his looks are irrelevant. We work together. It's part of his job to help take care of me under these difficult circumstances. We both want to make sure the guy who attacked me is caught."

"Of course," her dad said. "And Patrick looks like a really good source of both protection and hopefully catching the bad guy." He stood near the door now, as if he was attempting in this small way to protect her too.

In this short amount of time, she'd lost count of how many times she'd reiterated that Patrick and she worked together, and it was simply part of his job to take care of her.

And it was. Sort of. But... Well, she wasn't going to admit to her parents that she did in fact find Patrick good-looking and appealing in more than a professional way.

And his moving in with her for her protection...

Well, that did go above and beyond his regular duties, even if he had a logical professional reason to do so.

Okay, she could understand somewhat the reason for her parents making assumptions that her coinvestigator cared more for her than just as a professional colleague.

Although the idea... She forced herself to shrug off any thoughts that there could be anything more. Sure, she wanted a man in her life now as her child's father. And more.

Someone who'd really care for her and her baby.

Unlike the man who'd impregnated her: Emmett Sorel, her former boyfriend. They'd broken up as soon as she'd told him she was pregnant with his child. Things had turned horrible between them after that, even though she'd thought she really cared for him, which was why they'd slept together. But she certainly hadn't planned to get pregnant. Unfortunately though, their birth control method hadn't worked.

And she'd stopped caring for Emmett thanks to his attitude. But she hadn't wanted him to die—which he had, in a car accident two months ago. Not that he'd wanted to admit that her baby was his, but now there was no chance he would ever be in their child's life.

She knew that things would be better if the child had a loving daddy. And she certainly wouldn't mind having a loving mate who became that daddy.

She'd already been thinking about how to best meet the right man, even gone on a few dates thanks to using matchmaking sites. But no one—

"Honey, are you okay?" her mother asked, looking at her as if attempting to read her mind. Her mother had a knack for that—trying, at least.

"I'm fine. Just thinking again that I'd really rather not put Patrick to any bother, and I really can take care of myself."

"Nonsense." Her dad's tone was irritated. "You need help right now, Kyra, and it's a good thing that your partner from work will be watching over you. For now, and maybe for a good, long time."

Her father and mother both chose to read something that wasn't there into Patrick's kindness—and professionalism. She considered contradicting them again, letting them know she thought Patrick was a confirmed bachelor, but there was a knock on the door to the room where they all now sat on the bed.

Kyra froze, though she figured she knew who it was.

Fortunately, she was right.

"It's me, Kyra," called Patrick's highly welcome voice. "I'm coming in."

She noticed he didn't ask permission, but under these circumstances that was okay.

Unless, of course, their suspect had found and followed Patrick here...

No. She knew Patrick well enough to feel certain he would do something other than entering her room with the killer forcing him in.

He'd even fight the guy, endanger his own life, rather than do anything to risk hers—because she was the focus of his protection at the moment. And they were coworkers and friends.

"Come on in," she called, but he'd already done so, standing inside the room and closing the door behind himself. He appeared as he had before, no change of clothes and the same intense and concerned expression on his good-looking face as he regarded her.

"You okay?" he asked.

"Sure." She attempted to sound honest and upbeat no matter how nervous she felt about leaving the hospital and getting back into the world—with the Jewelry Slayer most likely searching for her.

But at least she wouldn't face him alone again.

Patrick would be with her.

"Let's get going then. I have my car here now and will drive us to your place, though you'll have to give me the address."

Not surprising. They'd worked together now for a while, but as coworkers they didn't visit each other's homes. She had a general idea of where Patrick lived but would need more information to get there if she ever needed to, just as he needed information now.

"We'll leave now too," Kyra's mother said. "And— well, I know you said you'd be staying at your apartment for a while, honey, rather than going to work, which is a good thing. We'll want to stay in touch and visit you there, and have you visit us at our place as well."

She had glanced at Kyra but now was looking at Patrick, as if seeking his okay.

"That should be fine, although we'll need to discuss timing and all," Patrick said.

Kyra interpreted that partially to mean that he'd want to be sure not only that she was safe on any visits, but that her parents would be as well. Nice guy, she thought again.

Preparing to leave, Patrick insisted on going outside the hospital room first to look around and maybe talk to anyone who happened to be there, or at least that was what Kyra assumed. He returned quickly and gave her parents the okay to go.

Kyra was immediately swept again into her mother's arms, then her dad's. "You be really careful, you hear?" her father said.

"We'll be calling you a lot," her mom added. "You can be sure of that. And feel free to call us anytime."

"I already do," she reminded her parents, hugging and kissing them both. "Now, you be careful too. Let's talk later tonight." She wanted to be sure they arrived home safely too. Their apartment was a distance from hers, in a nice part of the city as well.

"You ready to go?" Patrick asked her then. "I've parked in the doctors' lot here at the hospital. It's more secure than the one for the general public, and I got one of the patrol car drivers to make arrangements for me to get in. But will there be a place to park my car at your building?"

"Yes, it has a nice garage right next door, with extra spaces," she told him. Not cheap, but convenient, like the building where she resided.

Patrick had apparently also figured out the best way to leave the hospital without being overly conspicuous, staying inside till they could leave through a door into the doctors' parking lot.

She appreciated his caution.

She appreciated *him*.

Soon they were in his car, a black SUV that looked like a lot of other cars on the street, not like an official vehicle but not much different from her own. They were investigators, and the public didn't need to know who they were when they were driving between their current precinct offices and crime scenes. But she had already noticed the large equipment bag he carried, similar to the one she carried in the back of her car.

Kyra told him her address, an apartment building several miles away on East Fifty-Third Street near Second Avenue, near the precinct headquarters located in Midtown Manhattan on Forty-Second Street near Lexington Avenue, not far from Grand Central Station.

"I've got the app that can let us into the parking lot," Kyra added. "My space is available there since I left my car near where we were conducting the investigation. It'll probably get towed if it hasn't already been."

"We'll work things out to get it moved to the precinct lot for now," he told her, making her feel a bit relieved. "Eventually we'll have it brought to your apartment's garage—in a nonobvious way."

It sounded good, but she had no idea how efficient the Jewelry Slayer might be at ferreting out details, like which vehicle was hers and where she lived.

Well, they'd find out. And for now, she had a great guardian helping to keep her safe—like it or not.

She…and the child growing within her. So even though pangs of irritation and more sometimes sped through her, she would do whatever she had to so she could remain safe.

Especially because there was another being inside

her, and she wanted her beloved baby to develop and thrive and be delivered safely whenever it was time.

Nevertheless, life went on, and she had to consider some of the banalities too. For one thing, she'd want her car back soon. She hated not being able to get around on her own. She would already depend on Patrick for too much and didn't need him to be her ongoing chauffeur as well.

Right now, he drove slowly but carefully along the New York streets toward her apartment, between the usual street-level stores and taller department stores overshadowed by even taller apartment and office buildings. Traffic was as dense as usual this late in the day, and she noted Patrick looking from car to car, as if attempting to assess the occupants.

No surprise. She was doing the same thing. Would she recognize the man who'd attacked her? She'd seen his face, after all, so she hoped so.

But she also hoped she wouldn't see it here or now.

"How long have you lived at your place?" Patrick asked, apparently wanting to make conversation.

"About a year." She'd moved there several years after finishing her studies in criminal justice at the John Jay College of Criminal Justice in New York City and joining the FBI, in the hopes she would be selected to join the Criminal Investigation Division. She had met all the requirements, fortunately, and had become a criminal investigator a while back.

She had recently joined the CSI team she now ran with Patrick, and was glad their team now worked with the 130th Precinct of NYC on some particularly intense cases, since the captain of that precinct had requested the FBI's help to find some rampant serial killers. Fortunately, the nice apartment she now rented wasn't too far away from that precinct's headquarters.

And in the meantime she had met Emmett Sorel, a paralegal in a local law firm, and had fallen for him...

Never mind that.

"I assume it's in an apartment building," Patrick said. "Tell me about it."

So he could prepare to protect her there, she figured. He'd want to know the building's height, where her place was within it and anything else that could be important.

"The building's seven stories high. My place is on the fourth floor, and my living room windows overlook Fifty-Third Street. Nice view, in my opinion."

"I'm sure." His voice sounded wry, and she knew that wasn't something important to him.

"I know a few of the neighbors," she continued. "There are three married couples on my floor, and one has a child. There are three elevators, side by side, and all three cars fit about six people when full."

"Got it." He seemed more interested now. "And stairways?"

"One that goes from the lobby to the top floor. I've walked it now and then, though not recently."

She put her hand on her extended stomach and saw Patrick glance there too.

"Not surprising. So tell me a little more about the people on your floor. Do you know where any of them works?"

She described the two married schoolteachers with the six-year-old girl, the department store manager and saleswoman who were also married, and a couple who both worked in administration for a real estate company.

"I don't think any of them are dangerous, or likely to collaborate with someone like the Jewelry Slayer."

"Hopefully not," Patrick said. But she could tell he wouldn't make the same kinds of assumptions she did. That was probably a good thing. Who knew how friendly the Jewelry Slayer might be to other people—those he might use to find his victims who actually had expensive jewelry?

Someone on her floor? Elsewhere in her building? She didn't think so, but who knew?

She continued to watch the areas they drove by, as he did. Soon, they were a block from her building, in an area where there were other apartments around. "We're almost there," she told him.

"I figured. I want to park in the garage and stay with you as we walk in, rather than dropping you off."

Which was fine with her. She soon told him to make a right turn at the next intersection and go partially around the block until she could point out the entrance to the garage. When he pulled up to the entry gate, she took her phone from her purse and pushed the code into the app, and the gate rose.

Kyra then directed Patrick to her spot two levels down in the crowded, dimly lit structure that was underground and definitely filled with cars since most people there took public transportation to work and kept their vehicles inside. That's what she did when not out on an investigation assignment.

She felt bad her space was empty. It had made sense for her to be transported straight to the hospital for her checkup after the attack, but she wanted her car back.

With Patrick's help, she was hopeful. So far she'd no reason to believe he'd not accomplish anything he set out to do. She'd seen his successes on the job in investigating crime scenes and obtaining evidence that helped convict quite a few perpetrators, after all.

Getting her car back, and protecting her, were now other goals he'd added to his list of things to do.

"Okay," he said after he'd parked. "I'll get out first and check things around here, then let you know when we're ready to head to your apartment."

Another indication of his protectiveness. That was fine with her.

Another car was just pulling out of a space a few down from them. She recognized it as belonging to her neighbors a floor below hers, the Washbornes. It looked like Jessie was in the driver's seat. But Kyra couldn't tell for certain.

Surely, whoever it was didn't intend to harm her— or Patrick either. But in case things weren't how they appeared…

She put her hand on her stomach. Oh, yes, under the circumstances she realized she was probably a bit paranoid, but better that than ignoring danger and facing harm to herself and her baby.

And possibly Patrick too.

Sure enough, the driver waved as she passed by. Patrick still stood by the driver's door, but Jessie must have peeked into the car in Kyra's spot and seen who was inside.

She didn't talk to Jessie much, but Kyra figured she might have to explain some time that a coworker had driven her home—without going into any details why.

The car was soon gone. Kyra peeked out toward where Patrick stood and saw that his hand was on his hip—probably on the gun he'd undoubtedly stuck into his belt beneath his shirt. A precaution, but fortunately he hadn't pulled it out. He certainly hadn't had to use it.

He came around to the passenger's side and opened the door. "Everything appears okay," he said. "Let's go to your apartment."

Kyra led him to the door to the garage stairway. They were only a couple floors down, so she could walk the stairs as she usually did, even though there was an elevator not far away. She might need to use it as it grew closer to her time to give birth, but she was fine walking the steps now.

Patrick let her go first, but he stayed close behind, and he was the one to open the door at the top. They were soon in the lobby area of the apartment building, and Kyra let Patrick enter first.

She looked around the lobby when she entered. Even having a protector with her, she was a law enforcement officer in danger, so she remained fully cautious.

She liked the lobby area, which was large and open, with a marbled tile floor, textured beige walls and a tall ceiling. Several doors led off it, including one to the area where the tenants' postal boxes were, but Kyra didn't feel like checking her mail then. She doubted she'd gotten anything but junk mail anyway.

Another door led to the back of the building. But most important now was the bank of three elevators across from the entry. Kyra led Patrick there.

One of the doors opened as soon as she pushed the up button, and she headed inside. Patrick followed and quickly pivoted, looking at the area they'd just left, undoubtedly to be sure no one followed them.

All looked fine, fortunately.

"I'll get off first," Patrick said as they reached the fourth floor and the door began to open again.

Kyra wasn't surprised. She was actually grateful.

If her enemy had learned where she lived, he might be waiting there. Or even possibly in her apartment—and of course Patrick insisted on taking her key and opening the door first, then slipping inside and checking out all parts of the unit.

She stayed near the door for the minute or so it took him to look around.

"All clear," he said. "Now we can relax. Maybe."

His smile at her was much too sexy, even though she realized he was simply trying to be funny and maybe get her to relax.

But she felt anything but relaxed. Oh, yes, she still feared for the safety of herself and her baby.

But she also worried what it would be like to hang out here alone with Patrick for however long it took before they felt she could remain on her own again.

# Chapter 4

Patrick felt fairly comfortable that he and Kyra were alone in her apartment.

Or maybe not so comfortable.

He stood in the kitchen with her now, watching as she removed a couple bottles of water from the spacious metal refrigerator.

"Here." She handed one to him.

"Thanks." He screwed the cap off, taking a swig of the nice, cold water. He hadn't realized he was thirsty, but it tasted good.

He wasn't surprised when Kyra did the same thing. She probably needed to stay particularly hydrated, considering her condition.

Nice kitchen, though not very large. There was a small table with four chairs tucked under it beneath a narrow window with a decorative lacy drapery closed over it, along with the fridge and an electric stove, plus a microwave oven on the counter near the porcelain sink. The floor was decorated with floral tiles. The room was as attractive as the rest of the apartment.

At least Kyra didn't seem to be in danger here. He'd checked the place out as thoroughly as possible in the short time they'd been there. No indications of anyone else around. No indications that the place had been breached before they arrived.

No indication on the way here, or now, that the Jewelry Slayer was anywhere close, waiting to attack the woman who'd seen his face and most likely could identify him.

Patrick certainly hoped she could, when the opportunity arose.

But not now, when he had no backup nearby.

He'd call Captain Reeves in a little while and give her more information about what was going on. He'd already let Colleen know he intended to hang out with Kyra at her home for now, and where she lived had to be in the precinct's private records like everyone else's. But he wanted to make sure the captain set up patrols in the area, though not too obvious about their center of observation.

Of course concern about Kyra's safety wasn't the only thing that made him uncomfortable.

Staying here alone with her had its issues. He'd always found the lovely, sweet, dedicated and efficient woman he worked with attractive. Too attractive.

Never mind that she was pregnant.

But he would be here for at least one night, probably more. The place had two bedrooms, but as Kyra's mother had said one was decorated already as a nursery. Attractive for a baby, yes. But he wouldn't be sleeping in the crib.

The only bed was in Kyra's bedroom. Queen-size, yes, so two people could comfortably sleep in it.

But he definitely wouldn't hang out there.

No, fortunately there was an adequately large sofa in the living room. And hanging out there would more likely allow him to maintain Kyra's safety in this place.

"Let's go sit down," Kyra said. "We'll eventually want to have dinner, and I have some frozen meals we could eat, although we might want to order in tonight as long as we're careful."

"We'll figure it out," he said and followed her into the living room.

Like the rest of the place, it was quite attractive. He assumed the rent wasn't cheap. This was New York, after all.

The walls were covered in an attractive wallpaper with a white floral print, and the floors were laminate, in a moderate shade resembling slats of oak. The brown upholstered sofa was long and wide, with a moderately tall back. It faced an oval wood coffee table, as well as a flat-screen television mounted on the wall beyond.

The sofa looked large and comfortable enough for him to plan on sleeping there. The door to the outside of the apartment opened into the living room, so that would also be a good place for him to hang out for Kyra's protection. Windows along the farthest wall had thick, closed draperies over them.

They headed to the sofa now, since Kyra had indicated they should sit down to rest or talk or whatever she had in mind. Patrick sat at the end nearest the door, water bottle still in his hand. Kyra took her seat at the other end.

"I'm sorry I can't just cook us a nice dinner tonight, Patrick," Kyra said. "You've been so kind to come here to take care of me, but I just don't keep food stocked here much unless I know I'll be entertaining my parents."

Interesting that she didn't indicate she'd cook for any dates she might bring here. He knew things had gone wrong between her and the guy who'd gotten her pregnant and that something bad had happened to him, a car accident or something, so he was no longer in her life at all.

And maybe the fact that she was expecting a baby kept her from dating now. He could understand that—although Kyra was beautiful and nice and had a really good job, so he figured she would be sought after by lots of guys with good sense.

If there were any around here.

Well, it was none of his business.

"No problem," he responded to her. "I didn't come here for you to feed or entertain me. And I'll work things out to make it as safe as possible to have our meal brought in tonight. We can go shopping for future meals tomorrow—carefully. You don't have to cook for me though. I can cook for you. Or we can just take turns."

He was amused to see her laugh. "Oh, then you have more skills than just keeping me safe from a killer."

He laughed back. "I guess you could look at it that way. Can't say that I'm a super chef, but I can get along okay."

"Me too," she said, then seemed to hesitate as she regarded him with those wonderful deep brown eyes.

"Tonight, though… Is it safe enough to order in? Do you have a place in mind that can deliver? Or a delivery service that you particularly trust?"

"At this point," he told her, "I don't trust anyone. Time for me to make that call."

He pulled his phone from his pocket and pressed in a number. He put it on speaker.

"Patrick?" said a familiar feminine voice. "Everything okay?"

"I've got you on speaker, Captain Reeves." They usually were less formal while working with the precinct, but he used her rank to make sure Kyra knew who he was talking to. "Kyra is with me," he continued. "We're at her apartment now and will soon order our dinner. How are patrols outside?"

"Kyra?" the captain said first. "How are you doing?"

"Quite well, thanks, Colleen," Kyra responded, looking at Patrick with an expression that suggested relief and even amusement. "I appreciate your asking, and—"

"Of course I care how you're doing, and so does everyone in the precinct. I'm glad you've got Patrick with you under the circumstances. And you can be certain that cars, both marked and unmarked, will be driving around the area keeping watch. In fact, tell me what you two want for dinner tonight and I'll have someone in plain clothes pick it up and deliver it."

Patrick couldn't help smiling and saw that Kyra did too. "Thanks so much," he said. "That's really nice of you."

"No problem. So—what'll it be?"

Patrick figured that keeping it simple would be the best thing. "How about a pizza?" He looked at Kyra, and she nodded. In a minute, they'd told the captain their topping preferences.

"But anything will be fine with me," Kyra said.

"Same here," Patrick added.

"Sounds good," the captain said. "I'll put your official delivery person in touch with you in a little while so you can work things out. And both of you take care of yourselves, and keep me informed about how things go." She paused, then continued, "Unfortunately, though we've still got investigators out there looking, reviewing the crime scene and asking questions of people in the area, we haven't found where your attacker went, Kyra. We're still after that damned Jewelry Slayer."

"I understand." Kyra's tone was somewhat upbeat but Patrick saw the concern increasing in her expression.

"We'll ask some of your CSIs to get in touch with you tomorrow," Colleen continued, "since it would be helpful to get more details from you about how things happened."

"Of course," Kyra agreed, looking at Patrick. He nodded, not that she needed his opinion. But what the captain had suggested sounded appropriate. Helpful? He hoped so, but who knew what additional tidbit of information, if any, would help bring their quarry down?

"Sounds good to me," he said. "Meanwhile, we'll work from here for the next few days—" while he kept a close watch on Kyra for her safety, but he didn't have to say that "—and let you know if we learn anything new. And thanks so much for taking care of dinner for us. We'll repay the person who brings it."

"I assumed so," their boss said. "Enjoy. I'm just having a salad tonight so I'll think about how much you're probably enjoying your pizza."

Patrick laughed and so did Kyra. They soon said good-bye and hung up.

"Well, we have that figured out," Kyra said as Patrick kept his phone in his hand. "The captain had said she'd have whoever she sent to pick up our pizza and deliver it get in touch. That sounds good."

"Sure does," he replied, though he worried about how things would go. He'd be glad to talk to whoever Colleen contacted and get things worked out. Maybe even help choose the restaurant. And having someone show up at the apartment door downstairs, especially someone he'd talked to, was probably okay. He'd go meet them, then bring the pizza up here. But he figured that most likely he wouldn't know whoever it was, even if he talked to them, so he'd have to be damned careful.

"So now we'll have to decide how to work from here tomorrow without heading to the precinct or going out into the field. I especially want to try to at least make a sketch of what I remember of my attacker's face." Kyra looked determined, as if she had no thought about taking a few days off for her safety.

He appreciated that, and her intent to do something to show the face she had seen. Maybe there'd be something they could do remotely tomorrow while in touch with those continuing to check out the crime scene. Perhaps they could receive pictures, make suggestions, whatever, and decide how to get a computer tech to help Kyra get a sketch into the system for facial recognition. But as much as Patrick wanted to be out there to actually capture the damned Jewelry Slayer, keeping Kyra safe was the most important duty of all.

For now—hey, he was getting hungry. When was he going to hear from their special delivery person?

As if she heard his thoughts, Kyra said, "While we're waiting, I can get us some cheese and crackers as a snack. And—"

His phone played its song that said he had a call coming in. "Just a sec." He started to answer but as he looked at the screen he smiled.

Their delivery person? Maybe. If so, at least that would be one less thing to worry about. The call was from Craig Warren, one of their subordinate crime scene investigators on the FBI team.

"Hey, Craig," Patrick said as he answered. "How's it going?" He kind of hoped Craig was calling to say they'd figured out what happened at the crime scene and found the Jewelry Slayer. But his first thought had been the correct one.

"Going fine, boss," Craig said. "I'm heading for the pizza shop. I hope the one near the precinct is okay. Colleen told me to get and deliver your dinner tonight, and I figured I'd let you know."

"Sounds good. I assume she gave you the details about the order and where I'm hanging out tonight."

"Yeah," Craig said. "With Kyra. Is she okay? I'm helping with that crime scene investigation, as you know, and heard what happened."

"She's okay." Patrick wasn't about to talk about why he was hanging out with their coworker, but he figured Colleen had let Craig know that too.

"Glad to hear it. Anyway, I'm close to the pizza joint. I'll pick up your dinner soon, then head to the address I was given. Anything else I should know?"

"Not really. Just call me when you get to the apartment building entry."

"Good. See you soon."

When Patrick hung up, he told Kyra what was going on.

"Good, dinner soon," she said. "And we can feel safe with Craig as our delivery person."

"Right," Patrick said and hoped that was true.

Oh, he trusted Craig, but as a CSI on the case, he might have been seen by the Jewelry Slayer while investigating the scene after Kyra and Patrick were gone.

No reason to really think he'd been followed.

But no reason to assume that everything was okay either.

"Okay, then." Kyra remained on the far side of the couch, regarding him with her lovely dark eyes as if she wanted something from him.

But if so, why didn't she just ask?

"I guess we've got a long evening in front of us," he said, hoping that would get her to talk. "We could discuss how to handle the next few days if you'd like."

His opinion was that they'd just remain there, but she'd been right that they'd need some food to do that, rather than relying on Craig or anyone else as delivery people.

"How about a little TV news now to see if they've got anything about the murder?" she asked.

"Good idea," he said. "We can talk later, over dinner."

They both settled back on the sofa. Yes, the local news, including an interview of Captain Colleen Reeves, focused on the latest Jewelry Slayer murder—though they didn't call it that—but only the killing of Susanne Shermore as part of a theft, although they did liken it to several similar crimes. And when the national news came on, the story was there as well.

"Word is out there," Kyra said. "As it was with the

other murders. But that didn't help bring the perpetrator down. We can only hope that this time…"

"Oh, yeah," Patrick said. "With our help, the precinct will find him and get him into custody." But Kyra wouldn't be the one to do it, so not him either, most likely. He was going to make sure she remained safe while others found their target and brought him in.

In a little while, Patrick's phone rang again. Unsurprisingly, it was Craig. Patrick made sure the apartment was locked behind him, taking Kyra's key. He also carried a concealed weapon in his pocket, as before.

He let Craig into the lobby area. Craig was still dressed as if on duty, same as Patrick and Kyra—in a dressy white shirt and dark pants. But he had an unzipped jacket on top in the chilly November air. Patrick didn't spend much time talking to their coworker but paid Craig for the pizza—and they both took a quick check of the area outside to make sure nothing appeared to be a problem.

A few people entered the building, but they all had keys and, though they looked curiously at the strangers, they didn't say anything.

Nor did they appear particularly dangerous, although both Patrick and Craig kept an eye on them.

"Thanks again," Patrick soon said to Craig, back in the lobby. "Not sure how things will go tomorrow, but I won't be at the precinct and of course Kyra won't either." He would make sure of it, no matter whether she protested again. "I'll be in touch though, and maybe Kyra and I will work remotely somehow."

"Sounds good," Craig said. "Take good care of both of you." He turned to leave.

Patrick locked the building door, then hurried through

the lobby again, this time holding the pizza box. Soon he was upstairs. He unlocked the door with Kyra's key and entered.

She was still in the living room, standing beside the couch with the TV on. He didn't know how to read her well—not yet, at least—but she seemed glad to see it was him.

"Dinnertime?" she asked and came over to take the box from Patrick as he locked the door behind him.

"Yeah," he said. "I'm hungry."

# Chapter 5

The time was just past nine thirty that night, but Kyra was really tired.

The sound of TV news droned on the set against the wall, but she hardly paid attention. What the newscasters were talking about didn't involve the Jewelry Slayer, or even the Landmark Killer, another major case her FBI team was involved with. Just some bad road accidents and store robberies—sad, but not that interesting to her.

And so the stories weren't helpful in keeping her awake, especially since her companion for the night was watching, paying attention and not conversing with her at the moment.

She looked at Patrick. Damn, but he was one good-looking guy. Yes, her companion for the night—sort of. But only in a professional way.

When she wasn't pregnant, she was a bit of a night

owl, staying up late often to read articles on law enforcement and crime scene investigation and more, or reading crime novels by major authors, or even watching shows on television about chasing and catching bad guys—and sometimes chuckling to herself about how way off the mark many were. She did find some enjoyable though.

She got on to her laptop computer a lot too. She kept it closed on the coffee table most of the time but opened it when she checked email or worked on a report for work, although she did more of those at the office. Before.

Who knew how things would work out for the next day? Or week, or more?

Now, she still sat on the sofa with Patrick, where they'd spent most of the evening. Its comfortable nature wasn't helping her stay awake, but she was used to it—and she fought her urge to sleep.

Oh, she'd gotten up several times, once to help them get pizza slices on plates from her kitchen cabinets—no, Craig hadn't brought paper plates. But they'd eaten their pizza shortly after Craig brought it. And Kyra had gotten them both some more water, this time from the kitchen sink.She liked bottled water too and would need to buy tomorrow when they went grocery shopping.

At least she had some cereal and milk, so they'd be okay with breakfast.

If Patrick wanted coffee, she could make some for him. Since she was pregnant though, she wasn't consuming much caffeine, although maybe she would join him for a few sips.

She'd also gotten up to help clear away their plates

and put them in her dishwasher. Because she was pregnant, she'd visited the bathroom frequently.

"Hey, are you okay?" Patrick asked.

Despite all her musings, Kyra had nearly fallen asleep. She wasn't sure how long she'd just sat there without moving.

"Fine," she said. "But I am tired."

"I figured. Let's get to bed."

The way he phrased that nearly made Kyra smile. They weren't going to bed together. Patrick had already said he would sleep on the sofa, which was fine with her.

She didn't want, or need, the distraction of him sleeping in her bed with her, even to protect her.

"Sounds good. I've got some extra pillows, sheets and blankets I can bring out here for you."

"Just show me, and I'll get them."

She did show him where she kept them in the same closet where she also hung her jackets and other winter clothing. There were shelves in it, and she stored extra linens there.

She'd had a bed in the room that was now the nursery, since occasionally her parents had stayed overnight. But her mom had been really excited about the idea of helping her put a nursery together, and though Kyra had kept those linens around, her folks had taken the bed to their place.

Despite Patrick's protestations, Kyra helped to put the sheets and blanket over the sofa. She let him take care of the pillows though, since it was easier for him to carry them.

"I like to take my shower in the morning," she told him. "How about you?"

It would be helpful if they knew each other's habits—

but the idea of him being in her apartment with his clothes off…

She needed to keep her imagination in line.

It wasn't as if she'd be of any interest to him anyway—a pregnant coworker? Plus, this wasn't a time she should be thinking about sex, even in the future.

"Morning too," he said. "We'll work out the timing." He hesitated. "I put your keys on the coffee table before, but I'm going to get them again and just take a walk up and down the hall. I'll listen for anything that doesn't sound like it comes from the residents, but I'm not going to do any major patrolling in the hall or outside."

"Sounds fine," she said. She had an extra set of keys, but he wouldn't be around long enough for her to hand them over to him, she figured. "I'll open the windows for a few minutes though, and also listen for anything unusual from up here."

"Good."

Not that she expected any trouble that night, but who knew? Kyra waited till Patrick left before putting her pajamas on, and she listened from the various windows in her apartment, from her bedroom to the living room and kitchen, for anything out of the ordinary.

Nothing, fortunately. And Patrick returned soon.

"All looks fine out in the hallways," he told her. "Hear anything from here?"

"No. Hopefully all's fine outside too."

"Great."

He looked at her then, eyeing her because she had changed clothes, she assumed.

Those pj's she put on? Fortunately, she had gotten some to wear during her pregnancy and after, when she would be nursing her baby. The shirt had buttons, and the pants were loose, with ties at the waist that could be adjusted as needed. They had a floral print she liked.

Nothing suggestive, even though she would be hanging out at her place with this really great-looking man. At least he'd stopped observing her. She must not have turned him on—a good thing.

She didn't know what he would wear that night. Just his shorts? But he had brought in some zipped-up cloth bags he must have thrown into his car along with his bag of work items—including weapons, like she had in hers—when he'd gone home before picking her up at the hospital. The bags were now in a corner of the living room, so she figured he had changes of clothes there, as well as probably some night wear.

She doubted he'd be any sexier in whatever he chose than she was.

She hoped.

Sure enough, he pulled some things out of one of those bags and headed for the bathroom. She couldn't tell if anything was sexy, but at least what she assumed were his pajamas had substance to them.

Soon, he emerged, and sure enough he had on a plaid top and matching pants, somewhat baggy, not at all suggestive. Good.

Even so, with his thick brown hair somewhat mussed on his head, a bit of facial hair of a similar shade that had grown during the day and those hazel eyes that kept watching her, she couldn't help thinking that Patrick Colton was one good-looking guy—and she was going to spend the night in the same apartment as him.

Good thing it wouldn't be in the same room. And it felt very strange that she was attracted to him, notwithstanding the fact she was pregnant.

Not that anything would have come of it even if she wasn't expecting.

"Okay," Patrick said, "Ready for bed?"

That sounded somewhat suggestive, even though it wasn't.

"Yes," she said. "I'm tired. Are you ready for the sofa?"

He laughed. "I sure am."

He walked her to her bedroom door, flicked the switch so the light was on and glanced inside, as if wanting to make sure all was safe. It was, or at least nothing appeared any different from normal.

"Good night," he said to Kyra as she went inside.

"Good night." She closed the door but waited for a few seconds, then opened it again, leaving it slightly ajar.

She didn't anticipate anything bad happening in her unit that night, especially with Patrick out there watching over her, but she wanted to be able to hear anything out of the ordinary.

She assumed he headed for the sofa. She didn't hear the TV on any longer, so she figured he would be going to sleep too—although he most likely wouldn't allow himself to sleep very deeply considering that he was on assignment: protecting her.

And being a strong guy like Patrick, he probably could control how deeply he slept, at least to some extent.

She felt exhausted. Sleep sounded magnetic to her.

But she instructed her mind not to go too deeply asleep.

For her own protection, and Patrick's too, she needed to be prepared to wake up and be alert if there was any indication of trouble.

Still, she was undeniably pregnant. Undeniably tired. She really wouldn't have much control over how deeply she slept, she figured.

She would definitely be relying on Patrick for her safety, even though she doubted anything bad would happen that night.

Over the next few days?

Well, they'd see.

She soon hunkered down on her comfortable bed, hiked the sheet and blanket around her and tried to make herself just lie there and listen for a few minutes at least, but realized she was quickly falling asleep—and didn't stop herself.

Patrick made himself lie there on the sofa. He had his head on the pillows Kyra had made available to him and pulled the covers over him.

He listened for any noise around them.

Now and then he heard muted voices from different directions, probably from televisions of some neighbors, or perhaps the neighbors themselves. He listened as closely as possible, but nothing sounded inappropriate for a New York City apartment building in the middle of the night. The soundproofing of the walls wasn't perfect, but it wasn't too bad either.

He heard nothing threatening, and that was what was important.

Eventually, he allowed himself to fall asleep, but he primed himself to awaken periodically to listen some more and even prowl the apartment to check for any issues.

Somehow, the night went quickly that way. Yes, he got some sleep, but he also woke frequently and listened to the silence. He rose twice and walked around as quietly as he could, listening outside Kyra's door, but he didn't hear her and hoped she was sound asleep—although he did hear her head for the bathroom a few times while he was on the sofa.

After sleeping fitfully, he finally woke at six in the morning. Still lying on the sofa, he checked his phone, which he had plugged in to an outlet in the kitchen for a while when he had been walking around, but once it was charged he'd brought it back and laid it on the floor beside him.

Yes, that was the time. Back at his apartment, he had his high-tech clock radio's alarm function set to go off then, so he was used to it. But he hadn't set his phone to make any noise in case he didn't awaken when it went off, since he didn't want to disturb Kyra.

He figured she needed all the sleep she could get.

But him? Time to get up now. And stay as quiet as he could.

He got off the sofa, pushing the sheet and blanket to the back. He'd fold them later after Kyra was awake, again so he wouldn't disturb her till she got up on her own.

He had an urge to take his shower now but decided against that too, since she might hear the water running. Instead, he began checking emails on his phone.

He'd noticed Kyra's laptop on the table when they'd first come into her apartment yesterday, but he hadn't brought his own. Well, he should do well enough using his phone.

No exciting email messages had appeared overnight, unfortunately. The last he'd heard from the CSI people reporting to him who'd been conducting more of the investigation of yesterday's crime scene, they were still looking. No one had found any of the missing evidence.

No one had figured out where the murderer, and Kyra's attacker, had disappeared to. Not yet, at least.

Well, he'd talk to them further today, see what he could do from a distance, and—

"Good morning," said a sweet but groggy voice from behind him. He turned to see Kyra standing just outside her bedroom door, still dressed in the loose pajamas she had worn last night, her longish hair mussed around her face.

"Good morning," he said in return, wondering if he'd done anything to disturb her, despite his efforts not to.

"I usually wake up around now and assume you do too." Kyra approached and took the same seat as she had last evening. "Guess everything going on hasn't changed my internal clock, which is probably a good thing."

"Maybe," he said, "but it's fine if you want to try to get more sleep."

She certainly didn't appear wide awake, but even with her eyes and shoulders drooping she managed to look like one pretty lady. Her hands were hugging her baby bulge in front of her, and he hoped she, and the baby, were doing okay.

"No, I'm going to stay up, although I might want to nap later. But—well, I've been wondering how we're going to handle today. I know you don't want me to head to our office in the precinct and that you plan to hang out with me, but I still want to do my job and assume you do too. How can we do things from a distance?"

Patrick wanted to say something like she had no current obligations except to take care of herself, and his current obligation was basically the same.

But he figured that wasn't what she wanted to hear. And maybe there was something they could do remotely to help the investigation continue.

He wasn't sure what that was, though. At least the other three crime scene investigators who reported to Kyra and him, including Craig, could remain in the field and keep the search moving.

"We'll figure it out," was all he said. "Okay if I shower first?"

She seemed fine with the idea, so he grabbed some clothes from one of his bags as well as his electric razor and headed for the bathroom—after taking another walk around the place and peeking outside into the hall to make sure all still appeared okay. Fortunately, it did.

As he took his shower, he considered what it would be like to share one with Kyra someday, and he snorted in derision of himself.

They were coworkers. Didn't matter that she was attractive. And in a few months she'd also be a mother.

Both thoughts deflated not only his thoughts but a part of his body that had reacted as he'd briefly pictured being naked with a nonpregnant Kyra.

Dumb. He hurried out of the shower, dried off and put on the clothes he planned to wear that day, including a warm blue flannel shirt and blue jeans, gun in pocket once more. Then he shaved and combed his hair. Soon, he walked out of the bathroom and found Kyra in the kitchen in a loose pink robe, apparently putting things together for breakfast.

"I don't have anything too exciting," she said, "but hopefully it'll be okay for today."

"Anything's fine," he said and was glad to see she had a box of cereal out, a kind that wasn't overly sweet.

"Would you like some coffee?" she asked.

That definitely sounded good, but he said, "If you're going to have some."

"I'll make a pot," she said, "but it'll mostly be for you. It's not a good thing for someone expecting, like me, to indulge much in caffeine."

"Got it." Too bad he didn't know what was, and what wasn't, good for pregnant women. He'd try to protect Kyra in that way too. At least she seemed knowledgeable herself, and he would learn all he could from her on that front as well.

Well, he figured he had a lot to learn in many ways regarding this situation.

Most important was to figure out a way to encourage the other CSIs on their team, as well as cops in the precinct, to locate the Jewelry Slayer as soon as possible, hopefully today.

And of course for Kyra and him to do everything they could to help—as long as Kyra remained safe.

# Chapter 6

They didn't talk much as they ate breakfast at Kyra's compact kitchen table, which was fine with her, although she was used to talking a lot more with the man who helped her run their CSI team and was even more senior there than she was.

Most of the time, in the office and in the field, they discussed their cases, and sometimes even delved into some of the things they'd worked on before they'd joined forces at the FBI.

She'd always found him interesting.

She'd have liked to enter into a thought-provoking and enjoyable discussion now but wasn't sure where to begin. She didn't really want to talk yet again about why he was here.

Why she was in danger.

And all he would be doing to protect her…

Now, she mostly watched Patrick as he ate his cereal.

He appeared happy enough with it, and she didn't ask if he would have preferred something else.

If they took an expedition to a grocery store later, he could pick out whatever he wanted for tomorrow, and for however long he would stay here with her.

She could only hope it would end soon—that danger she was under.

But she had an odd wish that Patrick's presence here would continue for a while. Maybe it was her hormones, stirred up as she awaited another person in her life, her baby.

The thought made her take a sip of coffee. A tiny one. Only her second so far, and she doubted she would drink much more.

"Okay," Patrick finally said, looking at her rather than his cereal bowl. He too drank a little coffee as he continued. "I've been pondering what we'll do today, and I'm still not sure, other than stick around here. But we'll call the office around eight thirty when at least some of our CSI team should arrive. If none are there, that'll mean something's going on, so we'll call a cell phone or two. But assuming things are starting out as usual, even considering the vital cases they're working on, we should at least catch one person in the office and be able to discuss their plans for today—and see if they can suggest how we can help remotely. Or we can make suggestions to them as they occur to us. Okay?"

"Fine with me." But she couldn't help adding, "And you can always head into the office or out to the crime scene and just leave me here. I should be fine, and—"

"'Should be' is the underlying issue." His hazel eyes glared at her, adding to his message of irritation. "I'm staying here with you, at least for now. I said so yesterday, and nothing has changed today. And if either of us goes anywhere, the other will come along. I intend to be with you for the foreseeable future, until—"

Before Kyra could interrupt and protest—or thank him—her phone rang. She pulled it from her pocket.

Her mother.

She loved her mom and figured she'd be questioned, as usual, about how she was feeling. And, not as usual, about how things had gone last night and if she was safe.

If Patrick had kept her safe, as he'd promised…

"Hi, Mom," she said after answering the call.

"Hi, dear. How are you today?"

"Fine," she said, and she was. She felt the baby moving inside her, but nothing out of the ordinary for now. In fact, she'd decided that she felt well enough not to insist on going to see her doctor, at least not today.

"And everything's okay?" her mother persisted.

"It's good, Mom. Patrick and I are just eating breakfast. He's been making sure nothing around here is going wrong." And he was, or at least he'd been checking inside and around her apartment, the best he'd been able to do for now.

"That's great. I just wanted to tell you that your dad and I are heading to the grocery store down the street from us and want to bring you whatever supplies you'll need for the next few days. Just tell me what you want, and what Patrick wants."

She hadn't put her mom on speaker, but Patrick wasn't sitting far from her and she believed he could hear what was being said.

"That's really sweet of you. But—" She'd been about to say they were fine and were going out later, but the expression on Patrick's face caused her to stop. And in fact, on reflection, the idea sounded good.

Assuming the Jewelry Slayer wasn't observing her home and might wind up attacking her parents.

That thought shot through her. "But—" she continued.

"That will be very nice," Patrick said loudly. He reached out and put his hand over her phone so her folks couldn't hear what he whispered. "If you're worried about them, just remember we've got patrols around here. And it'll be good for you. We won't have to go out." He removed his hand, still watching her as if waiting to gauge her reaction.

He was right. For today at least, maybe it would be better if she didn't leave her apartment, especially since members of the precinct were watching over it—and would watch over everyone who entered her building, she figured.

That would include her parents, especially if Patrick and she made sure to notify Colleen what was going on, and who else needed to be protected.

And so she nodded at Patrick as she said into the phone, "Yes, Mom, that would be really nice. I appreciate it. We haven't come up with a list but we can put one together quickly and call you back. When are you planning on going to the store?"

"We're driving there now, so yes, please, call with your list as soon as possible."

"Thanks so much," Kyra said. "We'll get back to you soon."

After Kyra hung up, it took a few minutes to put their list together, but it included at least three more days' worth of food and water, including breakfasts, lunches and dinners.

"I really hope we won't hang out here long enough to finish it all without going outside," Kyra told Patrick. "And I'll pay my folks back immediately. I don't have that much cash, but—"

"I do," he said. "I always plan ahead, just in case. I picked up some money when I got my other things at my apartment." His grin was somewhat mischievous and certainly didn't do anything to ruin his handsome appearance. Kyra found herself smiling back.

"Sounds good," she said. "And I'll pay you back my half with a check, though if you prefer cash we can visit an ATM once we start going back out to work." And once she started living again on her own, she thought, but didn't mention that.

She hoped it would be soon since it would mean she was safe again. But she appreciated that Patrick would undoubtedly hang out with her as long as there were any doubts—or threats.

"We'll see," was all Patrick said, and Kyra figured she would have an argument with him when it came time for her to pay him back. One she intended to win. Sure, because he was somewhat senior to her on their CSI team, he probably earned more money, but she had always been thrifty and even with the baby coming figured she would remain comfortable with what she brought in.

And she intended to keep on working even as a mother. Her mom had offered to become their nanny, and Kyra loved the idea.

They soon called her mom back with their requests. Kyra had found it interesting that, for breakfast, Patrick wanted more of the low-sugar cereal that she had around.

Midday meals would be sandwiches with lunch meats and cheese as well as healthy, low-salt chips, plus fruits such as apples and bananas.

And for dinners, Patrick promised to cook hamburgers with salads and other meals now and then. Well, Kyra could help with that too. She also learned he wasn't against her putting together meals based on her Indian background, such as tandoori chicken and lamb vindaloo.

She'd love to cook for him... Where had that come from? They were working together, and he was protecting her, that was all. She didn't have to entertain him despite how he was caring for her safety.

But she did enjoy cooking, so she'd at least ask her parents to pick up the ingredients, and if she didn't use them now she could cook for her folks sometime soon.

"All of that sounds good," her mom said when Kyra was finished letting her know their list.

"Sure, but it's a lot. Feel free to whittle it down a bit. Hopefully we won't be hanging out here long."

"We'll see." Her mother sounded hopeful they would be. "And it will be so nice if you can make some meals for that kind, sweet man who's looking out for you."

"Right." Kyra wasn't going to argue with her mother.

And in fact she'd clearly had the same idea, or why ask for the kinds of food she would have to prepare for them?

"See you soon, dear." And her mom hung up.

"I'm done eating," Patrick said. "You too?"

"Yes," Kyra agreed.

"Good. Let's put our dishes away. Then we'll call

Colleen and check on the patrols around here. After that, we can get in touch with our gang and learn what's going on with the investigation."

"Great." In a few minutes Kyra had rinsed off their cereal bowls and spoons and stuck them in the dishwasher. They both kept their coffee cups, though Kyra doubted she'd sip much more.

Instead of going to the living room and its sofa, they sat back down at the kitchen table, where Patrick used his phone to make the first call. He put it on speaker.

"How are you both?" Kyra recognized Colleen's voice immediately.

"Last night went fine," Patrick assured her. "No indication our target knows where Kyra lives."

"Glad to hear that. And you'll be glad to know we had cars patrol the neighborhood at different times, marked and unmarked, and no one reported seeing anything out of the ordinary either."

"And I'm glad to hear that," Kyra said. "But has anyone located anything helpful at the crime scene or otherwise?"

"If so, they haven't told me," Colleen replied. "Of course I'll be in touch with your fellow CSIs today."

"So will we." Patrick looked directly at Kyra over the table as he added, "From here. We won't join them in the field or at the office, for now at least."

"I figured. Anyway, stay in touch and I'll do the same. And—are you feeling all right, Kyra?"

Kyra smiled, even though their captain couldn't see her. "As well as possible under the circumstances, with my insides being kicked now and then."

Colleen laughed. "Well, take care of yourself. And Patrick, you continue to take care of her." A pause, then the captain said, "We'll get the Jewelry Slayer. You can count on it."

"Absolutely," Kyra said. But would they get him before he could steal and murder again?

Or find and kill her?

Patrick stood, walked to the nearby counter and refilled his coffee cup. He also picked up Kyra's and put a little additional coffee into it, mostly to warm it, though he figured she might not drink any more.

"Okay," he said, sitting back down. "Let's try calling our gang."

He took his phone out of his pocket, looked at his recent calls and pressed CSI, then put it on speaker. It was answered immediately by Craig. "How you guys doing?" he asked, sounding concerned, good guy that he was.

"All's well here," he said. "How about there?"

"Fine too. Rosa and Mitch stopped in first thing at our precinct office and now are back out at the crime scene, although there's no indication we've missed anything. But everything just happened yesterday, so you of all people know it's too soon to just step away, especially since we haven't figured where our perp went."

He was referring to FBI Special Agents Rosa Benckler and Mitchell Alberon, coworkers to him and subordinates to Patrick and Kyra. Both were also excellent crime scene investigators with good records of finding evidence to convict perpetrators, so having them out in the field now was a good thing.

"Glad to hear they're out working, but keep us informed about when and if they find anything."

"Fine. And is it okay to let them know they're free

to call either or both of you if they have any questions, as they're looking over the crime scene even more carefully now?"

"I think that's a good idea," Kyra responded, and Patrick could hear her unspoken words, that she would like to be out there with them, especially if they found anything at all that needed more detailed investigation.

"Okay, then. I'll let them know. And I'd imagine you'll let us know if anything else comes to mind that we should check out."

"Of course," Kyra said. Her expression suggested she was frustrated, and Patrick wished he could figure out something helpful to tell her.

And in fact he did, after they hung up. "Okay," he said as they moved back onto their favorite place since he'd arrived here: the sofa. And took their same positions once more. "Now, here's what I'd like for us to do. Let's go over all that happened yesterday moment by moment, then call to figure out who's spending the most time at the site right now. We'll talk to whoever it is like it's happening all over again so they can put their eyes and minds on it as if they were there at the time, and see if there's anything else they can come up with that we might have missed."

"Wish we could do that," Kyra said thoughtfully, looking downward as if toward her stomach. "I was pretty emotionally involved as I was attacked, so despite the fact that I'm a good CSI, the distraction could have kept me from figuring out what our perp was up to— besides stealing the evidence I'd collected. But maybe if I considered it more, I'd remember something he said or did besides that."

*Unlikely*, Patrick thought. But he said, "Yep, you're

one heck of a good investigator, but considering what the guy was up to, you—or I—could have missed something helpful. Maybe one of our more neutral coworkers who wasn't there can figure something out."

"Exactly."

Patrick figured it was a good idea, a remote way to at least attempt to get more answers.

Would they accomplish anything though?

The only way to find out would be to give it a try.

"Oh, and though I'm far from being a good artist, I want to make an initial sketch of the guy who attacked me. I have to assume it really was the Jewelry Slayer and not just someone he hired. And hopefully someone in the precinct office can use my sketch to create something more official to do some facial recognition in the system. Or if that doesn't work, they can run it through the FBI system."

"Sounds good," he said, "but let's talk first." He realized some of what they would discuss would be repetitious—but still, hopefully, useful.

Even so, he described how he'd first gotten the call from Colleen and notified Kyra—although he didn't mention he'd been concerned about whether to set her on this assignment, thanks to her condition. But under the circumstances he wanted the best CSIs on their team on the job, and that included both of them.

After he'd described the situation, Kyra had definitely wanted to help out. They'd driven quickly to the scene, and Kyra began collecting evidence from the park where the murder had been committed.

Patrick listened now as she described the items she had first seen, then, after donning rubber gloves, began picking evidence up and placing it carefully into the evidence bags.

He asked a few questions, though he didn't have to. She described it well.

Then she got to the difficult part—after he had joined her and they both heard the woman scream. That was when Patrick rushed away, concerned that someone else was being attacked, but it was just the opposite.

He'd been had, and Kyra had been attacked.

Her voice shook, though it remained strong. She sat looking down at her baby bump, and he had an urge to draw closer and put his arm around her.

Heck. Why not? "I'm so sorry, Kyra. I should never have left you. And—"

"Don't." She didn't pull away, which made him feel good, but she looked him in the face. "None of this was your fault. Or mine. Now, tell me your story before we call whoever is at the scene now, ask if they've found anything and walk them through it. Then I'll try my sketch."

# Chapter 7

Kyra was doing her best to act professional. And calm.

Even though she was quaking inside and had been since she started to tell her tale again and relive the situation.

*Again* was the operative word. It wasn't as if she hadn't discussed the details of what she recalled from yesterday's debacle before with Patrick, and with her fellow CSIs—though not in person with the others.

But they needed to know about it.

And they didn't need to know the extent of her emotions. Her fear for herself and her baby. Her anger about not controlling the situation—and finding a way to bring the Jewelry Slayer down right then. Or at least prevent him from stealing the evidence she had been working so hard to collect.

Now though, it was Patrick's turn—once more, again.

They'd discussed what he'd gone through previously as well.

And Kyra had easily sensed his fury that he had been hoodwinked, and that he hadn't been with her to prevent her attacker from grabbing the evidence.

She also had the sense he was angry with himself for not protecting her then. But his taking on her protection now more than made up for it.

She appreciated that he'd put his arm around her as if to comfort her as she talked. And she had an urge to hug him even more as he expressed his anger and concern that he hadn't been there for her, at least not at the exact moment she needed assistance.

Even as he went over, point by point, what he had done at the site while first checking the area, then regarding her evidence collection.

Next, his reaction to the woman screaming.

Kyra knew him well enough to recognize that Patrick Colton wasn't about to let someone get hurt if he could do anything about it.

And the fact that it had been a hoax?

And that she'd wound up getting confronted and attacked while Patrick was off on a false tangent?

She didn't blame him, but he clearly blamed himself as he talked now about what he wished he had done.

His description was cut off by his phone ringing— probably a good thing. He looked at the screen. "It's Rosa," he said, referring to Rosa Benckler, one of the CSIs who reported to them.

Kyra immediately went on alert. Had they found something?

Unfortunately, that wasn't why she had called.

"I'm just wondering," Rosa said over the phone's

speaker as Patrick continued to hold it, "if you could walk me through how you examined the site for evidence, Kyra, and describe as much as you can what you saw and what you did."

She had done just that, sort of, with Patrick. But Rosa explained she was at the site now, and so was Mitch. They were taking pictures, making notes, doing all they could to examine the area and locate any clues as to who had attacked Kyra and anything else they could find, including any evidence previously missed—but so far, they hadn't found any. And considering how careful Kyra had been, she suspected they wouldn't find anything she'd overlooked.

Rosa continued, "We figured your telling us what went on might add to our ability to find something new."

Maybe. But Kyra was getting tired of not only rethinking the entire horrible situation but describing it. Reliving it.

But she was a crime scene investigator. A damned good one. She would simply deal with it.

And one of these times she might recall something important that she'd forgotten. Even if she didn't, letting other people in on details might lead to the result they wanted.

"Of course." She cleared her throat, knowing she felt, and sounded, rather choked up. Then she added something else on her mind—possibly a reason to not stay home, dangerous or not. "We need to figure out a way for me to work with a tech expert so I can attempt to identify the person whose face I saw."

She was looking at Patrick now. She knew it would be better if she went to the nearby precinct office quickly and worked on a computer with a tech expert so they could show her various facial recognition details and she could point out parts that fit or ask them to try something else. Or the FBI office, but it was farther away.

Sure, it could be done remotely. And she would try a sketch in a little while. But she really believed being one-on-one with an expert would make things go better and faster, and possibly more accurately.

Patrick's expression didn't change, and she figured he might be considering what she said but suspected it didn't modify his intent to keep her confined here for her safety.

"Sounds good to me," Rosa said. "But you should figure that out. Meanwhile, I understand that you ended up working on the street curb just outside the park to pick up possible evidence, right? I'm standing right now where I believe you were."

She described the place further and Kyra agreed Rosa was in the appropriate location. They talked longer about items Kyra remembered picking up and placing into bags, from the pen and nail file to the sunglasses, the piece of fabric and more.

"And the dirt here along the curb. There's still a surprising amount of it," Rosa said.

Kyra shuddered as she recalled how her attacker had not only grabbed the evidence bag but also rubbed his feet over that dirt, as if to be sure he left no footprints or anything else.

She recalled how she had attempted to stop him, as if she had ever forgotten.

And grabbed his hood and pulled it away from his face...and saw it now again in her mind. In enough detail?

She must have been reacting more than she realized, since Patrick, who had been staring her straight in the eyes as she'd talked, suddenly said, "Okay, Rosa. How about if you describe everything you see right now. I think Kyra has told you enough."

Kyra felt herself smile in gratitude. Oh, yes. Her recollections, recounted even just this one extra, detailed time, had made her feel terrified again.

Not that she needed to feel scared now.

That episode had been yesterday, and it was over. She was a good distance from the crime scene.

And her wonderful coworker was with her, protecting her.

She listened now as Rosa described the site pretty much as Kyra remembered it—and had just described it herself. But some things were different. Although crime scene tape remained to block off some areas, Rosa said, a lot of the area was open now and people were visiting the park and walking along parts of the sidewalk, probably somewhat like the place usually was.

Except for the most critical areas, which were appropriately blocked off.

"Anyway," Rosa finally said, "I'm going to look around a bit more and connect again with Mitch, who's closer to the building where that woman who yelled out apparently disappeared." Yes, they'd been told the whole story.

"Sounds good," Patrick said.

"Keep us informed," added Kyra. She knew her voice still sounded raspy, as it had during a lot of their conversation. "And watch out for a guy with a thin face, dark brown eyes and sparse black facial hair." Oh, yes, she recalled what he looked like, but in enough detail? She

hoped so, and that she'd be able to describe him sufficiently to get appropriate techs to come up with a visual
on the computer. But she would try a sketch anyway.

And it was unlikely he'd be back there today—right?

"Of course," Rosa said, then added, "I hope it was
okay to ask you to go over what you recalled, Kyra. I just
figured that since you couldn't be here, your discussion
and description might help us as much as if you could
point things out, and I think it has, at least to some extent. But are you okay?"

Their coworkers were aware of Kyra's pregnancy.
And they might be concerned about her anyway, considering the fact she'd been attacked while on the job.

Kyra appreciated their concern and said so. "I'm fine,
Rosa. Thanks. And talking about the situation in a way
that will hopefully help lead to a good resolution makes
me feel even better." She paused, then added, "And I
hope Mitch and you and everyone else are being careful too. We know the Jewelry Slayer is capable of some
pretty bad stuff."

"We certainly do," Rosa said loudly. "And we're absolutely being careful. Now, you take good care of yourself, Kyra, and you take good care of her too, Patrick.
And yourself."

"Will do," Patrick responded. "And keep in touch.
We'll call you often to see how things are going, and
feel free to contact us as well." He didn't make any of
what he said a question, Kyra noticed, nor should he.

He was in charge of their team, and so was she.

And they definitely would want updates.

Oh, how she hoped their team found something and
brought the Jewelry Slayer in quickly. Never mind if

she didn't get any credit for it. She'd done her job so far, and hopefully that would be enough.

If not, she wanted to do her best to identify the guy who'd attacked her, who she believed had to be the Jewelry Slayer, by attempting to use what she had seen of his face to point out his features. Or do anything else necessary to locate him and bring him in.

He needed to be stopped before he could hurt anyone else—or even steal more jewelry.

Damn, but Kyra wished she could be out there doing more.

But for her baby's sake even more than her own, she would listen to Patrick and stay home.

At least for this moment.

Patrick wished he could do more than physically protect Kyra.

He could tell from her demeanor, the tone of her voice, her clear determination to be professional as if attempting to hide what she was really thinking, that the ongoing conversations about all that had happened yesterday, with him and now with Rosa, were grating on her, even keeping her frightened.

Not that she would admit it.

Yet another reason to admire this beautiful and skilled coworker.

And there were plenty of other reasons, which he attempted not to dwell on.

Now, he joined the conversation with Rosa, assuring her he'd been listening and thanking her for her cogent questions and hard work. Then he reminded her to keep in touch, and have Mitch call them too. He and Kyra said goodbye, and he hung up.

"You okay?" he couldn't help asking.

"Of course, though I wish things were obvious to Rosa and Mitch so they could help track down the Jewelry Slayer right away while they're at the crime scene."

"Agreed," Patrick said, knowing it was a longshot. But not having Kyra need to get further involved—or in more danger—would be a major plus.

"But that would mean they're even better CSIs than I am, so maybe that wouldn't be such a good idea." Kyra's smile told him she was joking, or at least trying to, so he decided to play along.

"Better than me too, obviously. So maybe it wouldn't be such a good idea after all."

Her sweet smile turned into one of frustration. "I just wish I'd done something different when I could have caught the guy, not just gotten a good look at him. Even at that, I really want to do something as soon as possible to make sure my memory stays intact about what he looked like, and hopefully even figure out, with the help of our techs who work on identification, exactly who he is." She sighed. "I was kidding, or trying to, but I really wonder now if I'm as good a CSI as I thought I was."

Again Patrick gave into his urge to take Kyra into his arms. Okay, it wasn't entirely professional. But his colleague needed to have her morale boosted. That was all it was.

But the feeling of her in his arms as he drew her against him felt anything but professional, especially the way parts of his body reacted, not unexpectedly, but highly inappropriately.

"You're a damn good crime scene investigator, Kyra," he said brusquely. "There's no reason to think otherwise.

You were in a difficult situation. Yeah, the guy played both of us. And sure, after the murder committed there, we knew that whoever it was would probably do anything to save himself. But what he did, somehow getting that woman to scream and run away, and attacking you… No way could we have anticipated that. And you were already doing one hell of a good job grabbing up the evidence in a totally skilled manner. I'm just glad he didn't—"

He hesitated. He was definitely glad the SOB had only played Kyra and hadn't really hurt her, except for her ego.

It could have been a whole lot worse. And it might have been, if he hadn't shown up when he did.

Kyra threw her arms around him now too. They were facing each other, so he felt her baby bump against him—close to where his body was overreacting.

He should pull away, but that might only call more attention to himself, so he held her even closer, moving his head down till he felt her soft hair against his cheek.

"Yes," Kyra said softly. "I'm glad the Jewelry Slayer didn't slay me too. Yet. But since he knows I saw him… Well, I'm the one in this room who's really glad. Glad you're here to make sure I remain okay."

She pulled back and looked up into his face with her lovely dark eyes.

Good thing her phone rang or he might have done something even more inappropriate and kissed her.

Kyra glanced at her phone screen, then put it up to her ear. "Hi, Mom. Where—"

She paused, and Patrick figured her mother was answering her question without it being complete.

"Great," Kyra soon said. She glanced at Patrick.

"Yes, we'll come down and let you in." Apparently her mother said something else since Kyra paused, then said, with her eyes boring into Patrick's with the message she clearly intended to impart. "That's right. Patrick will come and let you in. I'll stay safe locked in my apartment and wait for you here."

Smart lady, Patrick thought. She obviously wanted everything to go well for her daughter's safety.

Well, so did Patrick.

As Kyra pressed the phone to end the call, he said, "You wait right here. I'll make sure everything's locked up and check the hallway and around the rest of the area. Then I'll go meet your folks."

# Chapter 8

Kyra appreciated that her parents wanted to do what they could to make sure she stayed safe—like meeting her protector at her building's doorway and letting him guide them in. Neither of them had been in law enforcement, but they seemed proud of her yet highly concerned about what she did and often asked questions about how she protected herself.

Previously, she had been able to laugh it off. But now—well, they also knew she had been in a dangerous situation, even if her trip to the hospital, where they had come to see her, had turned out to be almost unnecessary.

Fortunately.

She waited now in her kitchen, looking around to determine where to store the provisions her parents brought, assuming they'd picked up the things she'd requested. And knowing them, they had.

She wondered what they were saying to Patrick right

now. And what he was saying to them about her welfare and how he was ensuring that she, and her baby, remained okay.

Also knowing her folks, she figured they would take this short opportunity outside her presence to interrogate the man currently in charge of making sure she stayed safe.

Which made her wish she was with them now to make sure they weren't bombarding Patrick with demands. Oh, in the nicest of ways, of course. Both her parents were sweet and caring and very polite.

But they also both would do anything to ensure she was well taken care of, even under better circumstances.

And now—

She went into the living room and sat down but rose almost immediately as she heard the key at the door. In a moment the door opened. All three came in—her mom, then her dad and finally Patrick—each carrying large paper bags.

"Hi, honey," her mom called, as her dad also said unnecessarily, "We're here, Kyra."

"Hi, Mom. Hi, Dad. Glad you've arrived."

They smiled and headed past her toward the kitchen. She followed and saw them put the bags on the counter, then take off their jackets and lay them on a chair. In moments, they joined her in the living room. She was soon wrapped in warm parental hugs and hugged back, watching around her folks as Patrick grinned at them.

As usual when she was being casual, her mom wore a long shirt over dark slacks. This time, it was a pink floral print. And her dad had no problem looking like any other local man, in a long-sleeved denim shirt over jeans.

"Hey," Patrick said. "Good to see you both…and all the stuff you brought."

"Are you jealous that I'm getting all the attention?" Kyra couldn't help joking, but her mom evidently took it seriously.

"We can't leave this wonderful man who's protecting our daughter so thoughtfully out of this."

Kyra figured she should have stayed quiet, since in a moment Patrick was smothered in a hug from her mom. Not her dad though. No hugs, at least. But when her mom backed away, Sam Patel stepped forward and shook Patrick's hand.

"I thank you too," her dad said.

And as Patrick shook his hand back, he just said, "No problem."

Which was definitely untrue. It had to be a problem for this head CSI, working on a major case, to be away from the crime scene and hanging out with a coworker in her apartment, and dealing with the gratitude expressed by that coworker's overly zealous parents.

Yet another reason to appreciate Patrick. Not that she needed one.

"Come into the kitchen," her mom said. "I want to go over the things we brought. We got everything on your list, I think, but added some others we thought you might need."

Kyra wasn't surprised. Her parents always tried to go overboard in caring for her, from the time she'd been a child.

And now that she was expecting their first grandchild, they had become even more generous.

They put things on shelves in the freezer side of her refrigerator first, including some frozen vegetables that would last longer than the fresh produce, which had also been brought in plentiful amounts. Then things went into the fridge itself—that produce, including lettuce and tomatoes, milk for their cereal, meats and more. Other things went into kitchen cabinets, like bottled water. Kyra was happy that among all of it were items she would need to make some of the Indian dishes she hoped to cook for Patrick while they hung out here.

When they were done, Kyra asked, "Would you like me to boil water for some tea?" That was their preference over coffee, and she hoped they would stay at least a short while.

"Of course," her mom said. "But you sit down. I'll take care of it."

That wasn't a surprise either, but with a glance at Patrick she did as her mother requested, and so did he. In a short while, the four of them sat at the kitchen table with tea in front of them, as well as cinnamon and pecan sweet rolls—not of Indian origin, but Kyra had shared some with her folks previously and knew they were tasty. They'd brought fixings for lunch sandwiches along with everything else, but it wasn't quite time for that yet, so this snack was good.

The conversation her mom started wasn't so good though. Watching Patrick as she held a roll in her hand, Riya said, "As you know, Patrick, we really appreciate your watching our girl, since we know she's been in danger. But what do you know now? Is whoever attacked her coming after her again? Here? Even with you here, are the police also doing things to protect her? As I said, what do you know?"

Kyra kept her eyes from rolling in frustration. She wanted to tell her mom that everything was fine, that she didn't need to worry. But she knew her mother well enough to recognize that no matter what she said, the worrying would continue.

"Unfortunately, nothing is resolved yet," Patrick said, taking a sip of his tea. It was a good herbal tea, but Kyra had no idea if he liked it. It certainly wasn't as strong as black coffee. "But you can be sure the investigation is continuing in full force," he continued, obviously wanting to reassure her parents—a very good thing, Kyra thought. "We're in touch with others in our FBI department and the local police force. There's been more investigation of the crime scene, as well as the homicide that led up to our needing to find the evidence we were seeking there. And everyone who is investigating knows what happened and is working even harder to get things resolved."

That all seemed true, Kyra thought. Yes, the investigation was continuing and was one of the main focuses of the precinct where they currently worked, as well as the local FBI.

"I get it," her dad said. "And you can be sure we appreciate all that's being done—especially what you're doing, Patrick. Please keep us informed, both of you. I think it's time for us to leave, Riya." He looked at Kyra's mom.

"Okay," she said, though her tone sounded reluctant. Kyra understood that her mom was protective too.

All the more reason for her folks to leave. Not that she anticipated an attack here this afternoon—or hopefully ever. But if the Jewelry Slayer did learn where she lived and decided to get revenge for her seeing his face, Kyra would feel a lot better if it was just Patrick and her here facing him, and they didn't need to protect her parents too.

Even though that wasn't why they intended to leave before lunch, she was sure. They might have things to do that afternoon—more shopping, maybe.

Or maybe they wanted to give Patrick and her more alone time, and not just because he was protecting her.

In this short amount of time, it had become obvious that they considered Patrick not only her bodyguard but a man who had the potential of becoming more in her life.

Not going to happen, but this wasn't the time to talk to them about that.

They all stood up around the kitchen table, and her mom, being her mom, immediately bussed the teacups and paper towels her dad and she had used, tossing the towels and putting the cups into the sink.

While her mom did that, Kyra saw Patrick attempt to give her dad some money, undoubtedly to pay for the groceries. They had a bit of a disagreement, but not a nasty one.

"It's okay," she said to Patrick, then told her father, "Thanks, Dad. But you know that's not the end of this."

"Oh, yes, it is, honey," he said.

Kyra aimed a glance at Patrick, then back at her dad. "We'll see. In any case, we appreciate your bringing everything and spending time with us." And she really did.

"Oh, honey," her mom said as she walked her parents to the apartment's door. "You know Thanksgiving is soon. We'd love to have both of you join us." She managed a glance around Kyra toward Patrick, as if wanting to make sure he heard.

Kyra was sure he did. But she wasn't sure it made

sense for them to get together at her parents' place, or even here.

They'd just have to see how the investigation—and capture of the Jewelry Slayer—progressed.

"Thanks, Mom," Kyra said. "We'll see."

She hugged both her parents—and was glad when Patrick said he would accompany them outside.

Patrick joined Kyra's parents in the elevator going down to the first floor. Unsurprisingly, they chatted again about how glad they were that he was here and watching over their daughter. He came from a family where people watched out for each other, so he understood their concerns.

His situation was very different though. His father had been murdered by a serial killer when he was very young, and his mother had never gotten over it. But at least he had two brothers and a sister plus some close cousins. And he and his siblings had decided to dedicate their careers to tracking and capturing serial killers.

Like the Jewelry Slayer.

When the elcvator door opened, Patrick got out first. He checked around and didn't see any people, or even any movement, on the ground floor. He nevertheless walked outside with them to their car.

"You're protecting us too, aren't you?" Sam Patel asked him.

"Just keeping an eye on things around here," Patrick replied.

"And we definitely appreciate all you're doing," Kyra's dad said. Her mother nodded vehemently.

"We can tell you two really care about each other,"

Riya said. "And that's a good thing. We hope we see you again soon, hopefully for Thanksgiving if not before."

She'd mentioned that previously. Would it be a good idea for them to get together with Kyra's family for the holiday?

Patrick had to assume, since Thanksgiving wasn't far off, that he would still be living with Kyra.

If not, that would mean things had gotten a lot better than he anticipated, and the killer they were after had been taken into custody.

Well, he could wish, but he knew better than to assume things would go well. They'd just have to see if it made sense when Thanksgiving arrived to turn the holiday into a family affair for her. And the more they got together with her family, the more likely that her parents could be endangered too. At this point, Patrick had told Colleen about Kyra's folks but hadn't requested any patrols be sent to keep an eye on them and their home—just around here. But that could change.

No, better that they not spend Thanksgiving together with the Patels, although he would have to see how things worked out.

The Patels got into their car, an aging sedan, and Patrick watched as they drove off.

He also watched the street around the building. A black SUV drove by, and Patrick glanced inside. There were a couple of uniformed officers inside.

Good. The area remained subject to patrols, as he'd discussed with Colleen. He nevertheless stood there for another moment, then walked around the apartment building, just to make sure nothing appeared amiss.

No indication that the Jewelry Slayer was hanging

around, ready to burst in and harm the investigator who'd seen his face.

But that didn't necessarily mean the guy didn't know where Kyra was, or that he wasn't anywhere near there. He'd not done a great job of hiding at the murder scene, but since he hadn't yet been arrested he must have some smarts about keeping away from the authorities.

Maybe he had decided to flee. Not that Patrick wanted the jerk to get away, but that would at least be safer for Kyra and everyone else around there.

Patrick had walked up the steps, and he opened the door to each hallway as he got there and peeked down it. He saw people at the end of the hall on the third floor, but they included kids, so he assumed they were residents, a family. In any case, he had no reason to believe the guy with them was anyone but the father.

Not the Jewelry Slayer.

He soon reached the fourth floor and headed down that hall to Kyra's apartment.

He had brought the key and let himself in. He didn't see Kyra immediately, and his heart jumped in concern. That was silly, he told himself. She could be in the bedroom or bathroom, not necessarily waiting in the living room where he could see her right away.

Wherever she was though, he had to find her.

It didn't take long. She was in the kitchen, sitting at the same place at the table where she'd been earlier.

Her cup of herbal tea was near her—no surprise. But what she was doing was somewhat surprising.

Or not. He figured she would get started on attempting to sketch the face she'd seen of the Jewelry Slayer soon, even though she wanted to have a more technical rendering done since she considered herself a bad artist.

But anything might help.

"Hi," he said softly, hoping not to startle her. But she didn't even look up. She just waved her left hand in his direction.

He gathered she'd already known he was there.

"I called Colleen," she said, "and confirmed the patrols around here would keep an eye on my folks as they left. And right now, I want you to see this. It only vaguely resembles the face I saw. But at least it's a start, and it'll hopefully help me keep it in my memory."

He walked over toward her and looked down over her shoulder.

And made himself stop breathing, at least for a moment.

She might not be the best artist. He recognized that.

But somehow she had gotten into her sketch a rendering that suggested one nasty, furious butcher of a man, glaring at her with angry eyes and clenched, even, large white teeth.

A black hood around most of his face.

A hint of dark hair along his cheeks.

No, not a perfect picture. But Patrick figured it might help them identify the Jewelry Slayer if they found someone during their search.

And get the damned killer, and attacker, convicted of his crimes.

## Chapter 9

Kyra wished she had more skills in sketching.

Even so, she believed she had gotten at least some of the most important features she'd seen of the Jewelry Slayer's face down on paper, using a pencil since she sometimes erased things that didn't seem quite right and tried again.

But this would not be enough to get him convicted, even if they found someone who resembled her drawing. Unless he happened to be holding the evidence he grabbed. But she figured the Jewelry Slayer would have hidden most of it, maybe disposed of it.

Although he might be holding on to the most valuable items he stole, at least till he could sell them. Still…

"I'm sorry," she sighed to Patrick. "I tried but know it's not the best possible rendering—and I don't believe I'm capable of much better. At least it shows I have some recollection of what I saw despite my tension at the time. But—"

"But it's quite good," he said, sitting down beside her at the table. "We should be able to discern the features you depicted if we see anyone like that. Better yet, it shows you not only got a good look at the guy, as we knew, but you can recall details of what he looked like. And I've been pondering what to do to follow up on your viewing of him, and now I know it makes a lot of sense. Let's call Walt Elderson. I've got some ideas about how he can help even if we don't go to the precinct to have him use his dedicated computers to add more detail to your drawing."

Walt Elderson was the 130th Precinct's Deputy Commissioner of Information Technology, a civilian who was nevertheless part of their force. His name, Elderson, seemed a misnomer, since Walt was fairly young, especially for his superior position—maybe in his late twenties. He was a Black man who had apparently been working in technology since he was a kid, and was quite skilled with his knowledge and use of it for police purposes. Kyra had also met him when they started working with the precinct.

"Okay. I hope he comes up with something. You too. But otherwise, I really want to go to the precinct, even just a short trip, to work with him or one of the other techs on the computer. They can at least scan my drawing in and maybe use it to come up with something a lot better."

"Let's see," Patrick said. He had pulled his phone from his pocket and now pushed in a number that Kyra assumed was the direct connection to the tech department.

"Hi, this is Patrick Colton of the CSI team," he said quickly. "Can I speak with Walt?"

In a few seconds he was connected. "Hi, Walt," he said. "I'm going to put you on speaker. I want us both to talk to Kyra Patel, who's with me." He pushed another button, then held his phone in his hand with his elbow resting on the table.

"I heard there's something going on," said a moderately deep voice Kyra recognized as Walt's—not that she'd worked with him a lot, but when she'd recently needed guidance with a technical issue, he was the one she'd talked to. "Is Kyra okay?"

"Yes, and we want your help."

Kyra listened as Patrick explained the situation about her being attacked at the crime scene while collecting evidence against the Jewelry Slayer.

"Yeah, I heard about that," Walt said. "How can I help?"

Kyra decided to talk. "Well, I pulled the perp's mask off while we were struggling and saw his face. And I've done a preliminary sketch of what I saw. I want to get a much better version that actually looks like him on the precinct's computer."

"Wow," Walt said. "Got it. Yeah, I can help with that. But are you really okay, Kyra?"

"Yes," she said.

"But for now she's not able to go to the precinct," Patrick added, "in case our target is watching for her there. So far, no one has spotted him around here or anywhere else, or at least no one who knows who he is."

"So where are you hanging out?" Walt asked, then said, "Never mind. I don't think our phones are tapped, but just in case…"

"You can get that information from Captain Colleen," Patrick said. "Assuming you've got a way to bring some kind of computer equipment to us when I tell you in general where we are, and work with Kyra on getting the face she remembers onto the system."

"Oh, yeah. I can do that," Walt said. "I've got a laptop with special programming we can work with, and then I can upload what we come up with onto the precinct's system."

"That's wonderful," Kyra said. "Can you come here this afternoon?" It was only midday now. There was still time today when they could actually get something done—she hoped.

"I do have something important scheduled later," Walt said, dashing her hopes. But then he added, "Tell you what. Give me a few minutes to try to change it. If I can, then I'll be glad to come to wherever you are a little later."

Kyra's hopes had momentarily tanked, but now she felt a bit better—assuming Walt actually could modify his schedule.

"Let us know as soon as possible," Patrick said. "Talk to you later." He hung up.

Kyra looked at him. "Well, if he can't make it today we can aim for tomorrow." But she wanted to get this done right away to give those out there hunting the Jewelry Slayer this additional help.

And make sure she worked on a rendering that was a lot better, especially while her memory of what he looked like remained strong.

"Yeah," Patrick said. "That's what we'll do." But he sounded as potentially frustrated as she felt.

"Tell you what. If he can't make it today, let's go to

the precinct very briefly and carefully tomorrow. We can work with him then if he's available, and if not we can get one of the other tech experts, or visit the FBI, or—"

Interesting that Patrick's face looked just as handsome when he was clearly angry. "You know we're not leaving here for now. I don't know when that will change, but—"

His phone rang again before Kyra had a chance to rebut what he was saying. He continued to glare as he answered after checking the phone screen for who it was.

Fortunately, it was Walt. He wasn't on speaker then, but Kyra figured she knew what he was saying, or at least the gist of it. "Great," Patrick said. He put the phone on speaker then as he looked at her. "Walt said he was able to change his plans and will head here soon."

"But I need to know where *here* is," Walt said. "Though I can guess since you said to check with our captain."

"My home," Kyra replied without a hint of where it was. She still didn't think anyone was eavesdropping, but just in case…

"Okay," Walt said. "If I have any problem finding it, or feel the info will get compromised as I check into it, I'll let you know. Otherwise, expect me there in about an hour, assuming you're not too far from the precinct offices."

"Great," Kyra said, feeling both relieved and a touch concerned, just in case. "See you soon."

It was around two in the afternoon, and Patrick had just received another call from Walt, the second in the last hour. The first had been to tell Patrick he'd be heading there soon. Yes, he had gotten the information about Kyra's address from Captain Colleen, who'd gotten their personal info when the CSI team was formed.

And in the call he just received, Walt said he was parked nearby and soon would be at the apartment building. Patrick had already informed him about the process of getting inside—call him again when he was right outside, and he would come downstairs to accompany Walt to Kyra's apartment.

Patrick was fine with the precinct's top tech guy being the one to help them, even though his sister, Ashlynn, also with the FBI, was a tech expert too.

"I'm going downstairs to meet Walt now," Patrick told Kyra. She was again—still—sitting at the kitchen table with her drawing in front of her, occasionally making another small change to it. They'd taken time out for a quick lunch—sandwiches with some of the meats Kyra's folks had brought, plus bottled water.

Patrick had sensed Kyra's mood was excited that she'd soon have someone to help come up with a really good picture of the man who'd attacked her. And frustrated that she hadn't come up with a better picture herself.

Never mind that he'd tried to reassure her that what she had done already was amazing, certainly a wonderful start to a picture that should help law enforcement zero in on the man who had attacked her.

"Great." Kyra's smile really did appear relieved. "And are you doing your usual walk around the building and yard first?"

He had done that a couple of times since they'd last talked to Walt. It was a major reason why Patrick was there, after all: keeping track of their surroundings.

Making sure no one was there to hurt Kyra.

"My last one was recent enough," he said, hoping it was true. And he would take a quick check of the halls, as well as outside near the door, as he let Walt in.

"Okay. I'm looking forward to seeing the electronic version of my picture of the guy who attacked me that we can come up with. Hopefully, it'll be realistic—and whatever I see on the screen won't cause me to change the image in my mind of the features I saw."

Patrick wanted to give Kyra a hug, and this wasn't the first time, nor the only reason. But he sympathized with her. He'd already seen how detailed her nevertheless incomplete pencil sketch was. Could she keep that going, help Walt come up with a perfect rendering of the Jewelry Slayer's face?

Even if she did, how would they know it?

Well, whatever it looked like, it would be better than nothing, and most likely an improvement on her basic sketching.

They'd see...

"I'm looking forward to it too," he responded to her. "Right now, I'll head downstairs."

Which he did, after locking the apartment door behind him. He had brought Kyra's key and put it back in his pocket—near where he kept his gun. He'd have to ask her if she had a spare set, then hang on to it, but this remained okay for now. He checked the hallway around him. No one was there. No doors were open, or any indications of anything amiss.

He headed to the stairway again. And yes, he did peer out at the other hallways on the way down. There were a few people toward the end of the third floor, and a couple more on the ground floor, but no one near him—or appearing to be heading upstairs toward Kyra's apartment. Best he could tell, they were probably residents, including a family with kids.

He reached the front door and turned the switch to unlock it. Walt stood there, a large computer case on the ground beside him. "Greetings, Patrick," he said. "You ready for me to do my thing?"

"I've been ready for hours," Patrick told him, waving him inside.

Walt picked up his bag and moved around Patrick, who took a step outside to look around yet again.

All seemed okay. He saw no one staring at the building and just a few cars driving by at a normal speed.

He didn't allow himself to feel perfectly safe, but at least nothing made him any more worried than usual at the moment.

Locking the door behind them, he looked at the new arrival and smiled. "Have you ever gone on the road before to use your technology this way?"

"Nope," Walt said. "There's always a first time. And I'm looking forward to seeing how this works out."

Walt Elderson was a couple inches taller than Patrick's five feet ten. He wore a long-sleeved blue shirt over black trousers, a typical outfit for those at the precinct who weren't in uniform. His dark hair was short, framing his good-looking African American face.

"I've been using the stairway," Patrick told him, "but let's take an elevator. I'll bet your bag is a bit heavy."

"It is, but whatever works best is fine with me."

Patrick figured that getting to the fourth floor the fastest way was the way to go. He let Walt carry his own bag, showing him through the large, decorative lobby to the bank of three elevators. The car in the middle arrived quickly, and Patrick held the door for Walt to enter.

Soon, they were headed up to the fourth floor, and when they arrived and the door opened Patrick got out first and looked around, just in case.

He saw no one there, so he held the door while Walt got out with his bag. "Fourth door on the right," Patrick said, and when they arrived he pulled out the key to open it.

Walt glanced at him before entering, his eyes wide and somehow suggestive. "You're right at home here, aren't you?"

"I'm doing all I can to keep my coworker safe," Patrick replied, trying not to sound gruff. He knew Walt was prone to joking and figured that was what he was doing now—not really implying Patrick had anything going on with Kyra. He hoped. "Now, go on in." He thrust the door open and pointed inside. Walt preceded him as he should, and Patrick followed, pulling the door shut behind him and locking it once more.

Kyra stood up from the sofa to join them at the entry. "Hi, Walt," she said. She looked down at the bag he carried. "I hope that contains some really good technological stuff to help get a respectable view of the face I recall."

"Why else would I be here?" Walt grinned at her. "And I hope you actually got a good view of that face, so you can describe it to me and maybe recognize someone as I bring pictures up on my computer."

"That's certainly my intent," Kyra said. "And here's the start of what I've done so far."

Patrick had noticed the piece of paper in Kyra's hand as she approached, and now she held it up to show Walt.

"Hey, that looks like a pretty good start," the information technology expert said. "But I'll bet we'll come up with something a whole lot better."

"I hope so," Kyra said. "Let's go into the kitchen to put your equipment on the table and work from there."

"Sounds good." Walt followed Kyra, and as they sat down, he said, "I don't think I'll try coming up with what your baby looks like just yet though."

He was looking at Kyra's baby bump, and Patrick kept his hands from forming into fists. Their techie coworker was just joking again. And Kyra laughed without seeming embarrassed or angry. Patrick realized his own irritated reactions to that joke and Walt's earlier one were somewhat inappropriate, probably a result of the stress of the situation they were in.

"Too bad that won't work too," he joked back this time. "Now, why don't we get started?"

# Chapter 10

Was this going to work? Kyra certainly hoped so. All she could do now was rely on Walt and whatever equipment he had with him, and see what happened.

"Okay," he said. "Glad we're sitting beside each other. And here's the very expensive and formidable facial recognition gadgetry I brought."

She watched as he removed a fair-sized laptop computer from his nylon bag, along with a small electronic tablet.

"Can we plug this computer in? I charged it before I left the office, but it may need a lot more power before we're through." He also brought out a long extension cord.

"There's an outlet right behind us," she said, but before she could point to it, Patrick, who'd sat across from them, came over and took the cord, plugging it into the outlet. "Thanks," she told him.

"Ditto," Walt said. "Now, here's what we'll do. Just so you know, there are several similar kinds of software to help do realistic face sketches, even better than most artists."

"Definitely better than me," Kyra couldn't help saying.

"I think so, though what you've done so far should help a lot. In fact—" Walt took the paper Kyra had laid down on the table and set it beside his computer, which he had booted up. He ran the tablet gadget over it, and in moments her sketch was reproduced on the screen. Some parts were lighter than the rest, but it looked pretty much like the original.

"Wow," Kyra said, and once more Patrick rose to join them.

He looked at the screen too. "Yes, wow," he agreed.

"Okay, then," Walt said. "We've got a good start. Now, I gather from this area that the guy was wearing some kind of scarf or hoodie." He pointed to where Kyra had attempted to show how part of the perp's neck remained hidden, despite how she had pulled off most of his hood. She'd tried to sketch what she hoped resembled fabric that only covered some of the lowest portion of his face, as had been the reality.

"That's right," she said. "But I was able to see most of his face anyway when I pulled at it."

"Looks like," Walt said. "Okay, let's start with what you could see. Tell me his complexion—white, Caucasian, I assume from this."

"Yes," she said. "Maybe a touch dark, as if he was slightly tanned, although it is November so at least some of whatever tan he might have had in summer would have faded."

"Got it." Walt did some manipulation on the keyboard, and the pencil sketch now on the screen resembling Kyra's picture on white paper became a color picture of the man's face. "A little lighter? Darker? Other coloration?" he asked.

"That looks about right." She was amazed at how what had been her sketch had begun to resemble an actual in-color picture of her attacker's face, with some of the pencil tracks removed. But more detail was needed.

And… Well, she knew she remembered her emotions and at least some of the features. But she couldn't be certain everything was correct. Those emotions that were triggered by what happened might also have created at least partially incorrect recollections.

"Let's try those eyes next. They look pretty furious, right?"

"Oh, yes." Kyra felt herself shudder as she recalled the rage she had seen as the man looked at her, clearly infuriated that she'd gotten to see his face rather than just let him steal the evidence, destroy what might have been left on the ground and run off, as he had clearly intended.

No doubt about her remembering that.

She wished she could just shove it all into the past now and not even think about it. But it wasn't as if the man had only confronted her.

He had murdered someone.

He needed to be caught and incarcerated. He needed to pay for what he'd done.

Including what he had done to her, but that was only a tiny portion of the crimes he had committed.

"So what color were those eyes?" Walt asked.

"Brown. Very deep brown." She recalled that well.

She also recalled, "And I'm not sure my drawing is clear enough about how thick his brows were. Black brows, and they were bent, curved, in more than a scowl."

"Oh, yeah, fury," Walt confirmed.

"Definitely," Kyra said.

And in moments, after puttering with some keys on the computer, Walt had made the angry face even closer to what Kyra thought she remembered.

She felt herself shudder now despite trying to remain calm.

"How's this?" Walt asked.

"Very similar to what I recall," she said. "His hair was as dark as his brows, and that's depicted fine." In her drawing, she had shown the guy's hair as thin but longish at the top and along his sideburns.

Patrick now stood behind her, also looking at the computer screen, and Kyra felt his hand squeeze her shoulder gently, as if in sympathy. He must see how this highly difficult memory was affecting her.

Hard. Very hard.

But not only was Patrick protecting her from this man, her nemesis, whose picture she was attempting to help Walt get perfect. His touching her that way showed he was also attempting to protect her from her own fear and the emotions she tried to control, but not entirely successfully.

"Okay, next," Walt said. "The mouth. From what you've shown it was partly open, teeth gritted. Is the shape pretty much as you recall?"

"Yes, but of course this just represents a moment in time, right after he turned and I was able to pull his hoodie off. If I did additional drawings, I'd also try to depict how he looked as he threatened me before he ran off." At least how she recalled it. "That mouth of his was open even more."

"Well, if we try more drawings later I'll want you to describe that better too. But for now—talk to me about his teeth. I see you tried to sketch them. Were they as perfect as you depicted? All in a row, no gaps?"

"That's what I recall," Kyra said. Her nervousness was apparently affecting her body more now, as the baby was moving. She put her hands on her stomach in an attempt to calm the poor thing, even while she moved her shoulders forward slightly as she looked even more closely at the color picture derived from her black-and-white outline. "I think his front teeth were a little longer, but that could be just because I focused on them as he frowned at me with all that obvious anger."

"Well, let's give this a try," Walt said as he again leaned over the keyboard and moved his fingers on the touchpad. Sure enough, those teeth grew a bit longer. "Better?"

"Yes," Kyra agreed. "And—well, I don't think they were quite that white."

Walt played some more with the picture on the computer and the teeth on the glowering face grew a bit more beige. "Again, better?"

"Yes," Kyra said.

For a while, they discussed every detail, including the minimal dark facial hair that most likely indicated the guy had shaved that morning.

Then they were through. "I'll get this to the precinct and run it through our digital shots in our multiagency facial recognition computer files," Walt said. "And— well, I think you did a great job here, Kyra. You should know though, that I've done similar things before and the pictures as created here aren't always in the system, but sometimes the person trying to identify who they saw does recognize a face that is in the system who's a bit different. And… I've heard that changes in hormones thanks to stress while someone's viewing a suspect can make a difference in what they see too—and the fact you're expecting could be a factor. Let's just see how this works out, okay?"

Kyra felt herself deflate a bit internally. She'd seen the guy, yes. And as someone in law enforcement she felt she'd learned at least a bit what to look for in features of someone she was observing and wanting to remember.

But was she certain the picture she'd sketched, now more detailed on the screen, was identical to the man who'd attacked her?

Close, at least. Or so she hoped.

But as she had already considered, it still might not be perfect. And the idea of her hormones affecting what she saw…

She tried not to feel frustration. But so far, all she was doing was hiding. And trying to do something to help catch the Jewelry Slayer.

But she hadn't been successful yet, and neither had others in and around the precinct who were actually out there looking for him and the evidence he had stolen.

"So… Just in case," Walt said, "if we don't find a match in the system for this picture, when can you come in to look at our online files in case the perp's picture does happen to be there?"

Kyra felt a bit irritated as Walt moved his gaze from her to Patrick, now beside her. He was asking her protector what came next. But she was in charge of her life. She always had been, and that was true now.

Yet she still felt relieved, and grateful, that this brave coworker had dropped everything to protect her from the fiend whose face she had seen—and who might now be out there, who knew where, possibly trying to find and kill her.

"Why don't you just see if the picture here, Walt—" Patrick pointed to the screen "—if it looks like any of the pictures already in the system. If not, then we can talk about how best to get Kyra there for a short while to check out those other pictures."

Irritating, yes. Kyra had an urge to tell Walt she'd be there tomorrow—maybe *they'd* be there tomorrow—but assumed Patrick would take control even more. And for her own safety, and that of her baby, she couldn't do what she really wanted to and live her life as she used to.

"Sounds like a good idea," Walt said. He glanced at Kyra as if looking for her response.

What could she say, at least for now? "It's finc with me." She didn't look at Patrick to see his reaction. She figured his ego might be stoked by her going along with what he said.

Or maybe he was just doing what he was supposed to, what hc had promised—everything he could to ensure she was as safe as possible.

Okay, irritated or not, she appreciated what he was trying to do. What he was doing.

Even if he recognized she wasn't exactly on board with all he was inflicting on her.

Or maybe, despite herself, she was.

Patrick was highly appreciative of Walt's assistance, and let him know that as he accompanied their welcome visitor downstairs after he'd packed up his computer, and to his nearby car, all the time watching their environs for anything or anyone unusual—like someone with the face Walt had worked on depicting with Kyra.

"I just hope having a portrayal like this helps our precinct locate this guy and stop him from hurting anyone else," Walt said. The young tech expert put his bag on the passenger seat of his car and turned to Patrick, holding his hand up for a high five, and Patrick participated.

The residential street around them had some traffic, both pedestrian and vehicle, but nothing appeared amiss. Patrick walked with Walt back to the driver's side of the unmarked silver SUV, most likely a vehicle provided to him for his job, and watched as he got inside and locked the doors. He rolled down the window.

"We'll be in touch one way or another," Walt said. "I hope Kyra and you can safely visit our offices soon, but I'll do my damnedest to match this picture to someone in the system—and in any event will send it to those out on the street around the crime scene and otherwise hunting this guy, and warn them to look for someone similar even if not identical."

"Sounds good," Patrick said.

"Now, you be careful." Walt made it sound like a direct order, and Patrick appreciated his caring nature.

"You too," he said. "And I also hope we get to see you at the station soon."

He remained on the sidewalk, watching as Walt drove away—and watching his surroundings even more carefully. He was of course close to Kyra's apartment here. And again—still—he saw people walking around both alone and in groups, none appearing threatening. Just a regular day on a regular busy and building-lined New York street.

Maybe.

And though no one was particularly close by, Patrick kept his eyes mostly on the men's faces, but he saw no one resembling the picture they'd been working on that morning.

Not surprising. If the guy happened to be around, he knew Kyra had seen him and would probably be in disguise.

Patrick let himself into the building once more with Kyra's keys. He didn't think anyone was hanging out or watching, or, worse, attempting to barge his way inside.

And hopefully he was nowhere around—especially not already inside the apartment building. But Patrick couldn't be sure. So, once more, he walked up the steps to the fourth floor, still looking around.

Still being as cautious as he could.

As he reached Kyra's door, he looked around yet again before opening it then locking it behind him.

So what would they do next?

Kyra was in the kitchen, apparently putting together a lunch for them from the food her parents had brought.

"Are you hungry?" she asked.

He hadn't thought about it, but it was far enough into the afternoon that eating wasn't a bad idea. "Sure," he replied and started to help her.

"You don't need to do that," she said. "There's not much I can handle these days, but this is one of the few things."

"I understand," he said. "But it's in my blood to help with whatever I can, whenever I can."

He couldn't quite interpret the look she shot him but thought he saw both frustration and gratitude in it. "I figured. Okay, there's not really much to do since I already have the sandwich fixings out, and we can put our own together. Is that okay with you?"

"Sure."

Soon they were back at her kitchen table. Although Patrick wondered what she would ultimately do with some of the items her folks brought that appeared to be Indian food, for now they were just eating sandwiches with sliced turkey, cheese, lettuce and mayo—stuff that was normal to him.

He remained glad to be hanging out with her. Making sure the murderer she'd confronted wasn't confronting her.

Things around here seemed fine, but he didn't think what he was doing was unnecessary.

Someone as clearly ready to kill as the Jewelry Slayer was probably planning some revenge.

Oh, sure, he could be fleeing now that he'd been seen, especially by a member of law enforcement who might have skills at identifying him—which was true.

But they couldn't count on that.

"What are you thinking about?" Kyra asked from across the table. She had a portion of her sandwich in her hand, and a puzzled expression on her lovely face. "You look worried to me. Maybe a bit angry. Why?"

He didn't want to worry her any further, at least not right now, when it wasn't necessary. Still—

"Hey, I didn't think we knew each other well enough for you to read my mind. But you can probably guess who I'm thinking about."

"The Jewelry Slayer."

It kind of bothered him that his thoughts were so apparent. But not a lot.

This was one smart coworker. And having her read his mind about something like this made sense.

"You got it," he told her and laughed. He made himself stare down at his plate, then back up into her face with a grin of his own. "So tell me what I'm thinking now."

"That you're enjoying your lunch?"

"Close enough," he said. "And I'm especially enjoying the company."

Okay. Too much information, he realized, even if it was true.

"Me too." Her voice was low, and in a moment she rose. "I need another drink of water. How about you?"

"I'm fine," he said.

But once she reached the refrigerator, she turned back toward him.

"I'm also fine, not just about drinking water. Can't we plan on heading to the office tomorrow, just for a short while? I mean, we've seen no indication the Jewelry Slayer is around here. And if he is watching, maybe it would be a good thing for me to draw him out somehow."

"No way!" Patrick hadn't intended to sound so vehement. But for her to throw herself out there to tempt the guy to possibly kill her…

"I understand," she said and was suddenly hidden behind the refrigerator door. When she appeared again with a bottle of water in her hand, she continued, "But for us to hide this way…for me to hide this way… It doesn't seem natural."

"Time for you to change your nature then," Patrick found himself growling. "Hiding to stay safe? It's where we are at the moment, and for as long as it takes for our coworkers to catch the guy."

# Chapter 11

Change her nature? No. Kyra would never do that. She felt content with who she was.

Especially now, as she prepared to become a mother.

But she did understand what Patrick was saying. It was what he had continued to say since he had promised to protect her. She might not like hiding, but for Patrick to ensure her safety, hiding was of course what he wanted—and she recognized why. It would make things easier for him, for them both, perhaps. As if any of this could be easy.

She opened her mouth to object anyway but realized that would be fruitless. Maybe she could change the subject.

"I understand what you're saying," she said as she handed him one of the water bottles she held. She sat back down at the table across from him and began opening her own new bottle, looking at it rather than him as she continued. "And I hope you understand why I find all of this so difficult—and not just the fact I'm now potentially the target of someone who may want to kill me to shut me up. But I chose to go into law enforcement, and even though I'm a federal crime scene investigator and not a detective or someone out in the field hunting perpetrators of the crimes we're investigating, I'm really not used to just hiding and not getting out there and doing at least something."

"Not so far, at least," he said.

Had his tone changed from anger and irritation? Maybe. Kyra looked at him. And believed she saw some understanding there, a touch of it, at least.

Okay, maybe he did understand. He had chosen to go into law enforcement too, after all.

And at the moment, she wondered why. She was aware of some difficulties that had arisen with his family, thanks to rumors around the precinct, but didn't know the details.

Maybe this would be a good time to ask.

"I just chose law enforcement, especially crime scene investigation," she began, "because I'm addicted to solving puzzles. Figuring things out by research and not giving up till they're resolved. Helping to catch suspects in some terrible crimes is a major plus. How about you? Why did you become a federal CSI? And why did you decide to go into law enforcement at all?"

She looked straight into his hazel eyes as he raised his brows and glared at her. He didn't want to answer? That expression, as much as it made her wince inside, didn't make him appear any less good-looking. Only more challenging.

And Kyra was used to dealing with challenges...although not the kind that was her worst at the moment, staying safe despite a clear threat against her life, and therefore her baby's.

"Okay," he finally said. "I guess it won't hurt for you to know what got me into this, since maybe it'll also explain why I'm determined to make sure you remain okay, and why I've taken that on as my current challenge. And yes, I'm fine with taking on challenges— like hunting serial killers. It's what I do, and what my siblings do too, in case you're interested in hearing that as well."

She was definitely interested now. She knew Patrick had a couple brothers and a sister who were also with the FBI, though she didn't know why and she hadn't met them. Maybe she would hear the facts now.

"Yes," she said, still looking him in the eyes. "Please tell me."

Patrick looked away, taking a swig of water. Then he said, "I won't go into detail, but my dad, Desmond Colton, was murdered by a serial killer when I was very young. My brothers, Brennan and Cash, and sister, Ashlynn, were pretty young too, especially Ashlynn. We heard the story from our poor mom, who had to raise us herself, and even from other family members as we grew up without our dad and did more digging into the situation as we got older. As a result, we all went into aspects of law enforcement with the primary goal of helping to catch as many serial killers as we could to stop them from killing others."

"Wow," Kyra said softly, understanding his rationale now, though having no idea what it must really feel like to have had that kind of hurtful background. "What do

Brennan, Cash and Ashlynn do? They're all with the FBI too, right?"

"Yes, they are. Brennan and Cash are special agents, and Ashlynn is a tech expert."

Then maybe Ashlynn could have helped with the facial recognition picture of the Jewelry Slayer that Kyra had begun and Walt, with the NYPD, had helped to clarify. But that was irrelevant now.

"That's so sad. And so impressive," Kyra said. "And have you all stopped any serial killers so far?"

"We're all still working on it, although each of us have had some success."

He obviously didn't want to divulge details, which was okay with Kyra. But what a family!

And what a terrible situation that had brought them all into law enforcement.

"I admire all of you," Kyra told him, and she did. She'd chosen her profession based on an interest in stopping bad guys, sure, but she loved to work on investigating critical items of evidence, finding them at crime scenes, bringing them in carefully and solving those puzzles—a different kind of detail. Going after suspects who happened to be serial killers? Maybe, especially now. She had wound up doing more than just working the crime scene and collecting valuable evidence.

She had seen the man who had dropped it there. Who had killed not only the poor woman whose body had been found there, but others as well. And why?

Because of greed. He deserved to be brought in and tried and convicted of those murders. To spend the rest of his disgusting life in prison.

"I appreciate your admiration on behalf of all of us." Patrick moved from across the table and sat in the chair beside her. As he faced her, he was actually smiling, despite a somewhat haunted look in those eyes of his that she sometimes found mesmerizing. Like now. "And, hey, we all admire you too. I definitely do."

His proximity now made Kyra want to reach out and hold his hand. Hold *him*, though there was nothing she really could do to help with his difficult childhood.

And it didn't look, from his expression, like she had to do anything to cheer him up now anyway. He and his siblings had all found ways to deal with their past, or at least it appeared that way.

Still, when she next spoke, she kept her tone teasing. "Are your siblings inside your head at the moment telling you what to say?"

Patrick laughed. "I know them well enough to know what they actually would say if they happened to be here. They'd all want to make sure you achieve payback for what you experienced." He stopped laughing and reached out, taking Kyra's hand. "Me too, but you undoubtedly know that. And—well, one way or another I'm going to be there, to help bring in that miserable lowlife, the serial killer who finds pricey jewelry more valuable than human life. And who dared to threaten you."

Warmth, gratitude and more poured through Kyra. She appreciated that. And, oh, yes, she appreciated Patrick on so many levels, including this one.

Even though a tiny pang of hurt edged through her as well. She now knew he considered protecting people part of his law enforcement job despite being a crime scene investigator—and that included protecting her. She might be starting to care for him more than was appropriate, but it was clearly one-sided.

Nothing inappropriate from his side, at least.

"Let's both do that," she said, taking a firm and professional grip on her emotions. "And I thank you again for not only wanting to protect me, but for wanting to catch that slimeball." She hesitated only a moment before asking, "So what can we do here this afternoon, even if we don't go to the precinct or crime scene, to help bring the slimeball in?"

The sound of his deep laugh again amused her. Why did she like hearing him laugh that way?

Because it helped to cheer her up a bit in this difficult situation? Sure. But there was something about the sound, and the fact it made her feel good to have amused this great-looking, caring, protective guy so much.

"You and I are on the same wavelength, which isn't surprising," he said. "My idea is to call at least one of our fellow CSIs and get as much of an update as we can. Maybe they've caught the guy and forgot to tell us."

"Right," Kyra said. "Just like we forgot to tell them the Jewelry Slayer showed up here and you're the one who took him into custody before he could hurt anyone else."

"Don't we wish?" Patrick asked with a sigh, and he held out his hand. She put hers into it and loved the feel of his strong, warm grasp as she squeezed his back.

"Well, I certainly wish," she agreed.

"Not the showing up here part though," Patrick contradicted. "Okay, let's give Craig a call."

Kyra felt a shot of sorrow as he pulled his hand away, but their touching had simply been a short act of recognizing yet again that they had similar ideas. And calling Craig Warren, who'd been their main contact before and who'd seemed to step in above the others on their team to coordinate who was doing what, seemed a good idea. Even if he didn't bring them a pizza this time.

They remained seated at the table as Patrick again pulled out his phone and pushed a button, then put it on speaker.

Only one ring before Craig answered. "Hey, boss, how's it going? How are you and Kyra doing? I was going to give you a call a little later."

Kyra immediately wondered why but let Patrick respond. "It's going fine. Kyra and I are doing well, and why were you going to call?"

"To keep you updated on our progress."

Really? They'd made some progress? Kyra was delighted and wanted to hear more.

"Great," Patrick said. "So update us."

"And the answer is," Craig said, "we've gotten nowhere so far. Not really."

Kyra felt her heart plummet. Some update.

"What's going on, then?" She couldn't help jumping into the conversation and asking the question.

"Oh, hi, Kyra," Craig said. "I figured Patrick was still hanging out with you. Have you seen or heard anything from our target?"

"The Jewelry Slayer? Where is he? How would we have seen or heard from him?" Patrick was demanding those answers now.

"Hold on. Let me just tell you what's been going on, okay?"

"Yeah," Patrick said. "Tell us." He looked Kyra in the face, and she could see he was as angry and puzzled as she was.

"Okay. First, we've been told by our senior officers to give up for now on collecting more evidence from the crime scene, since it appears there's nothing left. Kyra did a good job to begin with, but what the creep stole might have had the only clues that might have been there for finding him. Nothing now, at least nothing we found. And there've been a couple more crimes committed in the precinct that the three of us CSIs left here on our team have been told to jump in on and find any evidence we can."

"What kinds of crimes?" Kyra had to ask. She leaned on the table, staring at the phone Patrick had put down between them, wanting to grab it and squeeze further information from it, from Craig.

As if that would help.

"Nothing more from the Jewelry Slayer," Craig said. "Or at least no jewelry thefts or serial killings, but since we're working here we're helping out. Just a bank robbery, where a customer yelled at one of the guys, who then grabbed him and threw him on the floor before they ran. Fortunately, the good guy wasn't hurt bad, and there appeared to be some items that could have fingerprints. The other might have been related—theft of a car nearby. The woman driver and her kid were pulled out but again fortunately not hurt badly. She grabbed her purse back, so—voila!"

"More fingerprints," Kyra surmised.

"You got it. We're still trying to figure out if they're in the system."

"But those are now occupying your time," Patrick said.

"Yep. But before you hang up and cry about our lack of progress, I want to let you know about one little thing that's stuck at the back of my mind about the jerk who attacked Kyra."

"What's that?" she asked immediately.

"Well, when Walt Elderson arrived at the precinct a little while ago, he showed all of us the picture you and he came up with, Kyra. Good job—I assume. In any case, there's a lot of detail. But so far—well, that face hasn't been found in our system."

She wasn't surprised. Surely, if they'd already figured out who their suspect was, they'd have let Patrick and her know.

"Sorry to hear that," she said, which was true.

"Same here," Patrick said. "But why are you bringing it up now?"

"Well, the thing is, apparently Walt didn't want to scare you, but he's told our group that he talked to Captain Colleen about his visit with you and showed her the current version of the picture. He indicated that after Patrick watched him drive off, he drove through the area for a short while, then parked and walked in the vicinity a bit, looking around. He saw a few people out and about, and before he left, he showed some of them the rendering and said he was a social media junkie looking for a new film star said to be living in the area but wanting to stay private. He asked if any of those folks had seen anyone who looked like that."

"And?" Patrick demanded.

"One of them had, supposedly right in your area, but it wasn't made clear where, other than on one of the streets driving a car."

Kyra opened her mouth to ask more as her insides curled in fear, but before she did Craig spoke again.

"Before you get too excited about it, I really didn't get a sense of anything more than the person he talked with possibly wanting to get in the news himself. He might have made it up. Or whoever he saw might not have looked like the picture at all. But just in case… well, be careful. As if you haven't been already, I figure."

"You figure right," Patrick growled. "I know it's getting late, so tell Walt I'll want to talk to him tomorrow."

When they hung up after saying goodbye and getting Craig's promise they'd talk more soon, Patrick said, "That might all be nonsense. But just in case…"

"Just in case," Kyra said, "I'm a bit edgy about it."

Patrick definitely understood why Kyra felt nervous. So did he, to some extent—mostly on her behalf.

Sure, that story Craig had just related to them probably meant nothing. Walt had probably tried to do his part in ensuring things around here remained safe for Kyra. The description of his supposed conversation with the guy who claimed to have recognized the photo didn't make a lot of sense.

And yet… What if he actually had spoken with someone who'd gotten a glimpse of the Jewelry Slayer?

Even if he had, that didn't mean their foe knew where Kyra lived, except maybe somewhere in this area.

Even so—

"I think I'll take another walk outside now." Patrick attempted to appear at least a bit nonchalant as he again looked at Kyra beside him.

"That story got to you too." It wasn't a question, but a statement. But he already recognized how astute Kyra was.

"Just want to check things out again after hearing it," he acknowledged.

"Okay." She seemed to hesitate.

"Do I hear a *but*?"

"Not really. But—"

He laughed. He'd already risen and now stood near her chair. He wanted to reach down, pull her to her feet and take her into his arms as he asked, "What *but*, then?"

"Look, I really like my apartment, *but* I'm getting tired of feeling like I'm tethered here like a dog wearing a leash, or a horse wearing reins. I know that kind of restriction is for a pet's protection too. But I'm not an animal, a pet or otherwise. I'm a professional in law enforcement, and I want to do my job—and not just be harnessed in one location even if it's good for me. And notwithstanding stories being told around me that could, and do, make me nervous."

She had risen too, but taking her into his arms was out of the question. Her lovely face was scrunched into a look of frustration and possibly anger. With him?

Most likely with the situation. But he was part of it, even if his part was to obstruct her abilities to do what she wanted for, yes, her own protection.

"I understand," he told her. "Look, I'll call Colleen before I go out, make sure there are still patrols around the area, make sure Craig told her what he told us. And I'll get her take on how things are. As long as it doesn't appear you'd be in more danger—well, much more danger—if you went out, maybe we can take a short visit to the precinct tomorrow so you can check the faces in the system, and be brought up to date about the search for the Jewelry Slayer as much as they can tell us. I'll mention that to Colleen now, okay?"

"Okay," she said. "It's better than nothing, at least. So—let's call Colleen now."

# "One Minute" Survey

## You get up to **FOUR books** <u>and</u> a Mystery Gift...

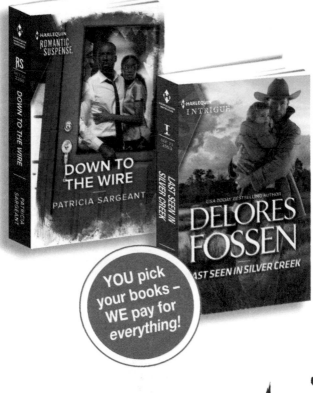

**YOU** pick your books –
**WE** pay for everything.
You get up to FOUR new books and a Mystery Gift...
absolutely FREE!
**Total retail value: Over $20!**

Dear Reader,

Your opinions are important to us. So if you'll participate in our fast and free "One Minute" Survey, YOU can pick up to four wonderful books that WE pay for when you try the Harlequin Reader Service!

As a leading publisher of women's fiction, we'd love to hear from you. That's why we promise to reward you for completing our survey.

IMPORTANT: Please complete the survey and return it. We'll send your Free Books and a Free Mystery Gift right away. And we pay for shipping and handling too! ← *We pay for EVERYTHING!*

Try **Harlequin® Romantic Suspense** and get 2 books featuring heart-racing page-turners with unexpected plot twists and irresistible chemistry that will keep you guessing to the very end.

Try **Harlequin Intrigue® Larger-Print** and get 2 books featuring action-packed stories that will keep you on the edge of your seat. Solve the crime and deliver justice at all costs.

**Or TRY BOTH!**

Thank you again for participating in our "One Minute" Survey. It really takes just a minute (or less) to complete the survey… and your free books and gift will be well worth it!

If you continue with your subscription, you can look forward to curated monthly shipments of brand-new books from your selected series, always at a discount off the cover price! Plus you can cancel any time. So don't miss out, return your One Minute Survey today to get your Free books.

*Pam Powers*

# "One Minute" Survey

## GET YOUR FREE BOOKS AND A FREE GIFT!

✓ Complete this Survey  ✓ Return this survey

**1** Do you try to find time to read every day?

☐ YES  ☐ NO

**2** Do you prefer stories with suspensful storylines?

☐ YES  ☐ NO

**3** Do you enjoy having books delivered to your home?

☐ YES  ☐ NO

**4** Do you share your favorite books with friends?

☐ YES  ☐ NO

**YES!** I have completed the above "One Minute" Survey. Please send me m
Free Books and a Free Mystery Gift (worth over $20 retail). I understand that I an
under no obligation to buy anything, as explained on the back of this card.

☐ **Harlequin® Romantic Suspense**
240/340 CTI G2AD

☐ **Harlequin Intrigue® Larger-Print**
199/399 CTI G2AD

☐ **BOTH**
240/340 & 199/399
CTI G2AE

FIRST NAME

LAST NAME

ADDRESS

APT.#

CITY

STATE/PROV.

ZIP/POSTAL CODE

EMAIL ☐ Please check this box if you would like to receive newsletters and promotional emails from Harlequin Enterprises ULC and its affiliates. You can unsubscribe anytime.

HI/HRS-1123-OM

**BUSINESS REPLY MAIL**
FIRST-CLASS MAIL    PERMIT NO. 717    BUFFALO, NY

POSTAGE WILL BE PAID BY ADDRESSEE

**HARLEQUIN READER SERVICE**
PO BOX 1341
BUFFALO NY 14240-8571

NO POSTAGE
NECESSARY
IF MAILED
IN THE
UNITED STATES

And they did. Colleen was her usual kind, concerned and professional self. "Yes, we still have patrols in your area—often. Nothing seems out of kilter, despite Walt's odd tale of showing the picture of the perp's face that you and he worked on, Kyra. So—well, sure, go check things out again tonight, Patrick. And if all still appears okay, your coming to the precinct tomorrow to discuss things with us is fine."

They talked a little more, then said goodbye.

Colleen ended the conversation with, "I hope I see you both tomorrow."

"Me too," Kyra said, then both sides hung up.

It was already past four in the afternoon, so sunlight was fading and sunset would arrive soon. There were plenty of streetlights in the area, but Patrick doubted he'd be able to see anything helpful.

Even so, he'd give it a try. He had to.

He started by taking Kyra's hand before heading toward the door. "Everything in here should be fine," he said. "But you take good care of yourself and your baby, just in case. I won't be long."

"You take good care of yourself too," Kyra told him, squeezing his hand. "Be careful."

He nodded, then put on the jacket he'd hung in the entry closet, stuck his weapon in his belt where it would be hidden and headed toward the door, taking the keys off the nearby table as before. He locked the door behind him, checking it carefully.

He saw a man and woman walk down the hall toward one of the last doors. Nothing too concerning there—although he wished he could look into the guy's face to make sure he didn't resemble Kyra's picture.

Not a chance, he figured.

As usual, he walked down the stairs. He saw no one else around. And as he carefully unlocked the downstairs door and went out he saw a few people nearby on the sidewalk. Maybe they were heading toward their own buildings or just taking a walk.

A couple were women, but three were men, and he just plastered a smile on his face and passed by—taking quick looks at their faces.

None resembled the important facial rendering now on the precinct's computer system.

He saw a marked police car drive by, which relieved him a bit, though the occupant probably wouldn't know who he was. And after they passed he crossed a street at the light—managing to look at the male drivers of a couple of cars waiting there.

Again, no resemblance.

He walked around the block twice, and as he did the sky above the moderately tall buildings grew darker, and the streetlights and lights from the buildings' windows provided most of the illumination. He smelled some exhaust from the vehicles driving around, including a few delivery trucks. Some cars were electric vehicles with no aroma though.

All seemed calm, a usual night on a regular New York City street.

No hints that the Jewelry Slayer was in the neighborhood.

Which didn't mean he wasn't.

Damn. Not that Patrick wanted to see the guy here. But where the hell was he?

Why hadn't any of the detectives or other cops in the precinct, or the FBI, found him and brought him in?

Maybe it would be a really good thing to go into

the office tomorrow with Kyra and talk to some of the others.

Maybe they could all come up with a good plan to follow to catch that dangerous murderer, using the representation of his face now on the computer system, or not.

He could only hope so.

And despite his concerns about having Kyra leave the shelter of her building at all, he would be sure to continue to watch over her and keep her safe.

## Chapter 12

Kyra directed herself to stay calm while Patrick was outside. There wasn't any real reason to believe the Jewelry Slayer was in the area, after all.

She nevertheless found herself worrying—about Patrick as much as herself. Maybe even more so. Yes, he was her protector. But the idea of him getting hurt—or worse—as he attempted to assure her safety... It horrified her.

Then there was her baby... Rather than just sitting around reading or watching TV, she went into the nursery and dusted a bit, even though she did so often enough that it was quite clean. Nor did she have to do anything with the few supplies she had already picked up such as diapers and clothing for a newborn, but she fussed with that as well.

She went to the nursery window and pulled back the drapes. It was approaching evening and becoming dark outside, although there was no difficulty seeing the apartment building across the street, of a similar structure to this one. She saw no windows or draperies open, which was a good thing. No one there was likely to be watching her, neither a neighbor...nor the Jewelry Slayer.

She closed the drapes and considered what to do next while she waited. And worried.

Oh, yes. She could start getting dinner ready.

Closing the nursery door behind her, she considered the possibilities and decided on lamb vindaloo tonight. She'd asked Patrick if he was okay with spicy dishes before she requested that her parents bring fixings for the lamb dish that she didn't already keep in her kitchen. He'd sounded fine with it, so she now, thanks to her folks, had all the ingredients needed. She'd keep the spiciness lower than usual though because of her pregnancy. Too much zest might not be a good thing for her and the baby.

One of these evenings she'd prepare tandoori chicken, but there wasn't enough time now to marinate it properly.

And she could always put together a good old American meal of pot roast or meat loaf or whatever if they did wind up hanging out here a long time and she needed to prepare a lot of dinners in the near future.

But for tonight, a special meal derived from her own background seemed a good thing.

Yes, something special for the special man watching out for her.

The recipe was in her head, thanks to her mother, so, standing at the wide counter near the sink, facing the window, blinds closed, she started putting together

her preferred sauce of ginger, garlic, some spices, sugar and vinegar, enjoying the aromas as she inhaled. She also sliced one small chili pepper, figuring she could add another later if she decided more spice was needed and acceptable to her. Then, she took some sliced lamb out of the refrigerator and began the short-term marination. Longer term would be preferable, but she'd had it this way before and it was fine.

She then put it all in a pot on the stove and started it cooking on a high temperature.

She next began cooking white rice, then putting together a small salad.

She then lowered the temp on the vindaloo so it would continue cooking and stay warm without being over-done.

Oh, yes, they would have a decent dinner, as she intended each time she wound up cooking for them.

Not that she was much of a homemaker. She liked to do what was necessary, what was important around her apartment, and figured she would soon be doing more as a new mother.

But mostly, she was a crime scene investigator and loved it. Or at least she had before...

Would she ever be able to get back into it the way she had previously, considering what had happened to her? She also wondered if her baby might come sooner than she'd originally anticipated, considering the increased amount of cramping she had been feeling.

Sure, it could have been a result of the stress she was under more than anything else, but she'd remain alert about the possibilities.

For now, she was nearly done with her food preparation. She realized though that she had no idea when they would actually eat. When Patrick would return.

It had been a while since he'd gone out. Was everything okay? If not, he wouldn't necessarily be able to let her know.

She considered calling him but didn't want to distract him, whether things were good or bad.

She realized it was her own currently worried nature making her fret like this. Usually, keeping busy, as she'd been, would let her maintain her mental stability.

It didn't help that the baby was now moving again inside her, as if he or she knew that Mama was upset about something. One way or another, that was probably correct. Her hormones, her nerves, might be irritating not only her but her little one too.

Her little one. She thought again, as she did often, about who was inside her. Yes, she could have had the sex determined but decided she wanted to undergo a traditional kind of pregnancy and wait to find out.

Not that her pregnancy really was traditional. No matter who her child was, there would be no daddy in the picture.

Well, there definitely would be a loving mommy. And grandparents too. And maybe someday the right man would come into their lives and become that special daddy...

Kyra shoved the image of Patrick's handsome, caring face from her mind. Yes, he was taking care of them.

But it was his job.

And where was he now? Was he okay?

Damn, but she wished she could call and find out without worrying about distracting him—

There. She heard a noise at the front door that sounded

like the key in the lock. She left the kitchen to watch, and sure enough the door opened and Patrick came inside, locking it behind him.

"Everything okay out there?" Kyra asked, hurrying toward him.

"Far as I could tell," he replied, discreetly not making a statement about it. Being a good, truthful law enforcement officer.

Kyra appreciated that about him—and everything else.

So much that she rushed up to him, much closer than she should have.

And suddenly she found herself in his arms. Had she initiated it? Had he?

Didn't matter. In moments, she felt him drawing her close despite the thickness of the jacket he still wore.

Then his mouth was on hers, the kiss hot and sweet and questioning and making a statement she couldn't yet read, but she threw herself into the embrace and kiss, getting even closer to him—despite her baby bump in the way.

"I'm so glad to see you, so glad you're okay," she whispered as she drew back just a little. "You were out there so long I started to worry."

"Hey, I'll have to get you worried again, even more." His voice was raspy, and he pulled her against him again, his lips again on hers, and they shared another heated kiss.

Then, as if they had each realized what had just happened, they both pulled back. Looked at each other.

And laughed. Sort of.

"You can tell me what you did and what you saw while we eat," Kyra said. "I have dinner ready."

"Gee, I'll have to go running around outside often," Patrick teased. "Assuming I like what you've put together. I appreciate the idea of dinner waiting when I get back."

"Don't count on it," she said. "I don't want to spoil you." That was a lie. She'd love to spoil him, in gratitude for everything he was doing for her.

While Patrick went to wash his hands, Kyra put their salads on the table, along with glasses of water this time. She'd like to have served him a good wine, which was her preferred drink at dinner—when she wasn't pregnant. Now, water worked just fine, and she figured Patrick would be okay with it too. He had been last night, after all, when they'd eaten pizza.

She also put two bottles of salad dressing on the table so Patrick could choose his preference, which turned out to be ranch. That was what Kyra chose as well.

And as they ate, facing each other over the table, she commanded him to describe his ventures outside.

"Oh, there were a zillion people walking around like zombies, and others driving by in cars," he told her, holding some greens on his fork, ready to stuff them into his mouth. "I looked carefully at all of them. None resembled your picture, which was a good thing."

"But what about the zillionth and one," she said, playing along. "Are you sure he wasn't the suspect?"

"Hmm," Patrick said after he finished his last bite of salad. "Guess I'd better go back out there when we're done eating to check him out."

Kyra laughed, wanting to give him a friendly jab in the ribs with her elbow but not close enough to do that. Instead, when she stood, she turned the heat off under the lamb vindaloo. She put rice on both plates first, then added the lamb dish.

She brought Patrick's plate to him. "Want to give this a try?"

"I sure do." And he did. She watched his face, and he appeared delighted, which delighted her as well. "Delicious," he said. "Not as spicy as I thought after you mentioned it before, but it's really good."

She explained she'd changed her mind about how spicy to make it. Soon, she sat back down and they both ate their dinners.

And Kyra thought about how wonderful this felt— sharing a meal she'd cooked with someone she cared about a lot, undoubtedly too much, in the pleasant environment of her kitchen, as if she'd simply invited a guy she liked to join her for dinner.

For the moment, she could act as if it was really that simple. Until—

"About tomorrow," Patrick said. "I don't think we should head to the office first thing, not without talking to Colleen or others first to check on how things seem and what those on duty will be up to that day. But do you have any preference about when to head there?"

Oh, yeah, she did. First thing. For the day. With a plan to visit the crime scene again, just to remind herself of everything that had changed her life so much.

There went the simplicity of her delightful meal with the man she was inappropriately attracted to.

And the reminder of who she was and why she was attached to her apartment.

But she decided to simply keep the dialogue going for now, so she responded, "I know I'm counting on you, and what you suggested sounds fine. But yes, let's go over what we want to accomplish at the precinct tomorrow so we can keep it in mind when we talk to Colleen first thing in the morning."

"That sounds good to me," Patrick said, taking a swig of water from his glass. "What I'd like is to learn what everyone else there knows or believes, and why. And their best take on how to find the killer, since they haven't yet. Some of them are detectives, after all. Crime scene investigators like us can sometimes find major, damning evidence, like at the scene of your attack. But more's needed."

"My sentiments exactly." Kyra looked beautiful as she nodded, which waved her lovely long dark hair. She also narrowed her deep brown eyes in agreement.

Which was fine, even though this change, talking business once more, somehow damaged the atmosphere Patrick had been temporarily sensing here as they ate dinner.

He had really been enjoying the meal.

And the company, the wonderful woman who'd prepared that meal and was sharing it with him? Oh, yes.

But Kyra was right. They'd been acting, for a short while at least, as if this was some kind of date between a man and woman who appealed to one another on a basis more like chasing a potential relationship rather than being on the job together.

Definitely not a good idea.

He'd felt a little relaxed after seeing nothing unusual during his somewhat lengthy venture outside, where he'd found no cause for worry. He wanted to believe Kyra's home was safe for her, and he wanted to keep it that way, to ensure her safety by staying here.

And now—well, Kyra had burst the little bubble he'd started to inflate. He'd already promised her a visit to the office tomorrow, at least a short trip.

He intended to follow up on that and make her happy, as long as nothing appeared that suggested it would be a dangerous outing.

But without knowing where her nemesis was, who could tell?

It would certainly be a good idea to discuss the situation with their coworkers tomorrow, those who'd been on the case and attempting to identify and locate the Jewelry Slayer.

But until they did, Patrick would always have to assume the worst: that the guy was somewhere near Kyra, knew where she lived, knew enough to follow her since he'd undoubtedly want to track her down and keep her from identifying him.

And the only way to do that was to harm her. Badly. Kill her.

"Tell you what," Kyra said. "We're almost done eating. Let me clear the dishes, then we can sit in the living room and talk for a while without distractions, okay?"

"Sounds fine with me as long as you let me help wash the dishes."

She smiled. "Thanks. I'll put almost everything into the dishwasher. But you can help bring things to the sink so I can stick them in and keep me company while I do it. Then we'll talk."

"We've got a deal," Patrick said, and Kyra laughed.

"If we were on the same side of the table, I'd make you shake hands with me to seal that deal."

Despite the nasty way his thoughts had been going, Patrick couldn't help laughing. He'd gotten to know

Kyra some as they'd worked together on the job, and he'd found her to be damned good at what she did, as well as a nice person. Smart. Always willing to talk about their assignments, make suggestions, do whatever she could to learn more.

But there had been nothing personal between them before.

Now, things seemed to have gotten very personal very fast. They were more than colleagues already. They were buddies.

And more.

And damned if he didn't want a lot more than this between them. More than the kisses they'd already shared.

Which wouldn't, couldn't, happen.

And not only because she was pregnant.

Pregnant. Having someone else's baby, even though the guy was no longer in the picture.

What would it be like to help Kyra raise her little one...?

Patrick would never find out, even though he would do what he could to help her, a fellow CSI who would need some time off to learn how to take care of a baby.

For the next few minutes, they did as they'd discussed, although after they brought some of their dishes into the kitchen Kyra took the time to move leftovers from the pan where she'd cooked the lamb dish into a large, covered container that she put into the fridge.

More for tomorrow, or whenever.

Soon, they went into the living room and sat on the sofa.

"I guess it's premature to talk about what I want to discuss tomorrow, since despite the little we've heard in our few conversations, we don't really know if anyone we haven't spoken with has more information," Kyra said. "But I'll want to hear what the crime scene looks like now, and if anyone who was in the area around that time has said anything or even verified that they were there and what, if anything, they saw."

"I agree," Patrick said. They talked a little more about the possibilities, but he had the impression Kyra didn't anticipate anything more helpful at this point than he did.

After all, if anything useful had been discovered, they'd surely have been notified, maybe asked more questions.

Maybe even visited more by others on the precinct staff—carefully, of course.

But none of that had happened, except for Walt's visit to work on the facial recognition likeness.

He added then, "We'll want to be sure Walt is there when we are, to find out what he did with the picture after putting it in the system, and what anyone else did to attempt to get any person who might have seen the Jewelry Slayer to ID him, or even just see if others in that neighborhood might have seen someone who looked like him before he stuck his hoodie over his face."

"I really hope so," Kyra said. She yawned then. "Oops. Guess I need to get to bed soon. I require more sleep these days for some reason."

That caused Patrick to smile at her yet again. He liked her sense of humor, even under trying circumstances.

"I wouldn't mind getting some sleep too," he told her. "Especially since tomorrow might be a busy day."

"Hope so." Then, as they both rose, she looked at him. "I think it's a good idea if you get a good night's sleep too. And hanging out on the sofa—well, I doubt you can sleep as well as if you were in bed." She took a deep breath and, hands on her baby bump, she said, "In fact, I'd like it if you hung out in my bed with me. You should be able to hear if anything goes wrong from there too."

His eyes widened. "Is that an invitation?" He kept his tone light. He knew that, even if it was, she wasn't requesting a night of hot sex.

Still—

"Yes, it is," she said. "The bed is big enough for both of us to sleep without touching."

And that was the answer he figured.

Soon, they'd both gotten through their bathroom routines, again intending to shower in the morning, but now they were in pj's.

Kyra let him know which side of the bed she preferred. And although it was a queen-size bed, she was a bit larger than she otherwise might have been, and he hoped he wouldn't crowd her.

He pulled the covers down on his side and began to plump up the pillows—and found Kyra joining him there.

In moments, she'd taken him into her arms. Or had he been the one to initiate it? They drew close and kissed, and despite himself Patrick felt the most intimate part of his body grow hard. As if he could do anything about it.

As if he wanted to… Well, he recognized that he might, someday. Later. As inappropriate as it was, the idea of sex with a nonpregnant Kyra really turned him on, and he kissed her even deeper—

But he heard the sound of a phone he recognized as hers, and they both drew apart quickly.

Kyra went to the dresser at the other side of the room where she had plugged her phone in to charge, his beside it. She looked at it and smiled but looked a little embarrassed.

"Hi, Mom," she said after picking it up and taking it off the charger. It must have been both her parents, since she added, "Hi, Dad. Yes, I'm home and about to go to sleep." A pause, then, "Yes, Patrick's still here watching out for me. He's in the other room." She looked at the floor as she lied to her parents, but Patrick could understand why—even though nothing could or would happen as they slept in the same bed that night. "I'll stay in touch, but all's fine. I'll still be home tomorrow." She unsurprisingly didn't mention their plan to visit the precinct. "Good night. And yes, the baby's fine."

She soon hung up. "I wonder if their ESP told them where we were and what we were doing."

"Really?" Patrick asked.

"No, but I know they're worried about me. So let's get a good night's sleep so I can confirm to them in the morning that all's still well."

# Chapter 13

Kyra did manage to sleep a bit, even with the sometimes moving baby inside her—and Patrick beside her in her bed.

She knew Patrick slept deeply at least some of the time, since when the baby's movements woke her she listened to the deep breathing beside her. No snores, which was a good thing. She couldn't swear she didn't snore when she slept, but she wouldn't ask Patrick.

Nor did she ask how things were around them the times she heard Patrick get out of bed and leave the room. She heard him going farther down the hall than the bathroom, sometimes into the living room.

Into the hallway outside? At least some of the times, since she used the opportunity for quick visits to the bathroom, more necessary now as the baby continued to grow. Patrick was somewhere beyond her then. She didn't know for sure if he went out, but she figured the cautious, protective man was at least opening the door to look out—with his weapon in his hand.

She woke around six thirty, a typical time for her when she was working, unless she had an unscheduled early morning visit to a crime scene. Her clock on the table on her side of the bed told her the time.

Beside her, Patrick lay there, but she didn't think he was asleep either. His breathing wasn't as deep as when she'd awakened in the night and he'd been sleeping.

She stirred a little, preparing to edge her way out of the bed. And she'd been right. Patrick's deep voice, a little groggy, said, "Good morning."

"Good morning." She turned, still lying on her side, to face him. "I won't ask how you slept, since I heard you get up now and then."

"I know you did, since I was aware you got up some of the times too."

Kyra laughed. "I tried to be sneaky, but guess I wasn't successful."

"Guess not."

Although Kyra, looking at Patrick's smiling eyes, had an urge to roll toward him and kiss him, she knew that wouldn't work with the baby inside her getting in the way. Instead, she just smiled back, and they both soon got out of bed.

Kyra let Patrick shower first so he could get dressed and do his watching-the-world thing while she got ready. While he was in the shower she laid out their breakfast—boxes of low-sugar cereal and some bowls. She'd get milk out later.

She considered cooking them a real breakfast—eggs, at least—especially since the lamb vindaloo meal she'd prepared last night had been received so well.

But she wasn't his cook or really anything but his coworker, under his protection, so she didn't have to do anything to feed him or otherwise make him happy.

Although the idea of making him happy… Okay, maybe her hormones were making her thoughts too wild.

Patrick soon exited the bathroom fully dressed, in the kind of clothing they wore to work: a nice, white, long-sleeved button shirt and black trousers, but without his suit jacket.

Which made Kyra both smile inside and sigh as she made sure the top of her pajamas were pulled sufficiently closed for nothing to show.

Yes, they would head to their precinct office that day, if all went according to the plans they'd discussed. She was glad.

She wanted to get back to work.

But despite all that Patrick was doing to protect her, would it be safe—for either or both of them?

Well, if he felt comfortable enough to give it a try, she definitely would too.

And she knew they both would be careful.

"My turn," she said and headed first to her bedroom to grab the clothes she would wear that day—underwear that fit notwithstanding her pregnancy, and an outfit similarly professional to Patrick's despite the looseness of her blouse. Then she headed toward the bathroom.

"In case I'm not here when you come back—" Patrick began.

"Let me guess," Kyra said as she grabbed the door and looked out from where she had begun to enter. "You'll be outside casing the area to make sure no one's out there threatening us."

"Now, how would you ever get that idea?"

Kyra knew Patrick was joking. He underscored it by taking the couple of steps to reach her and kissing her quickly on the lips, then turning to head out the apartment door.

Oh, yeah, Kyra appreciated the guy, and not only his protectiveness.

She enjoyed sharing kisses with him, even brief ones like that, no matter how inappropriate.

Well, if all went as she hoped, they'd somehow capture the Jewelry Slayer soon and her life could get back to normal. Patrick and she would just see each other at work, as they used to. No hanging out so much together that they subconsciously considered each other roommates—or more. Their emotions would tamp down to what had been usual.

Which in some ways would be a shame, she thought as she closed the bathroom door behind her and began, finally, to shower.

Patrick had only been living there now—what? A day? And it somehow felt as if he belonged there.

For her to sleep next to.

And kiss.

Ridiculous. They were both professionals. FBI agents and CSIs. They ran their team together, but that should be their only togetherness.

Except while he made sure her worst enemy didn't find and harm her…

Kyra, now in the shower, made sure to scrub herself as well as she could, including her baby bump.

Her baby bump.

If nothing else, that important and wonderful extension of her should be enough to keep her apart from Patrick.

Although—well, she couldn't help reminding herself that someday she would want to ensure her baby had a daddy, a great one. One who'd fit right into their family, help to take care of them as she also would help take care of him.

Someone like Patrick…

"Damn!" she exclaimed softly as she finished her shower, turned off the water and started carefully drying herself, making sure not to slip on the wet tile.

She was soon dry and dressed, standing at the still-closed door. She took a deep breath and opened it. Would Patrick be back inside?

One way or another, she would join him for breakfast. She had to act professional. Grateful? Of course. But nothing more than that.

Nothing that her out of kilter hormones generated…

She had just returned to the kitchen when she heard the front door open. She carefully peered out in that direction. It would of course be Patrick, but under the circumstances she had to make certain.

And it was exactly who she expected who walked in and shut, then locked, the door behind him.

"All okay out there?" she asked.

"Yeah, nothing unusual. A good thing—around here." He approached her, and his expression suggested it wasn't necessarily such a good thing. "I just wish—"

"Just what I wish," she interrupted. "That someone in law enforcement, preferably in this precinct, would have caught and arrested the Jewelry Slayer before he could commit any further thefts or killings."

"Exactly." Patrick stood in front of her now just outside the kitchen. His tall, well-formed body, even in his work clothes, seemed to take over the area. Definitely worth looking at. A lot. "I want him to pay right away for all he's done—especially for attacking you."

Before Kyra could object, could say that his attack on her was minimal compared with what he had done to the other women, those whose jewelry he had stolen—after murdering them—and even assuming the guy who attacked her was the Jewelry Slayer and not some minion, Patrick took her into his arms, tight against her baby bump, and kissed her.

Oh, yes. That wonderful, hard body against her now. What could she do but kiss him back? That shut her up from her intended contradiction.

It also made her feel…well, inappropriately special to this highly special man.

And inappropriate remained the key.

Kyra let go of him and stepped back. "Okay, then, let's grab breakfast before we call the office and confirm what we'll be doing today."

Patrick's eyebrows were raised, his wonderfully masculine lips still puckered a bit, as he smiled.

"Hey, I think that kiss made me a bit hungry. What are we eating today? Cereal again?"

"If that's okay." What if he didn't like having the same kind of meal on multiple days?

"Definitely. Cereal makes me feel strong and ready to face the day—and whatever it brings."

She knew he was joking but appreciated it nonetheless.

"Well, then, let's get you strong and ready to face all the nonsense we're likely to see today."

Kyra turned and approached the kitchen counter

where she'd put the cereal and bowls. She put them onto the table and said, "I'll make us—mostly you—some coffee again today, okay?"

"I can feel my caffeine craving growing, so bring it on." And Patrick went past her toward the refrigerator as she began brewing coffee.

This was turning into a routine, Patrick thought, after just a couple of days.

Only he knew today was unlikely to follow the routine of yesterday.

They'd already decided to possibly head to the office.

That would make it way different.

And hopefully not overly dangerous. But he figured it would still be better to wait till they were done eating before calling to check with their coworkers about whether there was anything new they should know before coming in. *If* they came in.

As soon as he finished his cereal, he took a sip of coffee from the cup Kyra had brought him, then said, "Okay, I'm calling Colleen now."

But she wasn't available then. Even though he had called her cell phone number, the system put him through to Sergeant Wells Blackthorn, Colleen's assistant at the precinct who was close to Patrick's cousin Sinead, and let him know who would be on the other end. Patrick immediately put his phone on speaker.

"Hi, Patrick," Wells said, his phone obviously identifying the caller too. "Everything okay with you? With Kyra?"

He'd obviously been informed about what Patrick was up to, most likely by Colleen, but maybe by Craig, or even Walt. After all, the picture of Kyra's vision of who'd attacked her, the Jewelry Slayer or, worst case, his henchman, was undoubtedly all over the station by now. Maybe everyone working at the precinct had seen it and heard about Kyra's situation—and how Patrick was now in charge of her protection.

"It's fine, at least for now. I take it you're aware of what's been going on."

"I think we all are."

Patrick could picture Wells sitting in his office beside Colleen's, although he didn't know for certain that was where he was. He was slightly younger than Patrick's age of thirty-three, a tall and smart guy who did a good job at the precinct. And Patrick couldn't think about him without recalling the scar on his cheek that he didn't talk about.

Patrick wondered if he would wind up seeing Wells in person that day. To help make that determination, he said, "We've been hanging out around Kyra's apartment but we're both concerned, and maybe a bit frustrated, that we don't really know how the hunt for the Jewelry Slayer is going right now. We're even considering coming into the office a little later today and talking to whoever's around about what information has been coming in—but only if things seem in order around there, and Kyra's likely to remain safe."

"Oh, yeah, I've seen that picture. I understand she actually saw her adversary and pulled his hood away from his face, right? That's the word around here, and the reason you're hanging out with her at her place while the Jewelry Slayer is less likely to know where she is—assuming he hasn't figured out where she lives. And you're there in case he does."

"Exactly. So what's the story there? Are a lot of people talking about the situation? Have they also seen the computer rendering of the guy's face? And how safe do you think it would be for Kyra to show up there for a little while to go over what she knows and what anyone else has learned?" Patrick glanced toward Kyra beside him, who seemed to be listening closely. He wondered why she hadn't jumped into the conversation yet.

But he needn't have wondered.

"Wells, this is Kyra." She leaned toward the phone, which he had put down onto the table. Her long, dark hair drew forward, framing her lovely face. "I'm here with Patrick, listening to you. I'm sure you can understand why I want to know what's going on and to talk to anyone at the precinct with any information. But I appreciate Patrick's concern for my safety and agree with it under the circumstances. Do you think it would be okay for me to come in for a short while?"

"Has there been any indication of where the Jewelry Slayer is right now?" Patrick inserted. "I assume he hasn't been ID'd yet or we'd have been told."

"Not sure I'm as totally up-to-date on this situation as some of the others around here, like Colleen. She's in a meeting right now. She should be back soon though. How about if I have her call you, then you and she can decide if coming in today is a good thing?"

Patrick saw the annoyance on Kyra's face and identified with it. Not that he was as determined as she was to visit the precinct, but a delay like this, not being able to plan the day, was frustrating.

Still, waiting was preferable to being told a definite no. "That's okay," he said, ignoring Kyra's glare. "But be sure to have her call as soon as possible, okay?"

"Sure. And I hope she doesn't know anything I don't

that would keep you from coming in. I'd really like to discuss the situation with you and anyone else who knows anything."

"Thanks, Wells," Kyra said, her tone neutral and not expressing that frustration Patrick saw.

They soon hung up. Patrick reached over and took Kyra's hand. "Colleen should have the final say," he said. "But let's check in with Craig, okay? Our fellow CSI might have an inkling of what's going on and whether there've been any rumors or more of where our nemesis is at the moment."

Kyra's lovely face brightened. "Of course. I wanted to talk to any of our team members who were around there anyway to get an update of what's occurred at the crime scene most recently, and whether anything at all helpful was ever found there after—"

She hesitated, and Patrick could tell she was thinking about what had been done to her there, and how what she'd been collecting was stolen.

Patrick reached for his phone again and began to dial Craig's number, figuring if the guy who reported to them wasn't available now, he'd next try Rosa or Mitch.

But before he finished trying to call Craig, his phone rang.

He looked at the ID and smiled at Kyra. Colleen, he mouthed.

He answered the call.

# Chapter 14

"Hi, Colleen." Patrick looked at Kyra with his brows raised and an amused expression on his good-looking face, still sitting on the chair beside hers at the table. "We were just talking to Wells, and—"

"I know," Colleen replied. Kyra could hear it because Patrick had put his phone on speaker again. "He said you wanted our take on whether it's safe for Kyra to come into our offices, and that you're hoping to talk to at least some of us about how the hunt for the Jewelry Slayer is currently going."

"I didn't think we were off the phone long enough with Wells for him to tell you all that." Kyra knew she also had an amused smile on her face. Then she grew serious. "Part of the reason is that I want to make sure I've given all the information I can about what happened the other day. I think I have, but without a group meeting, talking to more than one of you and getting your questions, we can't be sure I haven't accidentally omitted something. Or maybe I can give more detail about something that'll trigger someone else's ideas what to do next. We can all brainstorm together—unless, are there currently any matters where some of our CSI team are out checking over any other crime scenes?"

"Not at the moment," Colleen said. "Things in the precinct seem fairly quiet."

"As if waiting for the next Jewelry Slayer's shoe to drop," Patrick said. "Or hoodie to be pulled off his face."

"Yes, that was a good thing," Colleen said. "That facial rendering now in our system will certainly help identify him…"

"If it's as accurate as I hope," Kyra said with a sigh. "I think it is, but it was so quick, and my fear and other emotions might have modified his features in my mind and therefore in my drawing and assistance to Walt in getting a really good version of it onto the computer. And of course we can't be sure the guy who attacked me isn't an accomplice like the woman who screamed to get Patrick's attention apparently was."

Kyra knew she was batting her head virtually against a wall, recognizing that even if she'd been wholly herself her recollection of whoever had attacked her might have had imperfections. And with her hormones always in overdrive at the moment, that might only have made things worse.

"Well, we'll just have to see," Colleen said, "when we apprehend the guy, which I hope is sooner rather than later. Really sooner. And—well, I'm glad you're feeling okay with the idea of coming in even just for a short while. I'd like you to look at renderings of faces in the system of known perpetrators to compare them with who you saw. I'll have some of our guys check out the area around here and inside the building, just to make sure everything looks as normal as possible. In fact, unless you hear from me within the next half hour, why don't you plan to come in at—" She stopped for a moment, and Kyra figured the captain was checking the time. "It's just a bit after nine o'clock now," she finally said. "Why don't you plan to be here around eleven unless you hear otherwise? I'll set up a meeting that I'll attend, and also the CSIs on duty here today and anyone else appropriate. We can ask questions and brainstorm and whatever else works, and maybe we'll come up with some further ideas what to do next to find our perp. Sound all right?"

It sounded wonderful to Kyra. She'd be on the job at least for a while and hopefully help her coworkers to do their jobs as well.

But first, she looked at Patrick, her protector. Was he okay with it? He'd undoubtedly come with her, watch over her on the way there and while their meeting and whatever else occurred there, then bring her back to her home.

At least she assumed that was what her defender would do.

Fortunately, he nodded, and Kyra felt relieved and even a bit happier than before.

After they hung up with Colleen, they sat at the table for a short while longer, then Patrick said, "So we've got about an hour and a half to hang out here before heading to the precinct. Anything you want to discuss right now?"

"What, like what it feels like to be expecting a baby? Or how about—well, I could always tell you more about how fun it was to be confronted by our suspect. And as far as my successes as a crime scene investigator— hey, you and I have worked together on that for the past months. Could be that you could tell me just as much about my successes as I could tell you."

Kyra was watching Patrick's too-handsome face morph from an amused expression to an exasperated one, and more that she couldn't exactly decipher, but she could guess.

"Well, I suppose you could start telling me everything about your life and even more about why you chose law enforcement and becoming a CSI," he said. "But I've heard a lot of that before too."

"Okay, then. I think it may be time to watch some TV news for a while."

"Sure," he agreed. "But before we leave I want time to go check the street again—and the garage where my car is parked. We'll drive it to the precinct. Sometime soon I want to make sure your car's still there, in good condition—and no one is there watching it."

"Fine," she said. She'd enjoyed the absurdity of some of the beginning of this discussion, but what Patrick just said, although clearly appropriate, was definitely disturbing.

But everything going on right now had the possibility of being disturbing, and she was working on learning to live with it.

Even as the little being within her must have somehow felt her apprehension and started stirring.

Which caused her to place her hands on that bump— and see that Patrick was watching her and what she was doing.

"Everything okay?" he asked.

"Oh, yes, although I think someone also wants things around here to become a bit more peaceful."

Patrick frowned slightly, appearing concerned. Even that expression looked good on his handsome face, and Kyra smiled.

"How's the baby doing?" Patrick asked. "I mean, I know you can't tell completely, but I understand you're over six months pregnant, right? I know it shouldn't be for a while, but will you be able to tell when it's time to give birth?"

"Don't know," she said. "I haven't been through this before. But I gather it won't be immediately, though I'm nearing seven months. I hope it won't be too soon though, since the closer to nine months I am when I give birth the better the baby's health is likely to be. But we'll just have to see how things go."

"Yes, we'll just have to see."

Interesting that Patrick included himself, although she'd phrased things that way so it wasn't surprising. But would he still be watching over her as the time drew near?

At this point, with all that was going on, she wouldn't be surprised—even though she really hoped the man who attacked her, whom she really believed was the Jewelry Slayer, would be captured long before she gave birth.

Patrick got up then, but it took her a little longer to rise, partly because of the movement at her middle. She was concentrating on that more than heading for the living room. But she soon joined Patrick at what had become their usual spots on her sofa, and she grabbed the remote and turned on the TV, making sure it was on the national news station she liked best around this hour.

Some nasty stuff was going on in the world, but that unfortunately was the norm these days. She changed the station to a local one that also still had news at this hour before going into daytime talk and game shows.

There were also some nasty things happening in NYC, but nothing about the Jewelry Slayer. Hopefully, the guy had backed off from robbing and killing. But if so, it might make it harder to find him.

Still, this crime had only been a couple of days ago, and the guy had committed murder three times now with time in between, not just one after the other.

Maybe, because he'd been seen, he was backing off for a while. Forever. But Kyra doubted that.

And she couldn't help but remain concerned that Patrick was right, and the perp was trying to figure out a way to find her and shut her up. He wouldn't necessarily know that law enforcement had ways of putting facial recognition pictures onto computers and sharing them all over the place.

Or even if he did, he wouldn't know she'd done her best to have a representation done of him.

Or—he might just want to get rid of her simply because she had seen his face.

Still watching TV and listening to broadcasters happily describing the news, she tried to move her mind to something, anything, not so frightening.

"You okay?" Patrick asked. Unsurprisingly, her protector seemed to always read her mind, her mood, as he hung out with her.

"I'll be a lot better once the Jewelry Slayer is in custody." She tried to shoot him a look that was more determined and professional than scared.

"Got it." Patrick pulled his phone out, apparently

checking the time. "It'll still be a while before we leave, but I'll go outside and start checking around the area."

"This not-so-new news is boring you too," she guessed.

"You're right." He stood and grinned down at her. "Hope you can stand it a little longer."

"I'll handle it," she said. But she rose and held out her arms. As he drew closer, she added, "Just be careful out there. As always."

His strong, hard body pressed against her, but the kiss he gave her was quick. He obviously wanted to go outside.

"Will do."

No surprise. He saw nothing out of the ordinary in the building, out on the street or even in the garage.

Always a good thing.

He went back inside to get Kyra, and they were soon on their way to the precinct, with him driving. The traffic wasn't too bad this time of day on the city streets. The sidewalks were crowded though. New Yorkers headed to and from work or to nearby stores to shop? Maybe. Some could be tourists checking out the area too.

Patrick kept his eyes out for someone who appeared to be checking things more seriously—other pedestrians as well as drivers like him.

"So how do you think we should approach this?" Kyra asked as they drew nearer to the offices.

"I think we should leave it to Colleen to start with, since she's putting together the meeting. She'll have explained why to those who'll be there, and once we're all together she'll get the party started. She'll know who to ask what."

"Like me, and maybe I'll have the fun of describing my favorite incident yet again."

"Most likely," Patrick said, "although I'd imagine our coworkers, especially those likely to be meeting with us, will already know at least parts of what happened."

"That's what I figure."

He watched as Kyra stopped talking and peered out the windshield even more, also toward people around them on the sidewalks and in cars. Her hands were on her stomach, as if she derived courage from touching as much as possible the little person she wanted to protect.

In a way it was a shame he was driving then, since he had an urge to hug both of them—Kyra and her baby bump.

"Are you feeling okay being out here in the world instead of the safety of your apartment?" Patrick had to ask her. Never mind that he was with her and would protect her with his life, if necessary. Even though she didn't want to be confined that way, she probably felt at least somewhat safer in her home, whether or not she believed he was doing the best job possible taking care of her.

But she'd wanted to come out and go to work. She'd said so all along. Now that she had gotten her way though, was she happy about it?

"Yes and no," she said. "I can't be sure the Jewelry Slayer hasn't determined where I live, but with the patrols around and you hanging out with me, I felt fairly safe there. And I should be fine when we're inside the precinct offices. But out here—well, I can't help but worry some more. Even so, though I know I don't have to mention my hormones anymore, I figure that whatever I feel now is affected by them."

"Good to know you're confirming what I've been assuming."

She looked good dressed up for the office. Heck, she looked good no matter how she was dressed—or wasn't, although he hadn't seen her naked, despite how intrigued he was with the idea, notwithstanding her pregnant condition.

Not going to happen, even living with her to protect her. But he could dream about the future… Not now though.

He soon pulled into the multilevel garage. "Let's go on in," he said after he parked.

"Can we go to our offices first?" she asked as they hurried past the other vehicles on the concrete floor toward the elevators. Despite being an outside team, they had been assigned offices at the precinct. "I'd love to visit my desk before we get to the meeting."

"Let's see how things go," he responded, liking the idea too. But Colleen's plans would take precedence.

## Chapter 15

It felt somewhat strange to Kyra to stand off to the side as the elevator doors opened on the floor where Patrick had parked and let him go ahead to look inside before she could get on.

But she wasn't really surprised. Not with the way he was watching after her.

When they reached the bottom floor and the doors began opening again, Patrick waved one hand gently toward her and she read it to mean she should stay there till—surprise—he checked the area. This was getting old quickly, but for the moment Kyra remained appreciative of all he was doing to ensure her safety, even though she couldn't help continuing to worry about his safety too.

Soon though he motioned for her to follow him outside, and they walked along the short path between buildings till he used his card to open the side door to the precinct office building and, after glancing inside, had her enter first.

The building was a nice one, smaller but somewhat resembling One Police Plaza, the headquarters of the New York City Police Department. Rectangular, gray in color, it had rows of windows for each of the seven floors inside, all of them indicating where offices or conference rooms were located. Even though they hadn't entered the front way, they both nevertheless had to scan their cards through security detectors before they could go beyond the entry. Visitors had to go in by way of a security checkpoint at the main building entrance that had a metal detector, which picked out the badges and weapons of visiting law enforcement officers as well as anything civilian visitors might be carrying.

Colleen's office and the main conference room were on the top floor, but their team's temporary CSI offices were on the third. Some of the greeting officers in uniform were walking along the tile floor. Kyra recognized most and nodded a hello.

She figured at least some had heard what had happened to her since their greetings were even more profuse and friendly than usual.

And those she didn't recognize? Okay, she was being paranoid, but that was okay under the circumstances. They were probably known by at least some of the other cops around. It would be gutsy even for the Jewelry Slayer to attempt to disguise himself as a police officer. And no one was being stared at or otherwise picked out of the crowd by the others who worked here.

She noticed that, beside her, Patrick was scanning the others around them too, as if he had suspicions as well, but that was just Patrick being his protective self.

Soon they'd gotten onto one of the closest elevators and exited on the third floor. The wooden office doors were all closed, and no one wandered the hall. Good. That felt safer to Kyra, even though she had no reason to feel this building had been compromised.

No reason other than her continuing concern for her safety.

The door to Patrick's office was just to the right of the elevators, but he accompanied her to the next one, which led into her office.

And yes, he opened it and went inside first to look around. This was getting repetitious and even a bit annoying—but she knew he thought it necessary, even in her own office.

Maybe more so in her office than anyplace else in the building, actually. If her enemy had made his way inside, he had probably figured out where her office was.

Fortunately though, it was empty. Hers. It felt as calm and peaceful as her home, at least somewhat.

She pulled her comfortable office chair from beneath her metal desk and sat down, sighing in happiness. Her desktop computer was at the side, turned off of course, since she hadn't been there in days.

That was where she recorded all her information, mostly after ensuring that all evidence she'd collected at a crime scene was at a laboratory downstairs or elsewhere at the NYPD or FBI facilities, being logged in and analyzed for whatever significant case she had been investigating at the time.

That was when she actually had evidence she'd collected in her possession at the crime scene before she left it.

Unlike her current difficult situation.

"I'll give Colleen a call," Patrick told her before she could get too comfortable, especially with her baby bump. That was appropriate. They had to learn when and where the meeting would be, although Kyra figured it was likely to be at the main conference room on the top floor.

Sure enough, it was. When Patrick put his phone in speaker mode, Colleen sounded glad to hear from them. "The others I've asked here are already arriving. Please come to my office first, then we'll join them."

"Be there in a few," Patrick said, his eyes on Kyra's face, and she nodded.

They took the elevator up to the seventh floor. Patrick wouldn't have minded walking, but four flights of stairs wouldn't be good for his pregnant coworker. And the elevators here were fairly quick.

When they exited on the top floor, they headed toward Colleen's office. The plaster walls here had more roughness than on other floors and were an attractive pale green that went well with the wooden floor. There were fewer doors here too than on the other floors. Offices and conference rooms were larger.

The door to the office that was their goal was already open, and why not? Colleen was expecting them, and maybe the others about to attend the meeting would also go there first.

Even so, Patrick made his way around Kyra—and yes, he'd kept his eyes open as they'd made the short walk down the hall. "Hi, Colleen," he called inside. "It's Patrick and Kyra."

"Come on in," she said, and they did.

As always, Patrick was impressed by the larger size

of her office, and he particularly liked the photograph on the wall near her desk, metal like theirs but also larger. The photo showed Colleen shaking hands with the man who had been captain of this precinct before her, both in uniform.

Colleen stood close by and didn't suggest they sit down. "Has everything been okay with you?" She was regarding Kyra, unsurprisingly. "Last we talked, I gathered there'd been no indication that your attacker has come after you, but that's part of what we want to talk about, as well as let you know more of what the investigation has been like so far."

Colleen was an attractive older lady, with intense blue eyes and straight white teeth set in a lined face with moderate makeup and framed by her longish blond hair. Her uniform fit her slim body well.

"That sounds fine with me," Kyra said. "But—has anything been found, like the stolen evidence, or more about who the Jewelry Slayer is?"

"We'll discuss that and more," Colleen said as she ushered them back out the door, holding a tablet computer in one hand. Patrick assumed the answers were largely, if not entirely, negative.

Once they were back in the hallway, he saw Wells Blackthorn enter the door to the conference room. Wells's office was next to Colleen's, just before where the meeting room was located. He wondered if everyone else planning to attend was already there, or whether they'd dribble in.

Turned out that everyone he'd anticipated being there had beaten them to it. In addition to Wells, the members of the CSI team reporting to Kyra and him were all present: Craig, Rosa and Mitch. They all sat around the long rectangular table in the center of the room. Several seats among them remained vacant, and Patrick wasn't surprised Colleen headed to the far end of the table.

As they said their hellos to everyone, Patrick let Kyra determine where she wanted to sit—across from the door, as it turned out, in the chair beside Craig. There was an empty seat at her other side, and Patrick chose that one.

He probably didn't need to do much to protect her here, but he preferred being near her. After all, they were the heads of their special CSI team. Plus, they had both been present at the scene of the Jewelry Slayer's latest murder, though their experiences there had been somewhat different. Even so, they could coordinate what they said and did, at least to some extent.

And it made sense for them to hear together what the others had to say about their portions of the investigation—and whether anything useful had come of them.

Once they were all seated, Colleen said, "Thank you all for being here. I figured it would be best for all of us to coordinate in our most recent efforts to find the Jewelry Slayer and the evidence that proves he was the killer at the crime scene where Kyra was attacked—and was also the one who attacked her. Because Patrick and she haven't been in the office since, I'd like the rest of you, one at a time, to go over what you've been up to and anything you've discovered, even if you've reported it to me, or even to Patrick and Kyra."

Sounded right to Patrick. It might be somewhat repetitious to them, but a recap was always in order.

He watched as Kyra sat back in her chair, her hands on its arms and not near her baby bump, and looked from one person at the table to the next, appearing as professional as usual.

"Okay," Colleen said. "Who wants to go first?"

"I think Kyra and Patrick ought to go first," Wells said, "since they were the ones there starting out and... and went through whatever they went through."

Patrick liked the tall sergeant who sat there looking expectantly from Kyra to him, then back again. But at the moment, he would have preferred kicking him in his skinny butt.

Oh, he didn't mind talking, but he'd have preferred not putting Kyra through that, especially not right away.

But she just nodded and leaned forward, putting her arms on the table after maneuvering a bit to do so. "All right." She aimed a glance at him first through her lovely dark eyes, then began describing all that had happened that day, from their arrival at the crime scene and her careful collection of evidence in plastic bags...to the moment of confrontation by her attacker, who Patrick continued to assume was the Jewelry Slayer rather than another patsy hired to distract, like the woman who screamed had apparently been.

Kyra's voice was strong yet hoarse, and Patrick heard the emotion in it. He wanted to stand and draw her close to somehow make it easier on her. But even if he could make it somewhat easier, acting unprofessional wouldn't help.

She finally ended with her description of the man confronting her, grabbing the plastic bags, wiping his feet along the dirt in the area to attempt to hide any additional evidence—and then confronting her.

How she had pulled his hoodie, which he'd drawn

down to obscure his face, away enough that she could see his face.

How he then had insulted her, snarled—and fled as Patrick approached.

Then it was his turn.

Kyra had seen the emotion on Patrick's face as she spoke, as if he wanted to both confront the jerk who attacked her—and to hug her in comfort.

She appreciated that—and she also appreciated that Patrick had acted completely professionally by saying nothing and swinging his gaze at least part of the time from one person here to the next.

He told his own tale of hearing a woman scream, assuming she was the one being attacked, and rushing to help—only to find she had disappeared and apparently had simply screamed to get his attention while the other person there went after the evidence being collected. And Kyra.

Kyra mostly watched Patrick as he talked, but she also glanced at the others in the room who all appeared to know the story, considering how they nodded as they looked somberly at her. And she had spoken with some of them before.

"Okay," Colleen finally said as Patrick finished. "I think we were all mostly aware of what they both said. Now, I'd like the rest of you to inform Kyra and Patrick of what you've been up to, even if you've already notified them."

One by one, they did. Craig started. He knew their story best since they'd related it to him when he'd come to check on them—and brought pizza. The guy, despite being in his late twenties, was slightly more senior on their team than the other CSIs reporting to Patrick and her. Like the rest of them, his shirt was white and his trousers black. But he still managed to appear a bit casual since he had light brown stubble on his face, as if his shave that morning hadn't lasted the day.

He described working at the crime scene with Rosa and Mitch, searching hard for evidence that was no longer there. Expressing his frustration along with the others.

Next, Rosa. Kyra remembered well their discussion when the excellent Black CSI, with short braided hair and a frequent smile, was on-site and called Kyra to ask a lot of questions.

But her answers apparently hadn't helped Rosa locate any remaining evidence—another indication that none existed.

And Mitch? The slightly overweight guy, with short dark hair and the usual outfit of white shirt and black trousers, was eager and attentive and seemed to describe running circles in the area attempting to help Rosa—but still not coming up with anything useful.

Darn it.

When they all were done, Colleen asked some cogent questions, but Kyra heard nothing to indicate any of them had done anything but an excellent job of attempting to find answers—anything that would help them or others to identify and locate the Jewelry Slayer. Which only frustrated Kyra more. And, glancing at the somewhat irritated expression on Patrick's face, she figured she wasn't the only one.

"All right, then," Colleen finally said. "We, and others in the precinct, clearly have a lot more to do to get the answers we need. And I'm going to come up with some additional thoughts and instructions to make sure we all keep working on it." She paused, then said, "So for now, why don't we head to the other subject we all need to focus on."

"The Landmark Killer?" Wells surmised aloud.

"What else?"

Kyra had been somewhat involved in that investigation too, though not as much as some of the others who sat there. She had even discussed it a bit with Patrick—and knew he had a vested interest in solving that one as well.

When she looked at him again now, she saw his expression had grown from irritated to even more angry.

And she wondered what he was thinking.

# Chapter 16

Oh, yeah. Patrick and his fellow CSIs, including Kyra, had been working with others on their FBI team specializing in serial killers to particularly deal with this one: the Landmark Killer. That had been one of their most important assignments over the past weeks, along with the Jewelry Slayer, and they had discussed the situation often together and with others.

Recently, the guy had even been identified. He was the local FBI director's former assistant, Xander Washer.

And Patrick was furious with the guy. He had murdered people at local New York landmarks, apparently in anger and retribution after Maeve O'Leary, another major crime suspect, had finally been caught.

In fact, last week, soon after they ID'd him, a text came in from Xander to the entire team. Took you long enough. Too bad so sad that I'll reach the end of the goddess Maeve O'Leary's name and you'll never catch me.

Which unfortunately could be the case, considering how many murders he had already committed.

Maeve was formerly a Black Widow killer. After she'd been arrested, Xander, who apparently admired her—a lot—had begun murdering people at various landmarks one at a time, choosing places that started with the letters in Maeve's name and in the same order, trying to get her released.

And Patrick's anger was multiplied because the Landmark Killer had also made it personal. After a recent investigation, he had sent Patrick that taunting text message about his not having found some DNA evidence in an Upper East Side hotel, and the killer had struck again. Every time Patrick thought of it and the taunt, he couldn't help thinking about his former colleague—and former girlfriend—Ursula Andrews, who'd missed that evidence. And that had led to their breakup.

It also made Patrick too aware of some of the problems dating a colleague could lead to.

What a mistake that had been. He was determined never to date a colleague again.

Although... He saw that Kyra was watching him with care and concern. Drat.

Oh, yes, he cared about her. He would do anything to keep her safe.

But enter into any kind of personal relationship with her?

As intriguing as that seemed, recalling Ursula and all the problems that had caused reminded him much too clearly that he had to keep everything with Kyra strictly professional.

And so he dragged his glance from Kyra and watched

Colleen as she described the latest information in the Landmark Killer investigation.

There hadn't been much news recently. The sad part was, although the detectives involved continued to investigate any and all evidence regarding the most recent murders, they recognized that Xander was likely to strike again. Soon.

And though they knew he chose New York landmarks with the same initials as Maeve O'Leary's name and so far had gotten through *M-A-E-V-E-O-L-E-A*, the discussion about the many possibilities there were for *R* reached no conclusions. Yet. But the group meeting now mentioned every place from the obvious like Radio City Music Hall, Rockefeller Center and Riverside Park to less likely locations such as Edward Ridley & Sons Department Store, the Robbins & Appleton Building, the Rogers, Peet and Company building and even the areas in Queens named Ridgewood.

Patrick joined in as much as he could, but giving opinions on something like this was fruitless and frustrating.

"Okay," Colleen finally said. "Let's keep in touch about this and tell one another whatever ideas we have."

A lot of positive murmurs followed.

Then Colleen said, "And let's keep trying to find the Jewelry Slayer and get together again soon to discuss our progress, preferably with Kyra here as long as that works for her."

Patrick wasn't surprised to see Kyra nod vehemently as she said, "Definitely."

He understood. She seemed slightly happier here, maybe more relaxed than at her home, though he felt just the opposite. Oh, he'd seen no indication she was in more danger here than elsewhere. But it was harder to protect her out in public.

Although here he'd have quite a team of others to help, if any problems arose.

But soon they would head back to her house, and who knew if the Jewelry Slayer knew where she currently was, or where she lived?

Meanwhile, Colleen was finishing. "You all know the rendering of the Jewelry Slayer that Kyra helped with is in the system. Keep checking it as you go into the field, in case you notice someone similar."

"Please do," Kyra said. "But also be aware I can't guarantee it's perfect, or even as close as I'd like. The stress I was under at the time, plus trying to recall enough for a sketch and then more—"

"We understand," Colleen broke in softly, and the others nodded.

The meeting broke up and those present said bye to Kyra and Patrick and promised to do their best to find the Jewelry Slayer—as if they hadn't been already.

Colleen, hanging out till last, walked out the door with them. "Tell you what, Kyra," she said. "How about taking a quick scan of some faces already in our system in case one strikes your memory, possibly looking a bit different from your rendering and its online version? That can happen, and in fact does happen quite a bit."

Patrick assumed Kyra would agree, and she did.

"I'd be glad to," she said as they stopped in the hall near Colleen's office. "Like I said, I recognize that, despite my efforts, the guy could look different from that picture."

The smile on their attractive senior boss's face looked appreciative and caring. "You're clearly more than a

CSI," she said. "You've got a good comprehension of law enforcement and finding the truth. And I suspect your recollection of the guy's face is pretty good, so the rendering might be as well."

"I hope," Kyra said. "So who should I check with now to look at the faces already in the system?"

"Our deputy commissioner Walt Elderson and you apparently worked well together before. He'd be a good one to work with again now. He's in his office on the second floor."

"Sounds good." Kyra glanced toward Patrick, and he nodded.

Kyra wasn't surprised that Patrick remained with her. As always, she appreciated it, even though she didn't feel particularly in danger here at the precinct offices. She nevertheless quickly stroked her tummy bulge as they walked, making sure no one appeared to be watching.

Patrick and she were soon in Walt's office. Most of the precinct's highly technical stuff was on that floor. Kyra knew there were a lot of different kinds of computers but didn't know what they all were designed for, nor did she need to know.

At the moment, what was important was to check out whatever faces of perpetrators of various crimes Walt could show her, just in case she happened to recognize a very important one.

"Hi, guys." Walt didn't sound surprised to see them. Colleen might have alerted him that Patrick and she were at the station, so he might expect they'd stop in. "Let's go down the hall to one of the main computers so I can put you into the system." The tall young technology expert, wearing his usual blue shirt over dark pants, led them through the hall to a door at the end. On the way they passed a couple of others whom Kyra recognized as part of the precinct's Department of Information Technology, who said hi and appeared to look at her closely. They undoubtedly knew what had happened to her and had been given information about looking at the current rendering of her assailant in their system. But no one said anything about it as they passed.

Soon, Kyra sat in front of one of several computers in the room at the end of the hall, and Walt set things up so she could scan through the database of mug shots. He particularly aimed her toward men of the approximate age she had indicated in her drawing and the subsequent computer rendering.

A few had some similar characteristics. Several could have been him—or not. But none caught her attention as clearly being the guy who had stolen the evidence and attacked her.

When she was done, she had to ask, "Is that everyone in the system?"

"Not really," Walt replied. "We've got a lot. But I tried showing you as many as I could who were possibilities. I compared our computer rendering with a bunch of them too. And if anyone else starts standing out, or if you think of any other characteristics we should look for, just let me know and I'll show some other faces to you next time you're around."

"Like tomorrow," she said, not looking at Patrick, who sat in a chair behind her, to her left.

At least he didn't object. But she couldn't be sure he'd go along with that.

Her intent? Her hope? To start acting as if she was returning already to her job, her life.

They soon returned to their CSI offices, and Kyra requested time to hang out at her own desk and check emails and any snail mail that might have come in.

"Fine," Patrick said, standing in her doorway watching as she sat down. "Let's stay here for another hour. I'll ask Colleen to have a patrol in unmarked cars follow us back to your place then, just in case."

"Sounds good."

When an hour had passed, Patrick returned to Kyra's office after spending the time in his own doing pretty much what she said she was going to do.

He didn't see anything too exciting in his email or otherwise in the stuff that had piled up over the past days. Now, he knocked on Kyra's door but didn't wait for her to ask him inside.

He wanted to observe her face as she presumably was still checking her computer or mail—just in case she had received a threat online or on paper.

She looked up at him immediately with an expression on her lovely face that suggested she had been concentrating on the computer and didn't seem particularly concerned. Certainly not frightened in any way, or otherwise appearing as if she had seen anything inappropriate.

Nothing from the Jewelry Slayer, presumably, even though the guy might have figured out who she was and where her office was. She was clearly a crime scene investigator who was working in the precinct where he'd attacked her, after all.

"So how's it going?" he asked, smiling—and hoping all was well.

"Just fine. Didn't see anything particularly exciting, though I noticed a few other incidents being investigated by the precinct that might involve serial killers and will eventually require a CSI from our team at the crime scenes."

"I saw them too," he said. "And I already contacted Craig to coordinate who'll go out in the field and work on them."

A stubborn expression appeared on Kyra's face. "I know you're doing what's right, but we're both running this team so I should be in on the designations as well."

"Yeah," he said. "I understand. But I'm also—"

"Doing what you feel is necessary to protect me. I get it." Her smile now was wry, and he had an urge to approach and stroke that smooth cheek of hers.

But he was not going to do anything like that. Not now, and definitely not here.

"So are you ready to go back to your place?" he asked. "I already checked with Colleen, and she'll have a patrol or several keep an eye on us."

Kyra clearly sighed. "Okay," she said. "And I know you're just…being you. Yeah, let's go home. But before we do—"

"I know. You've already made it clear you want to come back here tomorrow. At least you're not demanding to go out in the field on any of those cases. So—well, assuming all goes well tonight, let's try to return tomorrow."

And he hoped that wasn't a big, untimely assumption.

He maintained all the usual cautions going into the

garage with Kyra to get her car, which was where they'd been told it would be. They would leave his here for now. When he'd let Colleen know they were ready to leave, she had a uniformed officer accompany them, and Patrick also saw a couple of marked cars patrolling inside the garage. Kyra and he reached her car safely, and he drove them onto the street also without incident.

Nor did they run into any trouble on the way back to her apartment. She confirmed to him that she would put together another dinner for them that night from the groceries her folks had brought—maybe not as exciting or oriented toward her background as last night's was, but that was fine with him.

At one point on their drive he heard an alarm, and a vehicle went speeding by. He felt his heart rate accelerate and also saw Kyra touch her baby bump, but there was no reason for them to stop once the ambulance passed, and they were soon able to get into Kyra's garage and then her apartment—after Patrick took a quick but careful look around.

That evening was uneventful. And when Patrick climbed into Kyra's bed beside her and watched her sleepy smile as they traded good-nights, he resisted his urge to hug and kiss her, reminding himself of his stimulated memories of his long-ago ex and why he wouldn't let himself get involved with a coworker again, the same kind of reminders he'd been giving himself a lot over the past few days.

The next morning, Kyra was clearly feeling well and eager to return to the office. Patrick checked with Colleen, who seemed pleased to have them come back and promised to keep things around there as safe as the day before.

And so Patrick did his now usual thing of checking around the area inside and outside Kyra's building, and they again headed to the precinct.

They did pretty much the same for the next few days. Things seemed too quiet, Patrick considered often as he sat in his office—or walked slightly down the hall to check on Kyra.

No indication the Jewelry Slayer had committed any more robberies or homicides. Both Kyra and he spent a lot of their time in the office going over existing evidence, trying to nail down more of what the guy was about—and where he might be. Was he hiding out even more now that he knew law enforcement officers might think they had even better reason to track him down since he'd endangered one of their own?

But that wasn't entirely true. When there was a homicide, and especially a string of serial murders, the FBI and this precinct and all others were determined to locate and arrest the perpetrator as soon as they could. The fact that the most recent person to be endangered after a murder was a CSI shouldn't make a difference— though it did to Patrick. But he knew his fellow cops would also do what they could to bring the perp down as fast as they could.

No, he assumed the guy was biding his time, maybe planning another robbery and homicide if he couldn't get to the CSI who'd seen his face. Or even if he thought he could.

Kyra seemed a bit tired now and then but remained eager to go to their offices, though she mentioned she'd like to be out in the field conducting actual crime scene investigations, rather than only assisting at the office by reviewing evidence online brought in by their sub-ordinates or others, while the labs started their analysis.

He understood that. He would have liked to be out in the field as well.

But until the Jewelry Slayer was caught, Patrick's place would be at Kyra's side during times they weren't in the office, and in his own office next to hers when they were at work.

It was frustrating though. Things were too slow. Patrick had an urge to go out there to help…but if anything happened to the woman he was trying so hard not to be attracted to he would never forgive himself, particularly if he wasn't around her at the time.

And nothing would happen to her when he was around. He would make sure of it.

The days morphed into a routine. He could tell Kyra was as frustrated as he was.

She spoke to her parents a lot at night, and he knew she was trying hard to sound happy at how things were going.

But she wasn't.

Nights at home. Sleeping near each other in her bed. And yes, he did disobey his own self mandates and give Kyra hugs and kisses at bedtime—feeling, oh, so well, her baby bump against him.

During the days, they worked several hours at the office after clearing it with Colleen. Working at their desks rather than conducting true crime scene investigations. Discussing the Landmark Killer, but not as much as the Jewelry Slayer.

No indication, fortunately, that Kyra had been located by the Jewelry Slayer or was about to be attacked.

And then one morning, maybe a week after this routine started, they were both on his phone sitting at Kyra's kitchen table after eating breakfast, prepared to confirm it was okay for them to come in that day.

"It definitely is," Colleen said. "And you'll be interested to learn there's been a bit of evidence learned in the case that might finally help us determine the identity of the Jewelry Slayer."

"Really?" Kyra exclaimed, pushing her chair from the table and standing. "Can you tell us what it is?"

"I will when you're here," Colleen said. "It's something that might help you identify him at last."

"On our way now." Kyra looked at Patrick as if wanting his confirmation—although he had the sense she'd be on her way there soon whether he was with her or not.

"Yes," he told her, grinning at her return smile—and resisting the urge to take her in his arms now, during the day, as he did when they headed to bed. "We'll be there soon."

# Chapter 17

As it turned out, Patrick did not wind up staying with Kyra at the station, but instead counted on other law enforcement officers to ensure her safety there, at least for a while.

First, he drove Kyra to the station and parked her car in its regular spot. He called Colleen to let her know they'd arrived, and she told them to come to her office right away.

There, Patrick was a bit surprised to see his cousin Detective Rory Colton sitting in a chair facing Colleen's desk.

Rory rose as they entered. "Hi, cuz," she said. "And hi, Kyra."

Despite being younger than him and somewhat petite, Rory was known as one of the best detectives in this precinct. Her black hair was short, in a pixie cut, and her green eyes stared challengingly at him as she smiled, as if she was prodding him to say something.

Which he did. "Hi back, cuz." Was she involved with the evidence Colleen had mentioned? Why else would she be here now? "Are you working on the Jewelry Slayer case too?" He assumed she was. It was one of the most important cases in the precinct now, and a detective with her excellent reputation would undoubtedly be called in to help with the investigation.

"I sure am. And I thought I'd check to see if you wanted to accompany me to a meeting I have scheduled in an hour or so."

"Should I want to?" he asked, figuring she was goading him for a reason and wanting to goad her back.

She approached where he stood beside Kyra and looked up into his face. She was dressed in an attractive and somewhat formal black suit. "I think so. There's a possible informant I'm about to talk with, and I know you have a vested interest in the case since you at least got a glimpse of the Jewelry Slayer."

"Then I should come too," Kyra said, "since I'm the one who got the best look at him."

"Oh, the person I'm meeting with isn't the perp," Rory said. "He just contacted our office, probably using a burner phone, and said he has some possibly helpful information. But—well, in case things aren't what they seem, I think it would be wise for you not to be present." Rory's gaze dipped toward Kyra's baby bump, then back toward Patrick. "I just figured that if what he had to say was useful, it would be helpful for one of you two to hear it, but Patrick's the logical one."

Before Kyra could object, Patrick said, "Makes sense to me. I'll let you know what he says, of course," he told Kyra. "But you know how important it is for you to stay safe."

"But are you going to be in danger?" Kyra looked at him, then almost accusingly at Rory.

"He'll be fine," his cousin said. "I'll make sure of it."

Before Kyra could protest further, Patrick told Rory, "Great. Let's go."

Rory drove them in her black official SUV toward Grand Central Station and parked in a lot near there. After walking half a block along the busy sidewalk, they entered a pizza restaurant.

"I haven't met our contact before, but he said he'd get a table near the door to the kitchen."

When they made their way around the other filled tables and busy waitstaff, Patrick saw only one table with a single guy sitting there. "Him?" he asked.

"Could be."

It made sense since that man wore a thick, gray sweatshirt and a cap on his head that all but obscured his face—attempting to disguise himself? Or at least not have his identity too obvious.

They approached, and Rory leaned down toward the guy. "John?" she asked, and Patrick figured that was an assumed name so he wouldn't be identified too.

"Yeah." The guy stood, placed a twenty-dollar bill on the table and led them out the door. If he was attempting not to be easily identifiable, Patrick wondered why he wanted to meet in a restaurant. Or maybe he just figured he'd be easier for them to find that way.

Soon, they'd exited and were standing at the side of the restaurant's building. "You're that detective I was talking to?" he asked Rory.

"Yes, and this is one of my coworkers." Rory nodded toward Patrick without mentioning anything else about their relationship, or Patrick's position with the FBI as a lead CSI agent.

Or that Patrick had gotten a glimpse of the Jewelry Slayer.

"Okay," the guy said. "Like I told you, I don't know much, but I wanted to let the cops know that...well, no details about it, but my girlfriend has some pretty valuable jewelry that she likes to wear on the job. And I'm not going to tell you what that job is."

Patrick surmised it could be anything from a Broadway actress to a call girl, but didn't ask. It wasn't important.

But what did she know?

"John" soon continued, "She's been pretty nervous about that Jewelry Slayer guy and has been asking some questions of her friends and coworkers. Not much info is out there—but, well, she did hear that word on the street is that the guy's name is Pete."

"Pete who?" Rory asked immediately.

"That's all she learned. But I figured it would be a good idea to pass at least that along to you cops, just in case it helped you bring the guy down. I sure don't want him to go after my girlfriend. Now, I've got to leave."

Before they could ask anything else, John turned and hurried away.

"That's your confidential informant's information?" Patrick asked Rory.

"Hey, it might be better than nothing. Or not. But we can try to follow up on it just in case."

"Sure," Patrick said. "Just in case."

They talked more about Colton family things than their jobs as they drove back to the station, but nothing new there either.

"Okay, then," Rory said after she'd parked and they had reentered the station's large lobby. "I'm going to get my detective group busy checking out any crimes recently committed by anyone identified as having the name Pete, and I assume you'll do the same with your CSIs and any evidence they located where a Pete was in possession of it or otherwise involved."

"You got it," Patrick said. They took an elevator upstairs. Rory remained on it while Patrick exited on the third floor.

He went to Kyra's office. She didn't rise from her desk as he walked in, but she smiled at him, which made him feel all fuzzy inside.

Enough of that. He kept his own expression professional—mostly. But heck, yes, he did aim a quick smile at her as he jumped into telling what he'd learned.

"Hey," he said. "I'm not sure how helpful the lead will be, but Rory's contact let us know that word is out there that the Jewelry Slayer's first name is Pete."

He watched her face, but her expression, though interested, didn't change much. "If so, he didn't tell me."

He laughed. "Well, in case it'll help, I'll contact Walt right now and ask him to run you through the digital mug shots of those in the system whose first name is Pete, and we'll see if any look familiar. Okay?"

"Fine with me. I'm willing to try nearly anything to identify that sleaze of a guy."

Patrick pulled his phone from his pocket and called Walt, putting him on speaker so Kyra could hear.

Patrick quickly explained what he'd learned, acknowledging it might not mean anything. Walt immediately said, "Hey, I'll start bringing up all the mug shots of the Petes I can find in our system. You want to come here now so Kyra can check them out?"

"Definitely," Kyra called, and after Patrick hung up they got on their way to the second floor, passing the closed doors of the other CSI offices. Far as Patrick knew, their subordinates were out in the field—perhaps even checking more into scenes of the Jewelry Slayer's crimes. Or not. It had been a while since the last one, and that scene had been scrutinized carefully. He would talk to them all later to learn what they'd been up to that day.

"You okay?" he asked Kyra as the elevator door opened on the second floor.

"Okay enough. I don't really like looking for the guy, but I definitely hope I find him and identify him soon."

"Got it."

They soon entered the tech offices and immediately headed to where the computers Kyra had been shown previously were located.

Walt sat in front of the one Kyra had used the last time. "Got a few Petes here already, and there are more in the system."

Patrick noticed the grim way Kyra sucked in her lips. He was about to ask again if she was okay, but she beat him to it as she sat down. "I'm not looking for a good time here, but I'm glad to do this further check. I really want to nail that guy."

Patrick understood. He admired her. He knew this had to be difficult for her. She'd feel bad if, after all this, she still couldn't ID him.

And if she did? Would they be able to find him? Get enough evidence in addition to her identification to bring him in and get him convicted?

He could certainly hope so.

With Walt's assistance, Kyra began going through the mug shots one by one, each identified this time with the first name of Pete.

None apparently struck Kyra as familiar at first. She acted totally professional, letting Walt and him know which characteristics in each were similar to or different from the man she'd seen. They were mostly actual photos, although a few were artwork comparable to what had been done after Kyra's attempt to sketch the guy, then help make it a more realistic image online.

Some had different shaped faces or ethnicities. Others had different colored hair or styles that weren't the same as the man she'd seen. Different eye colors. More facial hair.

Patrick admired how precise and careful she was. But he knew she was getting tired. And frustrated.

So was he, but he wouldn't say anything to her. Maybe she didn't recall the face as well as she'd hoped.

Or maybe the guy just wasn't in the system.

Patrick kept observing her review of the computer, avoiding checking his phone or watch for the time. But—

"That's him!" Kyra suddenly exclaimed, half standing and pointing toward the computer screen. "I'm sure of it. That's the face I recall, oh, so well, especially now I'm seeing it again."

"Who is it?" Patrick demanded.

Walt immediately pressed some buttons on the keyboard and the faces stopped scrolling. "It's Pete Coleman," he said, squinting over Kyra's shoulder toward the screen.

Yeah, this guy resembled not only the picture Kyra

had helped with, but also the way she had described the man who'd attacked her at the crime scene: Caucasian with maybe a slight tan, deep brown eyes, curved, dark brows, hair somewhat thin but longish on top of his head, with sideburns. And also long teeth.

Patrick respected Kyra's judgment. This had to be the man who assailed her. The Jewelry Slayer.

"Okay, then," he said immediately to Walt. "What's his record? Why is he in the system?"

"Not because he's been identified before as the Jewelry Slayer, but apparently there were some incidents in the past where he attacked people, mostly women, and robbed them of jewelry, money, whatever. He was arrested and tried and found guilty of at least a couple, but he wasn't found guilty of hurting people badly, let alone killing them, and his loot was recovered, so he didn't get much prison time…then."

"It should be far different now," Patrick said. "We need to have him brought in. Do you have information about where he lives, or—"

Before Walt could answer, Kyra began to stand, grasping her stomach and moaning loudly.

"Are you okay?" Patrick asked in deep concern. He drew closer, putting one arm around her as he stared into her face.

Her closed eyes and agonized expression suggested she was in pain. Deep pain.

She slumped, nearly falling to the floor, but Patrick grasped her firmly, keeping her tight against him.

She gasped, then began panting, with her lips in an O. And then she stopped. At least for then.

"I think," she said, teeth clenched and tone suggesting she was hurting. Badly. "I think the baby is on the way."

\* \* \*

The pain in Kyra's middle was like nothing she had ever felt before—unsurprisingly.

Fortunately, the worst of it didn't last long. But she knew she'd had a contraction. The first, but it was a major one.

More would come, most likely.

Now? Surely not. This had to be false labor, right? The baby was approaching seven months, too young to be born.

But if it was born now, surely it was old enough to be healthy.

She appreciated how Patrick held her close, supporting her body—and her mind.

"Hey," he said, "we know the hospital, and they know us from your last visit. Let's head there right away."

She knew he was attempting to keep his tone light but also realized he was serious.

Should she go to the hospital?

Maybe so. One contraction didn't mean she was about to have her baby, but in case it was the first of many…

At the hospital, they could tell her what was going on and make sure the baby was okay. And it would be better than hanging out at the office, or even going home, without knowing for sure what was happening.

"I wouldn't mind seeing some of my new buddies at the hospital." She tried to keep her own words, and tone, light. But she knew things might be serious.

The pain she had felt was definitely serious. And if there were more contractions, *when* there were more, what would she do?

Having medical attention would be a good thing.

"Is there anything I can do?" Walt asked.

"How about accompanying us to my car?" Patrick responded. "I want to help Kyra, if she needs it, and you can too. And you can also be our eyes to keep watch in case that guy Pete happens to be out there."

At his words, Kyra's pain started again. Another contraction? Oh, yes, she realized, again grasping her midsection as if that would help.

A lot of pain.

She couldn't think for a minute or more as the pain increased, then started to ease. Oh, yes. She had no doubt she was in labor.

Was it because identifying the Jewelry Slayer had triggered some things inside her that had been unanticipated this soon?

Patrick held her hand as she bent over till the agony subsided enough for her to stand. To breathe.

"Let's go to the hospital," she managed to gasp.

"See if the station has a wheelchair," Patrick demanded of Walt.

"No need," Kyra said. She hoped. But after a minute she started walking toward the elevator. Patrick still held her hand, and Walt went ahead to press buttons.

When they were outside on the sidewalk, Patrick looked around them and told Walt to do the same, then wait with her while he got his car. He was back so soon that Kyra assumed he must have run.

After Walt and Patrick helped her into the passenger seat, Patrick drove quickly, telling her again they were headed to the same hospital where she had been examined after her attack. It was the closest to the station too.

No more contractions yet. But Kyra felt rumblings and movement inside that suggested more were on the way.

"Can you call your parents?" Patrick asked her.

"I don't want to worry them," she said immediately. But she knew he was right.

Even if it was false labor—and she was pretty sure it wasn't—her parents would want to know and be there with her.

"If you don't, I will, next time we stop at a light. But give me your dad's number."

"I'll do it." She got her phone out of her purse, on the seat beside her. But before she could press any number in, the pain began again. She stopped, trying hard not to gasp or moan, but she did anyway.

"Are you having another contraction?" he asked. "Never mind. I know the answer."

She took a deep breath, then began panting a little. She'd read that something similar was what women in labor were supposed to do but suspected she wasn't doing it right for where she was in the process.

Even so, it helped with the pain, if only a little.

What was next? Her water would break sometime, but hopefully not here, in Patrick's car.

Fortunately, it didn't take long to get to the hospital, thanks to Patrick's fast but safe driving. Somehow, lights and traffic seemed supportive. But she didn't call her parents yet, though at Patrick's request she programmed their numbers into his phone.

Patrick pulled the car up at the hospital's emergency entrance, and some people in scrubs, probably emergency medical technicians, hurried over to them.

One came up to Patrick's window and Kyra saw him open it. "Need some help?" the concerned-looking guy asked, then peered past Patrick to where Kyra sat. "Is she in labor?"

"We think so," Patrick said as Kyra felt another contraction begin.

The EMT immediately got a gurney, and they soon had Kyra out of the car.

"Please do call my parents," she managed to say to Patrick, although she hoped to keep her purse with her so she'd have her identification and medical insurance card with her. That meant she would also have her phone. But using it could be a problem.

"I sure will," he said as the EMTs began wheeling her away while her latest contraction continued.

She began breathing even heavier this time, again probably not the way she should do it. She wished Patrick could stay with her.

But she, and her baby, needed medical help right now.

Oh, yes. She was sure her baby was on the way.

# *Chapter 18*

Damn, Patrick thought. He wanted to stay with Kyra as much as he could, for her protection and his own concern about her, especially now. But at the moment he had to get rid of the car.

"How will I find her inside?" he called to the technician who'd spoken with him. The guy had started to follow the others.

"Just ask for her at the front desk," he called back.

Patrick wouldn't be able to claim any relationship to her except as a coworker, but hopefully he'd get to see her, or at a minimum check on her condition.

In any case, he parked in the lot along the outer wall of the hospital rather than heading into the garage. Fortunately, he found a spot.

And as he rushed in, he called Sam Patel and let him know what was going on, where they were.

"Kyra's in labor? We'll be there right away." Sam's

tone was emotional, and Patrick heard a woman's voice nearby, undoubtedly Kyra's mother.

He would have company soon as he waited to learn how things were with his colleague—and her labor.

Inside the hospital's main entrance, he stopped at the large entry desk. "Hi," said the receptionist who sat there. The middle-aged woman with light, wavy hair wore unbuttoned white scrubs over a green blouse. "Can I help you?" She appeared familiar, and Patrick assumed he'd seen her when he was here with Kyra the last time.

"Yes, thanks. I just dropped off a coworker who's in labor, and I'll want to hang out in an appropriate waiting room to make sure she's okay. Plus, her parents are on the way and will want to join me."

"I get it." The receptionist smiled. "Here's where you should go."

After her description of how to get there, Patrick headed for an upstairs hallway after stopping in the cafeteria for a cup of coffee. Something stronger, like a beer, would be more appealing but they didn't sell any there.

Soon, after checking with a nurse at a desk in the hallway on his destination floor to make sure Kyra was in the delivery room and doing okay, he went inside the waiting room to sit and stew. No one else was there, so he got his choice of chairs and selected one in a group so Kyra's folks could join him when they arrived.

He made himself sit rather than pace as he worried. Should he patrol the halls, in case Pete somehow knew what was happening and arrived to attack Kyra here? Unlikely. But Patrick did go back out and state to the nurse he'd just spoken with that he was working with this precinct of the NYPD, and he had some concerns about their patient that he didn't specify but asked to be notified if anything suspicious happened. No need to go into detail about his actual background with the FBI.

The nurse's expression turned horrified, but he reassured her that he just might be overreacting.

He hoped.

And while he stood there talking to her, Sam and Riya arrived. Kyra's mom approached Patrick right away. "They told us at the front desk that Kyra is okay and said we should wait here for more information. Have you heard anything?" The worry on her aging face didn't make her look any less like her daughter. As Patrick had seen her before, she wore a jacket over a long, flowing shirt, this time a solid shade of pink, and dark slacks.

"No," Patrick said, "I haven't heard anything, but I was told any news would be provided here. And that's even more likely with you, her parents. I'm just her co-worker, and I let them know that." And hinted there were things going on around her that shouldn't be, but he hadn't gotten into any details about that.

"You're more than that with our daughter." Sam Patel's slight accent seemed stronger as he eyed Patrick through his glasses. He was dressed even more casually than Patrick had seen him before, with a gray sweatshirt over dark blue jeans. They clearly hadn't taken time to change clothes before coming here, even if they'd wanted to. And they definitely had arrived quickly.

"I'm certainly watching out for her," Patrick admitted, without telling her parents why she had apparently gone into labor—after identifying the man who'd attacked her, the Jewelry Slayer. They might learn that later, but not from him.

Nor did he say anything that might trigger their earlier indications that they might consider him an appropriate mate for their daughter and father to her child.

That just wasn't going to happen.

No matter how attracted he felt to her sometimes. He wasn't about to let things go any further. And he certainly didn't want kids.

Kyra's mother asked the nurse if she could be with Kyra during childbirth and was told she would check with the doctor and Kyra and let her know. For now, they should go into the waiting room.

"Let's sit down for a while, okay?" Patrick asked them, and they did, leaving the door open so whoever would come and let Riya know if she could join Kyra would be able to enter right away.

In a few minutes a nurse came in and said Kyra did want her mom to join her. Patrick shrugged off a sudden pang of jealousy. There was no reason for him to be with his colleague then, as long as she remained safe.

In fact, the whole idea of being here while she gave birth was crazy. He should leave. He could make sure there were patrols around the hospital and even alert their security to keep an eye on Kyra.

Heck, he did that anyway, leaving Sam in the waiting room. He knew where hospital security was headquartered from their last visit, and let the people in the office know there were potential issues involving the law enforcement officer in labor.

He returned to the waiting room, where Sam sat on one of the chairs. There was fortunately a television and Patrick turned it on, putting on news. He hoped that was okay with Sam. He didn't really want to get into a conversation with him about what had happened to trigger Kyra's labor, or the fact she'd been going to the office for the past few days—although she might already have informed them.

But instead of just watching, Sam began to pace, clearly nervous about his daughter's situation. Patrick joined Sam after a while. He knew childbirth took some time, but the wait made him even more concerned—and nervous for Kyra too.

They both sat down eventually and yes, watched some news. Fortunately, nothing regarding the Jewelry Slayer or even the Landmark Killer was mentioned.

Eventually a doctor in blue scrubs came in. She looked familiar to Patrick, and he knew she'd been one of the doctors who'd examined Kyra when she was here in the emergency room after her attack by the Jewelry Slayer. She identified herself again as Dr. McGrath and said she was helping with Kyra's delivery. "Kyra's mom asked me to come here and give you a progress report," she said.

Interesting that Riya didn't come herself, but the doctor said things were progressing fine and Riya had wanted to stay there.

"How is Kyra doing?" Sam asked.

"Pretty well. But as you may know, labor can take a while. I suspect she has another three to four hours to go, at least. And our observation and help could be modified since the baby is a bit premature, about seven months, if I understand correctly. Anyway, if you want to stay here, that's fine. You can get something to eat in our cafeteria. But I'll check in with you again as it gets closer, if her mother wants me to. Or she can come here and give a report."

Three to four hours. Or more. Even though he wasn't a father, Patrick knew such things could take time.

And so he hunkered down with Sam to wait.

Sam soon went to the cafeteria and brought back sandwiches for both of them, but Patrick wasn't particularly hungry.

Four hours passed, then five. The TV was turned off. He talked to Sam a bit about his life in the US and in general, and even described a bit what it was like, in his point of view, to be a crime scene investigator—without getting into detail about any cases.

They both grew quiet, and Patrick realized he was starting to fall asleep—when the doctor burst through the waiting room door again. "The baby is here!" she exclaimed. "It's a little boy, and Kyra's now in a room with him, and she and her mother want you to come."

In just a few minutes, they were in that room. At a nurse's request, they all put on sanitary masks she gave them, for the protection of both the baby and his mother.

Kyra, looking exhausted but smiling and not wearing a mask, lay in the bed—with a really cute, tiny infant wrapped in a blanket snuggled up to her. Riya sat in a chair next to the bed, and Sam dashed over.

"Are you okay?" he asked Kyra. "Is the baby okay?"

"We're both fine, Dad," she said. "Although since he came early they're going to check him out in the neo-natal intensive care unit, maybe keep him there for a while. But they said I could have him now for a short while to greet him." She lifted the baby, and her father took him into his arms as Patrick watched. And again felt jealous.

For some reason, he wanted to hold that infant. The

little eyes opened briefly without looking at him or anyone else, but Patrick felt immediately hooked.

Did he want to become a dad after all?

Did he want to become this baby's father?

Heck, no. Right?

He should get out of there. And he would, soon.

But for now, he just watched as Kyra and her parents interacted with her new son. And hoped he would somehow get to know the baby better, as dumb as that might be.

Labor. It definitely hadn't been fun. Despite getting some anesthesia as things progressed, Kyra had hurt. A lot. And now she was sore. And tired. And remained in a hospital bed for the moment after being brought here from the delivery room, though she planned to get up soon.

But no matter that she'd had some pain. Now she was delighted. She was a mom. She already adored her adorable little son.

Watching how delighted her parents seemed only made her happier.

And Patrick was still here. For her protection? Probably. But the expression on his face as he looked at her baby, so sweet, so caring…

Did he like the baby? It certainly seemed so.

Would he make a good father—hey, enough of that.

Better that she worry not about that, but about the health of her premature son. At least the doctors must have figured he wasn't doing too badly, since they didn't whisk him off immediately to the neonatal ICU, though they did conduct what they said was an initial thorough exam in the delivery room and said there was more to come.

Her mother held the baby now. Kyra noted they'd all been given protective masks to wear so they wouldn't breathe germs on her little infant. Even Patrick had one on.

Did he want to hold the baby? Or was he just being protective in this way too?

Being protective was certainly who he was.

Her mom was crooning love words and moving her head close to the baby. Her dad was near them, also smiling behind the mask and clearly happy, especially when the little one was handed to him. He hugged Kyra's baby, but not too tightly, as he also began speaking loving words, this time in his own native language, Gujarati. He'd taught a little of it to Kyra when she was younger.

And then—her father took a few steps closer to Patrick and gently held the baby toward him. Sure, her co-worker was protective and caring, but would he hold her baby?

To her surprise, he took him and hugged him close, though only for a minute before handing him back to her mother. As her mom took the baby, she smiled at Patrick, as if inviting him to hold him more. To join their family.

No. That wasn't going to happen. Kyra thought she'd made that clear to her parents.

But still, the way Patrick had looked while holding the baby... She couldn't help wondering yet again what kind of father he would make someday. Not with her son, but surely someday he would marry, have kids...

"He's really a cute little guy," Patrick said, making Kyra wonder even more about his future as a father.

If only there was a possibility of his remaining in her life as other than a coworker. But she knew better.

"I assume you'll be staying here overnight, at least," he continued.

She doubted that he would. "I think so. They'll be keeping the baby at least overnight and most likely longer for further examination, and they want to keep an eye on both of us."

"Sounds good," Patrick said.

"We'll stay here too," her mom said, but she probably didn't know the primary reason Patrick was asking. He didn't have to hang out here to protect her, at least not now.

Maybe not again. Did knowing who their perp was make it easier for those appropriate in their precinct to catch the guy? Was Pete Coleman already in custody?

She doubted it. If so, someone would have let Patrick know, and he would have told her as well.

"Thanks," she told her mom, who still held the baby. She smiled at her father too. But she didn't look at Patrick. Not at that moment.

Until he asked her, "Have you decided on a name for the little guy yet?"

Interesting that he'd pose that question first. Her parents knew she'd been considering ideas, even running some by them. But they hadn't asked her decision yet.

She looked at Patrick, who had moved to her bedside. Damn, but his handsome face seemed intense, curious, as if he really cared about what she said.

"Yes," she said. "I wanted to pick a name that goes with my wonderful heritage." She glanced at her parents, then held out her arms toward her mother, who carefully placed the infant into them. "This little guy is

Ajay." She hugged the baby, gave him a kiss and said, "Welcome to the world, my wonderful Ajay."

And she was delighted, and surprised, to hear Patrick say, "Yes, welcome to the world, Ajay."

# *Chapter 19*

Okay. Time to leave, Patrick thought.

Otherwise, he'd want to give that cute baby another hug. How had it happened? That little tyke had somehow grabbed his heart. Held it now in a steely grip.

Ridiculous. He'd decided long ago not to have kids of his own, so why become so attached to one that clearly wasn't his?

No matter how much he was attracted to the mother. Too much. He admitted it to himself, but it would go no further.

Never mind that he wanted to hug the baby's mom even more than he wanted to hug the kid.

Kyra looked exhausted—but also exhilarated. Apparently having a baby agreed with her, even though she still lay in her bed, now with Ajay in her arms.

But what good would it do for Patrick to stay there? Apparently she'd remain in this room overnight, at least.

And she'd said the doctors would be giving Ajay further exams in the neonatal intensive care unit. That would allow Kyra to sleep.

She would surely be safe here, even without Patrick hanging around. He'd already notified hospital security to keep an eye on her, and he'd confirm that patrols would continue to go by overnight and as long as she was here to make sure nothing outside looked amiss either.

Oh, yes. It was time for him to go. And for the little that was left of tonight, at least, he could head for his own apartment.

He approached Kyra's bed again to say good-night. Little Ajay was apparently awake, his tiny eyes slightly open, his mouth rooting around as if he was ready to eat—and Patrick assumed Kyra would be nursing him.

Baring her breasts that were currently inside the hospital gown she wore.

Definitely time for Patrick to go—although the idea of watching the baby nurse that way was somehow intriguing to him, and not just because of what he would see of Kyra's body.

"I think it's time for me to leave," he told her, maneuvering around where her folks were.

"Will you be back tomorrow?" Kyra asked, as if it mattered to her. Maybe she figured she would be heading home, or at least hoping she would, and wanted his protection.

"Most likely," he said, despite wanting to shout he definitely would. "Let's talk and see how things are going."

Instead of coming here though, he should go into his office—and beyond.

It would be time for him to dig in and get involved

with the search not only for evidence, but also for the location of their target, Pete.

Get him off the streets before he harmed anyone else.

Get him incarcerated before he could harm Kyra again.

"Please—please let me know tomorrow how the investigation into Pete Coleman is progressing, okay?" Kyra's voice was low, as if she didn't want her parents to hear, but as alert as those two were, Patrick figured they'd heard. They didn't say anything though.

"I'll let you know whatever I find out," he told Kyra, also speaking quietly.

Patrick left then after one more goodbye to Kyra and each of her folks. He wanted to say something to Ajay too, but that would seem ridiculous—wouldn't it?

When he got outside, it was still dark, around five in the morning, and dawn was a couple of hours away. Well, he could sleep for a short while, at least, once he got to his apartment.

And he did get a little sleep. But he managed to get to the office around nine o'clock. He'd grabbed a cup of coffee at a shop along the busy Manhattan street after he parked, and he now sat at his desk.

Leaning on the metal surface, he pulled his phone from his pocket and called Rory. His cousin was the investigator who'd most likely be on the case of seeking the Jewelry Slayer now that he was identified.

Rory answered nearly immediately. "Hey, cuz. Walt and Colleen informed me late yesterday that Kyra ID'd one of the mug shots in the system as belonging to the guy who attacked her—Pete Coleman. We got an APB out on him right away. I wanted to let you know, but they also told me that Kyra apparently went into labor, and you took her to the hospital. Do you know how she is?"

Patrick knew he shouldn't feel embarrassed about hanging out with a colleague in labor who was potentially being stalked by the criminal she'd been attacked by, who might be attempting to find her now. Rory and others knew he was doing his best to protect Kyra.

"She's okay," he said. "I just left the hospital a while ago. We've got patrols in the area, and security is keeping an eye on her. Now, I wanted to be involved with bringing Coleman down."

"Got it. I'm about to go out in the field to help check on some leads about where he lives and might otherwise be, and you can come along. But I also want to know—and I'm sure others do too—did Kyra have her baby?"

"Yes," Patrick said, attempting to keep his tone professional rather than gushing over how cute the infant was. "A little boy. They're keeping him for a while at the hospital since he was premature, and Kyra's with him."

"Wonderful! Anyway, I suggest you check in with Colleen, then I'll meet you in the lobby and we'll get on the road."

After hanging up and taking a swig of coffee, Patrick called Colleen and also told her what was going on with Kyra. He additionally got her okay to accompany Rory. "I really want to be there, if possible, when the Jewelry Slayer is taken into custody."

"I figured." Colleen's tone sounded amused. "I also figured you'd hang out with your colleague till her baby was born."

"I wanted to make sure she remained safe." He tried to sound professional, hoped it wasn't too obvious that he'd also wanted to be with her during that amazing time of her life.

"Of course."

They hung up nearly immediately and Patrick rushed downstairs. Rory arrived a few minutes later, and they headed for her car in the same lot where Patrick had parked. She again drove her black official SUV, and Rory pressed the button to unlock it, then slipped into the driver's seat.

When Patrick was in the passenger's seat and Rory began driving, he asked, "So where are we heading?"

"We're meeting up with some uniformed officers to help in the search and arrest, if we happen to locate Coleman at his business or apartment."

"Where does he work, and where does he live?"

Turned out the guy apparently worked in customer service at one of New York City's most elite department stores, which might be a good way to spot women wearing, or buying, expensive jewelry. Some uniformed officers were in marked cars outside in case backup was needed. But when they went inside and visited the customer service department, and Rory asked to see Mr. Coleman, they were told he was on sick leave.

In Patrick's opinion, the guy definitely was sick, but not in the way his employer's staff probably believed.

"Let's try his home," Rory said as they left.

"Fine with me."

She made a call to the head investigator on the matter as they left. The police cars remained, but Patrick and Rory headed toward their next destination.

Coleman lived in Greenwich Village in an apartment complex that was also elite—which Patrick noticed right away when they arrived.

A couple of marked cruisers were already on the street, and some uniformed officers approached as Rory and he left her car.

"Any sign of our suspect?" Rory asked.

"Not out here," said the taller of the two officers who'd come up to them. "We assumed you have a warrant."

"Yes, I do." Rory nodded and headed toward the front door of the apartment building. It was locked, but there was a button to push to summon a manager, which she did.

The senior, nicely dressed guy who answered the door looked at Rory and Patrick, then the uniformed officers and also the warrant. "Please come in. I'm Michael Anderson, the manager here. I've no idea if Mr. Coleman is home, but his unit is on the second floor." He sounded eager to please the authorities, which was fine with Patrick.

But he wasn't surprised that no one was home. Rory was the one to knock on the door, and when they received no answer she requested that the manager, who'd stayed with them, open it.

Pete Coleman wasn't there. But Rory told the manager that they wanted to have a look around, and the warrant gave them authority.

"Of course," he said. "I'll wait right inside the door, in case you need anything."

And to make sure nothing got stolen, Patrick figured, even by cops.

They all looked around, Rory and the uniformed officers and him. And Patrick was stunned to see a window in the bedroom wide open, and a bedsheet was tied to one of the bed's legs.

Had Pete been there, realized they were around and escaped out the window?

Why else would it be open this way? It was November, after all, getting cold and rainy at times. Not a good time to keep windows open to air out a place, let alone hang a sheet out a window.

Damn! He and most of the others ran to look around outside. A couple of patrol cars were there, but only one on that side of the building, and the cops there had been out patrolling the area.

No one had seen Pete, if he'd just fled. They could send some other investigators who were already on their way here to check in nearby buildings with windows facing the area in case anyone saw anything, but no indication was found about where he might be at the moment. He might not know yet that he'd been identified, only that his face had been seen. But he'd undoubtedly figure it out if he heard there'd been a search warrant on his apartment, whether or not he'd been there when they arrived.

Would he leave town now?

Would he hang around somewhere else and attack more women with jewelry?

Or go after Kyra even more for having seen him and been able to ID him?

They didn't stay long, but all of them walked around the building and farther in the neighborhood, still looking for the face Kyra had identified, glancing up at some of the many windows in nearby buildings in case anyone was looking out, but no one was.

And Pete Coleman apparently was nowhere around here.

It was early afternoon when they headed back to the

offices. Patrick and his cousin stopped for a quick lunch on the way, still talking about the Jewelry Slayer—and also about the other big case keeping the precinct, and the FBI, on edge, the Landmark Killer.

"We've got to bring both of them down soon," Rory said as she ate her fast-food burger.

"I agree," Patrick said. He'd gotten a chicken sandwich. He ate it but wasn't particularly hungry.

Soon, they were back at the precinct. They met with Colleen to bring her up to date, and she held another meeting with some of the others who were in their offices. She praised them all for doing their jobs—and also made it clear she was hoping for faster results in both cases.

It was late enough in the day when the meeting was over that Patrick figured he could leave.

And where to go? He knew where he wanted to head.

He called Kyra's cell phone. She answered right away.

"How are you?" Patrick asked quickly, hoping the answer was favorable.

It was, and apparently Ajay was doing really well. "Surprisingly, I think they'll release us tomorrow." Kyra sounded happy.

"How about if I come now for a visit?" Patrick asked. No reason to think Pete knew where Kyra was—but if he'd fled his apartment as it appeared, he might be even more eager to locate the woman who'd seen, and now identified, him.

In any case, that was a good excuse to visit Kyra and Ajay.

"Sounds good to me."

Patrick grinned. "See you soon." And after another

phone call or two on the cases he was most concerned about, he headed for the hospital.

Kyra was alone in her hospital room now. Her folks had noted how tired she looked and decided to leave, though they promised to return the next day, or even that night if she called and asked them to.

After they left she'd gotten some sleep, but now that she was awake she wanted company.

Yes, she could have called her parents and requested their return, but she was pleased that Patrick was on his way.

Waiting in her bed for the nurses to bring Ajay back for nursing and more time with her before further medical observation, Kyra had already told herself she wanted Patrick to be there, to let her know that, thanks to her identifying him, Pete Coleman had been caught.

Of course Patrick could just have called to tell her that, but she hoped with all her heart that the man had been found and brought into custody so he could pay for all he'd done, and Patrick hadn't had time, while helping in the arrest, to let her know, and now wanted to let her know in person.

And if Coleman hadn't been caught?

She hated to think about that.

Even so, if that was the case, she looked forward to seeing Patrick again and hoped, if Coleman hadn't been caught, that her wonderful colleague would continue with her protection—hers and Ajay's. And her parents', although they were most likely fine if they weren't with her.

But as much as Kyra liked the idea of Patrick staying around her, professional or not, she really, really hoped Pete Coleman was now in custody. She and her son would be safe, and so would all Coleman's additional potential victims.

She continued to overthink this. She knew it. But Pete Coleman had affected her life in a lot of ways, including causing her to go into labor. And he'd made her worry about not only her own safety now, but her baby's as well as the other people she'd already been worried about.

Including Patrick.

Her cell phone rang then, and she lifted it off the table beside her bed where it had been charging again. She checked. It was Patrick.

"Hi," she said.

"Hey, I'm here at the hospital. Okay if I come to your room?"

"Absolutely!"

"Be there in a minute."

She was delighted it took him even less time to get there. He entered after knocking once, smiled at her, then looked around. Unsurprisingly, he was in the professional clothes he usually wore on the job. "You're alone." He sounded surprised, and maybe a little displeased.

"They're bringing Ajay back in a few minutes, and my folks have gone home."

"Well, I'll be glad to keep you company for now." He walked closer and sat down on the edge of her bed, near where her legs remained under the blankets. She somehow wanted him to touch her so she could feel as though he was really with her. "And I want to see Ajay when they bring him back."

Okay. She couldn't stand it. She had to know.

"So tell me. Have they caught Pete Coleman yet?"

She hated the way his face grew blank and knew the answer. "We found where he works and checked his apartment, but he wasn't either place. The precinct has an APB out on him and all officers are on the lookout."

"But he's not in custody." She made it a statement. It clearly was the situation.

"No. I'm so sorry. We don't have him yet."

It must have been at least partly her still-unbalanced hormones that made her eyes tear up, but she didn't say anything.

Patrick moved closer. Put his arms around her and hugged briefly, then backed off, though he remained sitting, this time near where the upper part of her body was raised by the bed. He looked straight into her face with his hazel eyes intense, as if he was about to assert something important. And he did. "But we'll get him. I promise. And in the meantime, when I can't be with you, I'll make sure you're still protected." He paused and moved closer, surprisingly planting a quick but caring kiss on her lips. "This will all be over soon."

He moved back, leaving Kyra with an urge that she didn't fulfill to hold out her arms so he would draw closer.

"I know," was all she said. And she hoped it was true—but didn't completely believe it.

# Chapter 20

In some ways, Patrick wished he could stay with Kyra all the time now. For her protection? Mostly. But he also really liked being with her.

That night, he hung out in her hospital room till nearly midnight, after she'd fed Ajay again and the infant was taken away for further observation, and Kyra was clearly falling into a deep sleep. Appropriate or not, he kissed her good-night and told her he was going home but would see her tomorrow.

When he left, he again made sure there were patrols along the street. He even asked to have some uniformed cops walk through the hospital again for Kyra's safety. Now that Pete Coleman would undoubtedly know she'd identified him, who knew what he'd try to do in revenge?

Patrick had already ascertained, from Kyra and the doctors in charge, that Kyra and Ajay would be released the next day. The idea was for her to remain for the morning and go home that afternoon.

Therefore, Patrick would head to the office first thing and maybe go out with those tracking Pete, then come back and help get Kyra and her baby home. And if all went well, he could return to work for a while afterward. That meant he needed to get some sleep that night, at his apartment.

When Kyra went home the next day, Patrick felt sure her folks would be involved too.

Which they were. Patrick returned to the hospital around one the next afternoon after a frustrating morning of learning no more about Pete's whereabouts—despite going out with Rory and some of her colleagues into areas considered most likely to be where their target might be at the moment.

No sign of Pete near the store where he worked or his apartment or other locations being considered that day.

And so Patrick did what he'd previously planned and went to help get Kyra home.

He checked with those in charge of the patrols he'd asked for including cops checking inside the hospital, as well as hospital security. All seemed fine there too. A good thing.

But where was Pete Coleman? Somehow, Patrick had to help find him.

Not that early afternoon though. He was determined to get Kyra home safely, then get back on the job. Later, he would return and hang out with her and her baby for the night.

Her parents were unsurprisingly in her room when Patrick arrived. "Hi, Patrick," Riya greeted him. Her pretty face glowed, somewhat like her daughter's, and she wore a long peach blouse that day. "Are you ready to help Kyra and Ajay get home?"

"I sure am," he said, smiling. He had come to like Kyra's parents. But he had to make sure to back off and not encourage them much. They weren't his family and never would be.

Kyra was soon checked out of the hospital, then they all left. Sam drove Kyra in her car with Ajay, now in a cute car seat bought by his grandparents, to her apartment, with Patrick driving ahead observing the area and Riya behind in their car. Strange procession, Patrick figured, but with the patrols on the street also watching out for them he felt relatively sure they could arrive safely, which they did.

Once they were inside Kyra's place, he hung out for a while, enjoying watching the new mom take the baby into his nursery and make sure all was in order there.

When it was nearly time for her to nurse Ajay, Patrick quickly let them know he was heading back to his office for a while that afternoon—but that he'd arranged for some precinct officers to not only hang out on the nearby street but also patrol the building now and then.

Fortunately, there was no indication Pete Coleman was around, but Patrick didn't intend to take unnecessary chances.

Still, he hesitated before leaving—and Kyra clearly recognized it. In a pale yellow shirt that could easily be unbuttoned when it was time to feed the baby, her hair framing her beautiful face, she sat on her sofa while her parents took Ajay into the nursery to change his diaper. "Go ahead," she said. "I really want you out there so you can bring down Coleman. I just wish I could be with you."

He wished he could be with her too—and he would be. He would return and planned to spend the night. "I'm certainly going to do my damnedest to catch the guy so we won't have to worry anymore. But if today's not the day, you can be sure I'll hang out here with you tonight."

"I figured." Her tone was droll, but the expression in her eyes looked grateful.

He couldn't help bending down to start giving her a soft goodbye kiss. Only, to his surprise and delight, it turned into something longer and hotter, which only made him more determined to return, as dumb as that was. But, oh, that woman, his beautiful colleague, turned him on. A lot. Which was ridiculous. Even if it wouldn't be totally inappropriate to have sex with her, the fact she'd just had a baby made it even more absurd.

Despite their holding each other close for several long seconds, Patrick finally left—after reassuring Kyra he'd see her again in a few hours.

He hoped yet again Pete Coleman would somehow get into their radar that afternoon and be caught so things could return to as close to normal as was possible under these circumstances.

But he wasn't.

So Patrick returned around six o'clock. Riya had made dinner, including enough for him, and he joined all of them for the meal.

"It's so nice to have you back again," Riya said as they sat at the table. "I feel so much better about going home tonight, knowing my daughter, and my grand-baby—" her tone grew even sweeter "—will have wonderful company, and your continued protection here."

"Same with me," Sam added.

Kyra just looked at Patrick and smiled. She held Ajay in her arms, even as she ate.

Patrick insisted on helping with the dishes afterward. Kyra offered to, but it was time for her to feed Ajay again.

Soon, her parents left, and Patrick was alone with Kyra and her newborn.

Damn, how he loved staying that night with them, even more than he'd appreciated hanging out to protect Kyra before—and not only because he was protecting her now. He really tried his best not to be enamored of baby Ajay—or even Kyra—but it was a losing battle.

He found himself really caring for them. Both of them. As absurd and unacceptable as that was.

And yes, he was there when Kyra was nursing Ajay for his midnight and several later feedings. He even wound up changing Ajay's diaper—more than once. And he laughed along with Kyra when he got peed on.

*It's all a damned wonder and miracle,* he thought. *What's happening to me?*

He spent the night beside Kyra in her bed, again glad of her current just-past-childbirth and nursing situation. They did kiss almost sexily before falling asleep, and he thought about what it might be like to do more, but of course they didn't.

What would the future hold?

Nothing more, he told himself. It couldn't. After all this was over, they'd remain colleagues.

And that would be that.


Kyra lay awake for a while with Patrick back beside her—not that she wasn't exhausted.

Was he asleep? She wasn't sure. He breathed somewhat deeply, but not necessarily in sleep mode.

She was amazed at how sweet Patrick was with Ajay—a man who'd made it clear he never wanted to be a father. But he'd helped pick Ajay up from his crib and put the baby in her arms so she could feed him— and didn't watch too closely as she bared her breasts one by one to provide that feeding.

Although just the little bit he did felt somewhat tantalizing to Kyra. Not that she felt sexually attracted— not now, with her hormones so out of kilter just after childbirth. And it couldn't happen later either.

But Patrick would remain in her life—the right way. She hoped to get back to work again soon, once she eventually got Ajay used to a bottle and worked things out for her mother, who'd promised to be their nanny, to help take care of him.

Once things were back that close to normal on the job, any attraction to Patrick would be erased forever.

But those kisses once they got into bed... Well, hormone issues or not, maybe there was some sexual attraction between them, but it would definitely go no farther for many reasons.

She soon fell asleep, but woke up for Ajay's next feeding—again with Patrick's help getting the baby ready. And again. And then morning came.

She felt Patrick stir beside her in bed. "Good morning," she managed to say.

"Good morning. Ready to start the day?"

She would have felt more ready if Patrick had come over, helped her up and shared another wonderful kiss with her. But that didn't happen, which she knew was a good thing. She did look over at him and enjoyed seeing him in his pajamas. Hey, she enjoyed seeing him no matter what he wore. And speculated what he looked like in the shower… "I sure am," she managed to say.

She wished in a way she could go to work with him. She'd been able to somewhat while she was pregnant, at least to check faces on the computer system and sometimes do a bit more.

But she wasn't ready to leave Ajay just yet, not even with her parents. Certainly not while she was still nursing him the way she was.

Someday? Sure, and she could look forward to it, even though she recognized she would miss her son while away from him—and wouldn't let it be for long periods of time.

"Time to feed Ajay again yet?" Patrick asked. It soon was, but Kyra showered and got dressed first, although she let Patrick use the shower before her.

Then it was time to feed her baby—with Patrick's assistance in bringing Ajay to her on the living room couch, where she sat after they'd woken the baby and Patrick—yes, Patrick again—had changed his diaper.

"Ready to eat, sweetheart?" Kyra asked, and her baby's answer was to drink eagerly, with Patrick sitting nearby and watching…which was okay.

Then, after making some sweet, cooing noises, Ajay fell asleep in his crib.

After that, the adults had their breakfast—and yes, Kyra made some coffee and sipped a little. They also ate the cereal they'd bought together and both enjoyed.

Then Patrick prepared to leave for the day. "Call me immediately if anything seems to be a problem," he said as he reached the door. Kyra got it. Even though she again wished she could be on duty too, that would have to wait.

Ajay was most important right now.

This was the first day, but she wasn't surprised when it turned into a routine. Things went similarly for a few days, then a week and longer. She got calls at various times during each day, some from Patrick and others from cops he'd gotten to hang out in the area to watch over her, keep an eye out for Pete, make sure she was safe. Several let her know when they were around, which she appreciated. She got to know who they were—all from the 130th Precinct. Patrick visited at least once each day and stayed a while.

Plus, she remained alert, as close to cop mode as she could while taking care of herself and her little son.

And she looked forward to Patrick's return each night.

His being with her for dinner. Checking around the area for her safety. Helping her prepare for Ajay's meals.

Changing her son's diapers some of the time.

Joining her in bed…and sharing such inappropriate, but wonderful, kisses.

Of course her parents visited often during the day, helped her with Ajay. Were glad to see Patrick when he returned. He sometimes brought dinner, after checking to see if her folks would be joining them.

And her mom and dad always seemed fine with leaving when Patrick was going to be there all night. Kyra knew they might be expecting a lot more from the relationship between her and her coworker than it was, and they were sure to be disappointed when things finally settled down—after Pete Coleman was finally caught.

She suspected she might be a little disappointed then too. But that was, or would be, reality.

She'd at least continue to see Patrick. He might even visit now and then to see Ajay. He seemed amazingly happy to be with her little son—despite his assertions that he never intended to become a father.

But even if he continued to drop in to say hi to her son, things would be different.

# Chapter 21

Impossible. Wasn't it?

But one of the managers Pete Coleman reported to at the elite department store where he worked apparently saw him walk in and notified police. They'd said Coleman was on sick leave, so why had he come in? As far as Patrick knew, no information had been given to those managers about why authorities were seeking Pete, but they had been requested to watch for him and call a particular number at the precinct in case he appeared—and they'd been warned he could be dangerous.

Apparently, he had gone in, maybe even claiming he was well now and attempting to report for work. Did he really think he had gotten away with all he had done so far? He wasn't living in his apartment now, but why go to work?

Hopefully, Patrick thought, they were about to find out.

Though they weren't aware of Coleman committing any crime there that day, FBI Crime Scene Investigator Patrick had been recruited by others in the precinct, including his cousin Rory, to go with them to attempt to take Coleman into custody. That was probably more because of his knowledge of the case than any other reason.

Fortunately, the call had come in after Patrick arrived that afternoon. Rory and others there knew how determined he was to help bring in the Jewelry Slayer who'd attacked his coworker, who had later ID'd the guy.

And now—was it finally time to bring Coleman in?

Patrick, wearing his usual outfit on the job plus a warm jacket, rode in Rory's car with her to the store. Being her passenger was becoming a bit of a habit, but Patrick figured it wouldn't last long.

Hopefully no longer than today.

Other official cars were around them. When Rory parked on the street like the others, Patrick hung out behind the officers going inside. He wanted to watch as Coleman was taken into custody.

"You okay?" Rory asked, hanging back with him.

"Bring him in and I will be," Patrick said, and, after slapping his shoulder jovially, his cousin joined the others who had been let into the store via a back door, thanks to one of the managers. *Go get him*, Patrick thought. Of course they would all have to be careful, since there were customers in the store and the authorities didn't know exactly where Coleman was—assuming he was still there.

Okay. Patrick wanted to watch it all unfold, but even though he was a CSI and usually assisted in getting a case resolved without being on the front lines, this situation was different. He at least wanted to watch, and if there was anything he could do to assist those in charge, including helping to make sure the civilians who were around remained safe, he'd do it.

And so he would go inside the store not just following the others, but entering from the front to observe— and watch out for Coleman.

The store was several stories high, with lots of columns in the architecture and picture windows on the ground floor where quite a bit of merchandise was exhibited. Some was interesting, including displays of rows of jewelry, although Patrick figured at least some was nice-looking costume stuff. There were probably alarms on the windows in case anyone broke in. The store management wouldn't want anything of value to get stolen.

A lot of people were on the first floor as Patrick entered. Couples dressed for cool weather, groups of women and men checking out displays of clothing and other items on that level. It was approaching the holiday shopping season. And there were always tourists visiting NYC who liked to check out stores during their visit.

Patrick watched for any sign of official activity but didn't know where the uniformed cops or investigators in civilian clothes like Rory—and him—were hanging out. Hey, he could maybe do a little shopping himself while he was here, for baby things. Appropriate or not, he wanted to buy a holiday present or two for little Ajay.

And for Kyra...? Unlikely but—

He stopped as he noticed someone on the escalator coming down from the second floor who was muscling in and pushing others ahead of him out of the way.

He recognized him immediately. Pete Coleman.

Patrick swiftly headed in that direction, moving around the patrons in his way and wishing he could direct them all to leave immediately. But that would give him away, and there was no indication anyone was in danger.

Although with Pete Coleman, Patrick figured everyone in his vicinity could be in peril.

Placing his hand on his waist where his weapon was in his pocket, hidden by his shirttail, he arrived at the bottom of the escalator just as Coleman got there too.

"Damn," the guy said, staring at Patrick and clearly recognizing him. "I know you. You were there when—" He didn't finish, but instead dove toward Patrick, knocking him over forcefully so he bumped into one of the patrons—and his arm hit a tall glass display case on a counter with jewelry inside. Damn, but that hurt. The glass didn't break, but the edge was clearly sharp, and the strange angle of the impact caused Patrick's arm to start bleeding, not too badly but enough to elicit cries of shock from the people around. A bright red stain to started appearing on his shirt. And the pain was definitely noticeable.

Patrick stumbled, but with all those people around, and Coleman now racing around them toward the doorway, he didn't dare draw his gun. Even if he could have aimed, the damage was to his right arm.

He held his shirt against his arm as he saw some uniformed guys racing around, as if they'd been elsewhere but now knew where Coleman was too. Rory and some of her fellow investigators were with them.

But as far as Patrick could tell, despite there being cops all around, probably even guarding the entrances, Coleman had escaped.

Again.

"Are you okay?" Rory asked as she reached him.

"Yeah," he said, but he knew his tone said otherwise. He'd pulled his sleeve up and saw the cut that was bleeding.

"I'll let the others try to apprehend Coleman," his cousin said. "We're going to the hospital to have your arm checked out."

The hospital. Again. But this time he'd be the one in the ER.

Well, Patrick knew he would be fine. But having an exam and getting some antiseptic on his arm and having it bandaged to stop the bleeding?

"Sure," he managed to say. "Let's go." He was furious with himself for not capturing the Jewelry Slayer when he was right there, letting him injure him instead, even though it wasn't serious.

Well, he might be on his way to the hospital now. But one way or another, he would bring down the vile murderer soon.

It was getting late. Sitting in the living room watching TV news, Kyra wondered where Patrick was. Her parents had come over that afternoon but had a commitment to visit some friends for dinner, though they had brought food earlier to make sure Patrick and she didn't go hungry.

Assuming Patrick was coming that night. He had been for many nights, but she didn't know what he was doing at work that day. Someday she would be back at work with him, but little Ajay would take precedence for a while.

She considered calling Patrick but figured he'd get

there when he got there. And she knew he would call if he wasn't coming. He was definitely a considerate person and would know she expected him.

She heard Ajay start crying in the nursery. He'd been sleepy last time she'd fed him, about half an hour ago, so she'd taken him in there and put him in his crib. He might need his diaper changed now.

Too bad Patrick wasn't there to do it. Her work colleague seemed to really get into handling such things for her baby son, as odd as that seemed.

She used the remote to put the TV on pause, then went into the bedroom. Sure enough, when she checked her crying baby's diaper, it was damp. "Come here, sweetheart." She picked him up, putting him onto the top of the special dresser that had a changing table at the top that could be removed when it was no longer necessary. She kept disposable diapers in the top drawer, and she quickly changed this one, putting it into the plastic bag in the waste basket with a lid that sat beside it.

"Okay, Ajay," she said, hugging her son close. "Let's go into the other room and see if you're hungry."

When they arrived in the living room though, her phone rang. Holding Ajay carefully, she pulled her phone from her pocket and checked it and wasn't surprised to see Patrick's name on the screen. She answered. "Hi, Patrick."

"Hi. I'm on my way there now. Sorry I'm late."

There was something blunt in his tone that made Kyra ask, "Is everything all right?"

"Yeah. See you soon."

But somehow Kyra doubted that everything was okay.

Patrick arrived in about ten minutes and let himself

in with the keys he now had—Kyra's extra set. Kyra was waiting in the living room.

He wasn't wearing his usual work clothes but a casual blue sweatshirt over jeans. He carried a tote bag. She figured he had gone home after whatever he had done at the precinct that day.

"You know," she said as she moved out of the way and closed and locked the door behind him, "as much as Ajay and I enjoy having you around, you could have stayed home this evening. I assume, from what you're wearing—"

"No way was I going to leave you two here without me." His tone was a growl.

A pang of fright rocked through her. "Has Pete Coleman been found? Does he know where I live?"

Patrick looked at her with an expression in his hazel eyes she didn't recognize, then aimed the gaze at Ajay before returning it to Kyra's face. "Kind of," he replied, "and I still don't know. But I saw him today."

He gingerly pulled up the sleeve of his sweatshirt, and Kyra saw a long bandage there. It looked like something official, like he might have gotten it from a doctor. At a hospital?

"Oh, no," Kyra said. "What happened? Did he hurt you?"

"In a way. But I'm angrier that I didn't grab him and keep him from running. He got away again."

Kyra wanted to hear what had happened—and didn't. Still, she said, "Come into the kitchen. I'll get our dinner served—and would you like some beer? I think I have some that my folks brought in case you wanted any. Although is it okay for you to drink…with that?"

"Yeah. I'm fine. I'm on antibiotics though, and had

it checked out at your favorite ER. Right now, dinner sounds fine. But no beer."

Suddenly, he grabbed her with his right hand, clearly being careful not to hurt Ajay in her arms, and gave her a strong but quick kiss. "I'm going to catch that SOB, and soon," he said. "Don't listen to what I'm saying, Ajay. But enough is enough."

At her command, Patrick sat down at her table. She put Ajay, now asleep in her arms, in the bassinette she had in the kitchen and got the dinner her folks had left ready—tuna salad, which she made into sandwiches. Then, as she sat down after giving them both water, she demanded that he tell her what had happened.

She was horrified, and scared, that the Jewelry Slayer had attacked and injured Patrick, even though he had fortunately not done any serious damage.

Patrick, this man who was taking care of her. Who kissed her a lot and hugged her and helped tend her baby, as though they had more than a professional relationship.

And Kyra let herself realize now, as she had been fighting off before, that she really did care for Patrick. More than cared for him.

No matter how inappropriate it was, she had fallen in love with him.

Not that she would tell him. She wouldn't. She couldn't.

But she did manage to make sure he got all the food he wanted that evening.

He even laughed when she offered to make him yet another tuna sandwich after he had eaten two. "Are you trying to get me to appear pregnant with additional weight?"

She laughed back. "Nope. And just gaining weight isn't all there is to a pregnancy."

"I figured."

Her parents called once they'd finished eating and Kyra had insisted on taking care of the dishes herself. They were back on the sofa, Ajay in Patrick's arms.

"You know Thanksgiving is next week," her mom said. "I assume you and Patrick will spend it together with Ajay, and your dad and I would like to come over early and bring you food, though our plans have changed and we'll eat with some friends who want us to join them so we won't stay long." She mentioned one of her close neighbors. "They'd love to meet Ajay but understand that it's too soon to bring him, which is why they didn't invite you."

Was it? Maybe. But in any event, Kyra didn't want to go out and about and potentially endanger even more people with Coleman still out there and possibly looking for her.

It was strange for her folks to not want her to join them even after mentioning Thanksgiving before—but she figured they wanted her to be with Patrick.

"Well, we'll enjoy seeing you for however long you can stay." That was Patrick. Kyra had put the phone on speaker. And he didn't object to spending Thanksgiving with Kyra and Ajay and keeping things fairly quiet around there.

They hung up soon after. Kyra wondered how Patrick would do when they went to bed that night. Yes, he stayed with her yet again. His pajama tops did cover his bandage—which he showed her again. "I'll have to be careful to keep it dry when I shower in the morning."

They kissed good-night. Hard. Emotionally, Kyra

thought. Oh, yes, she had begun to love this man, and she had the sense he really cared for—loved?—her too. But neither of them spoke of such things. Still, Kyra wanted to hug him even closer and longer. But she kept all her emotions to herself.

There was no sign of Coleman the next day, apparently, although they returned to their routine of Patrick going to the office for a couple of hours in the morning and in the afternoon.

She felt safe with even more backup of other law enforcement officers watching over Ajay and her, even dropping in.

And time continued to pass. Patrick's arm healed well, or so he assured her. He even showed her the wound once when he changed the bandage, and though Kyra imagined it still hurt, she could believe it had improved a lot from the time he was injured.

Patrick seemed frustrated a lot when he returned to her apartment. No sign of Coleman now.

"But our teams are still looking, and we will find him," he reassured her. She figured he was attempting to reassure himself as well.

Soon, it was Thanksgiving, and Kyra's folks came early in the morning with turkey and fixings—as well as some holiday toys for Ajay that he wasn't old enough to play with yet.

"Now, you have a wonderful holiday," her mom said as they got ready to leave. Kyra still thought it odd that they weren't staying to celebrate together.

Of course she understood why, especially when her dad said to Kyra at the apartment door, while Patrick watched Ajay, "We talked about enjoying more time with you today, honey, but figured this would be the first holiday that Patrick and you could really spend time together to celebrate."

"But we could have all celebrated together," Kyra protested, knowing her parents were hoping for way too much from this professional relationship.

Still, the idea of having Patrick and Ajay all to herself on a special occasion like this felt amazing.

And it was. The meal Patrick and she shared, thanks to her folks, was delightful.

The company even more so.

And when they finished eating, she fed Ajay again, changed him, bathed him and put him in his crib for a nap.

After that, Patrick and she watched a romantic holiday movie on TV, something she never did and figured he didn't either.

They sat together on the sofa, in each other's arms.

And Kyra couldn't imagine a more wonderful holiday.

# *Chapter 22*

Wow. This was probably his best Thanksgiving ever, Patrick thought as he sat on the couch with Kyra trying to make himself pay attention to the silly movie—but instead he was focused on the woman beside him. The woman who remained close enough that their sides and shoulders touched—just for warmth, they reminded each other now and then, even though the apartment was fairly comfortable.

Never mind that his arm on the other side still hurt a bit where Coleman had injured it. It was healing. That was what was important.

Right now, he appreciated that Kyra's family had brought their meal—then left. Oh, he recognized they expected, or at least hoped, for too much to happen between their daughter and him on this holiday night, especially if they didn't hang around.

And if Kyra and he weren't coworkers, maybe it

would. Certainly not sex, under the circumstances, but expression of mutual caring? That couldn't, wouldn't, happen either.

His mind slipped to memories. His Thanksgivings growing up hadn't been all that wonderful, not with him and his three siblings and a grieving, scared mother who never really recovered from the murder of her husband and having four kids to care for alone.

Their father had been killed by a serial killer back then. And as they grew, Patrick and his siblings wound up dedicating their lives to tracking and capturing serial killers.

That had been his story, growing up in the Colton family here in New York City. Things had improved for them, and he did spend some holidays with family.

Could he have Kyra and Ajay join them sometime? Unlikely. His siblings probably wouldn't want anyone to bring coworkers to a gathering like that.

That was all Kyra could ever be to him. Although…

Damn. Maybe it was time to start being honest with himself. He had really come to care for Kyra. His wanting to continue to protect her, take care of her, wasn't only because he wanted his work colleague to remain safe.

He focused on how she felt as they sat close together. Should he move over a bit? Maybe not now. She seemed to be enjoying the movie, or at least she was watching intensely. Why disturb her?

And hanging out there gave him the opportunity to watch her lovely face and the way her eyes seemed glued to the TV screen, the long fingers of her hands clasped in her lap over her silky blouse.

Her slimming body. Her beauty even in this kind of relaxed, casual situation.

His pleasure in studying her this way despite attempting not to seem too obvious about it.

He wondered if what he had started feeling for her could be love.

Love? Ha! He didn't even know what that felt like. He'd never experienced it.

At least not before...

He slid his gaze over her again, then made his eyes return to the television despite not concentrating. She must have noticed though, since she glanced at him briefly, then returned her eyes to the TV. That was fine.

He didn't want her to even imagine what he was thinking.

Love? The idea wouldn't go away, now that he'd thought of it.

Not that he would ever tell her, and he certainly wouldn't act on it. They couldn't have sex now, and even when her body had healed that still couldn't happen.

"Are you enjoying the movie at all?"

Kyra's voice startled him, and he looked at her again.

"Sure. Not my favorite, but it's definitely fine for a Thanksgiving evening."

"Good. I'm enjoying it a lot."

And to his surprise, she snuggled up even closer.

Smiling, he wrapped his arms around her and concentrated on her curves, her warmth, her nearness...

And made himself start watching the movie in more earnest so he wouldn't allow his hands to roam against even unsexy parts of her body.

The movie was a holiday romance, and it had a typical happy ending, where it seemed clear the couple was heading for a happily ever after.

Too bad reality wasn't like that. Or if it was for some people, it would never include Kyra and him, no matter how he had started to feel about her. Was she starting to care about him that way too? Even if she did, it wouldn't matter.

They both soon checked on Ajay, who was stirring. Patrick helped to change his diaper—damn, but that was becoming a habit. One he surprisingly enjoyed. Then Kyra fed Ajay again on the living room sofa, with Patrick watching.

And enjoying all of the view, including the baby's eager sucking. And what Ajay was sucking on—oh, yeah, he enjoyed watching that too.

Bedtime now, and Patrick performed his usual patrol, plus calls to those in nearby patrol cars.

Wherever Pete Coleman might be just then, he didn't show up around there.

That night, their routine remained the same too—sort of. They had gotten into the habit of good-night kisses, some of which were fairly hot, as surprising and inappropriate as that was. But that night, as he settled in beside the woman he still had the obligation to protect, he started to give her one of the same kinds of kisses they'd grown used to, although his mind couldn't help returning to his thoughts earlier of love.

He attempted not to factor that into their long kiss, but somehow it became even longer and hotter than they'd been sharing before. He thrust his tongue into her mouth, and they seemed to tease each other that way. Their bodies pressed even closer than usual.

If things had been different, Patrick knew he'd be

pulling her pajamas off and doing—what he couldn't do now. Or at least would be trying to, assuming his partner in this bed also wanted it.

But that wasn't going to happen now.

"Wow," Kyra whispered against his mouth. One more hot kiss though and she pulled away. "Good night, Patrick. I really want to let you know—" But she stopped.

"Know what?"

"Never mind. Good night," she repeated.

And it took Patrick a long time to fall asleep, particularly because the soft breathing beside him suggested that Kyra remained awake too.

She got up a few times to check on Ajay and to feed him, with Patrick getting up too, to look around the apartment and outside—again, their routine.

In the morning, more routine. "I really would like to go into the office with you again," Kyra said after Patrick performed his check of the area and returned to get ready for work. She had gotten dressed in a casual light green button shirt and jeans, certainly not sexy, but he still wanted to wrap his arms around her. Again. But of course he didn't.

"Soon," he said. "Once we figure out where Coleman is and bring him in."

"Yeah, really soon." Kyra's tone was sarcastic, but she gave him a quick kiss as he headed out the door without objecting further.

Before he left the area, he made sure a patrol was on the nearby street and that some cops on duty were patrolling now and then inside Kyra's apartment building—as he'd done before when he'd left, and would continue to do until the Jewelry Slayer was finally in custody.

That morning at the office was different than most recent ones. Yes, he talked to some of the CSIs who reported to Kyra and him and sent them out into the field to crime scenes, again mostly less major ones, which were the norm at the moment.

He also got called into Colleen's office—no surprise there either. She wanted to talk about the status of the attempt to find the Jewelry Slayer now, she said, and more. Patrick wondered what else was on her mind. She also had Wells Blackthorn in her office.

As she sat behind her desk, as usual in her uniform, Colleen's always-large blue eyes had a tilt to them that Patrick interpreted as frustration. He sat down in a chair facing her. Wells was in another.

"No indication yet of where the Jewelry Slayer disappeared to," he surmised aloud.

"You got it." Colleen's hand fisted on her desk. "But our force is still out there searching. And that's not all I wanted to discuss today. There's been some news about our other target."

"The Landmark Killer?" Patrick asked immediately. He was aware that the other serial killer, who was the subject of the FBI's and precinct's intense searches, had remained quiet during a lot of November, unnerving the entire team. Where was he? What was he up to? He clearly was lying low, maybe so he wouldn't make any mistakes.

Or maybe because he was planning something big and didn't want to get arrested first.

"You certainly can surmise what's going on around here," Wells said in response to Patrick's question. He leaned forward, the expression on his youthful yet resolute face grim. "Yeah, the Landmark Killer. You know he's been identified as Xander Washer, the FBI director's former assistant, right?"

"That's what I thought. I even attempted to meet with the guy to discuss some related stuff and check him out, but nothing came of that." That wasn't long ago—but before he'd gotten so involved in hunting the Jewelry Slayer. "Still, that's what I heard."

"Well, in any case, you've been coming here to the precinct every day lately, as we all have. And—well, the precinct's main phone line received a few texts you might not have heard about. The first, a while ago, got us all up in arms—and then there was another. They're anonymous, from a number that must be a burner phone. We can't find the source."

Patrick leaned forward, his elbows on Colleen's desk. "What do they say?" He didn't want to sound too demanding to these officers in charge here, but he really wanted to know. Right away. Even though that wasn't the case he was most involved in.

But he gave a damn and wanted to help if he could—while giving precedence to the Jewelry Slayer situation.

"You'll love this." Colleen looked on her computer, then pressed a few keys. "I want to be sure I get this exact," she said, "though I could probably tell you without looking." In a moment she said, "Here's the first one that got our juices flowing. It says, 'Took you long enough. Too bad so sad that I'll reach the end of the goddess Maeve O'Leary's name and you'll never catch me.'"

"Great," Patrick said sarcastically. His understanding was that the killer had gone through most of Maeve O'Leary's name already, but there were a couple letters left.

"And it's a lie." Wells half stood. "We'll definitely catch him."

"I'm sure." Patrick had to say that, though doubts washed through him.

But they had to find the Landmark Killer—as well as the Jewelry Slayer. And those in the FBI, as well as this precinct, were really skilled at what they did. Surely they could latch on to the Landmark Killer, and the sooner the better.

"We got that one a couple weeks ago," Colleen told him. "Since you weren't working much on that case I never got around to telling you. But—well, we got a second one just yesterday and figured everyone around here should know about it. The threat is increasing. We really need to get that guy."

"Yeah. The new text was even worse than the first." Wells was shaking his head. "But it gave us some ideas about what the guy may be up to now—though not his timing. And the fact he said what he did… He's taunting us."

"Tell me—" Patrick began.

"That damned latest one says, 'Off to sharpen my skates.'" Wells scowled.

Patrick, still seated across from Colleen's desk, stared at Wells. "That has to mean the skating rink at Rockefeller Center, right?"

"That's what we think," Colleen told him, and Patrick turned back to face her. "In fact, call your cousin Rory. Or go see her now. I think she's in her office, but she and some of her fellow detectives are on the case, checking into the possibilities. I want you to work with her."

Patrick promised himself to go see Rory as soon as

possible. But before he could leave, Colleen stood and started pacing. "At least we have some more help now."

"What's that?" Patrick asked.

"Well, for one thing," Colleen said, stopping to look at Patrick, "do you know who FBI Director Roberta Chang is?"

"Sure. I've met her in the FBI offices. Is she there now?"

"Yeah," Wells said. "She'd been off at some nation-wide meetings, but she just returned. We'd left her some messages, and she came in to check on what was happening. We told her more about what's going on."

"She was clearly horrified," Colleen said, "and she offered our investigative team anything the FBI can provide to help find the Landmark Killer."

But not Pete Coleman? Patrick understood that they seemed focused more on the Landmark Killer at the moment than the Jewelry Slayer, and though he understood he felt frustrated so he just said, "That's good to hear."

"Anyway, I'm glad you're on top of the Jewelry Slayer case, but like I said, I'd also appreciate your being active in helping to find the Landmark Killer."

"Of course. I'll do my best to stay on top of both."

He excused himself to go talk to Rory, who fortunately remained in her office on the floor below Colleen's.

She wasn't alone. "Hi, cuz," she said after Patrick knocked on the door and walked in. "I'd like you to meet Isaac Donner, my new partner. He's been with the NYPD for a while, but he's new to our precinct."

Donner, who stood near the door, seemed like an older fellow, although maybe that was because his hair was silver. Otherwise, he could have been around their age. He stared at Patrick with his blue eyes, and there was something in his expression that seemed arrogant somehow. Patrick wondered how long he had been with the department.

"Good to meet you, Patrick," Isaac said. "In case you're wondering, yes, I'm new to this precinct, but I transferred here specially to work on the Landmark Killer case."

"Got it," Patrick said. "Me? I'm on that one too. I really hope we get the guy fast, but my focus is more on the Jewelry Slayer."

"That's what Rory told me. Anyway, I'm out of here. Need to get out there to work on the investigation."

Patrick looked at Rory, who didn't look entirely pleased, but she said, "Sorry we don't have time to talk right now. Let's plan on catching up soon. I want to hear how things are going with you—and with Kyra."

"Fine," Patrick said. As he headed toward the door, they did too. Going to check how things were in Rockefeller Center?

Well, Patrick was intrigued by that and would be glad to hear more from Rory later. In fact, he asked, "How about if I join you now? Not sure whether you'll need any CSI specialists with you, but if there's anything I can do to help I'll be glad to."

"Why not?" Isaac asked.

Rory just shrugged. "Sure, why not?"

"This is so wonderful," Kyra's mom said. She sat in Kyra's living room on the sofa, with Ajay on her lap, wearing one of her long, silky blouses. She was feeding the baby some special formula from a bottle.

Yes, Kyra had requested they buy some, knowing her

folks were coming for a visit that day. Ajay was only about three weeks old, but she'd wanted to see how he did with some formula so she wouldn't have to feed him breast milk all the time—no matter how much she enjoyed doing it. But she had researched the possibilities, and the brand she'd requested them to bring was well recommended by noted pediatricians.

Kyra would continue to feed her little son mostly breast milk for a while. It was probably best for him, though she would wean him off it eventually, and this was a good way to start. And this way she wouldn't have to be with him all the time.

She could let her parents babysit for at least short periods of time. That would allow her to leave her apartment.

"I agree, Mom," Kyra said. "You're really good at that. Looks like you have experience feeding babies."

They both laughed. "I would say so," Riya said.

And Kyra's dad, who sat beside them in his casual jeans and sweatshirt watching them carefully through his glasses, added, "She was really good at feeding you, a long time ago, using her own milk and also whatever the formula was then. I imagine it's different now. Hopefully better."

"That's what I understand," Kyra said.

Her parents left soon after that. Little Ajay appeared exhausted so Kyra put him down for a nap.

Then she headed to her kitchen table, to think and to plan. At least the first part of her scheme seemed to have worked, regarding getting Ajay ready to be babysat. She drank some herbal tea. And decided what to do. How to approach Patrick.

She figured he would return that afternoon for a

while before heading back to the office—or into the field—as he'd been doing since Ajay's birth. But he wouldn't let her go to work with him now, even to stay inside her precinct office with Ajay while she got on the computer or had meetings with people who were there. He still considered Coleman too much of a threat.

But she wanted to go to crime scenes or other important sites soon, if only for short periods of time, since she wouldn't have to bring her son.

Most important: she really, really wanted to do something to help get Pete Coleman into custody so she wouldn't have to worry about him anymore. For her sake and Ajay's.

She continued to ponder what to say to Patrick that afternoon. She had an idea, one he'd probably hate. But it was better than what had gone on lately.

Well, figuring she knew what his response would be, she would insist on speaking with their supervisor at the precinct too.

And so as Kyra sat there, she planned somewhat how to approach the subject with Patrick. She was worried about him, after all.

Sure, the Jewelry Slayer had confronted her, and she had ID'd him, which resulted in her going into labor. But he hadn't actually hurt her—not yet at least.

But he had injured Patrick.

As the time approached when Patrick usually came back for the afternoon, Kyra brewed some coffee. She wanted him to sit there with her as she made her point.

She checked on Ajay, but her little son was still sleeping. That was fine for now. She sat back down again.

Around when she expected to, she heard a key at her door and Patrick entered. "Hi," he said. He looked damned handsome, as always, in his dressy work clothes. And he stared at her with his hazel eyes in a way that made her wonder if he actually cared about her the way she did about him as he asked, "How've you been today? And Ajay?"

But his looks, his apparent caring, were irrelevant, especially now as Kyra had something on her mind.

Something important.

"We're fine, thanks. Want some coffee? I have something I need to talk to you about."

His expression grew blank as if he anticipated what she was going to say and didn't want to hear it. "Is the coffee hot?"

"Yes, I just brewed it."

He went to where the pot sat on the counter, grabbed a mug from the cabinet near it and poured some.

Then he sat down beside her. "So what's on your mind?" he asked.

*You don't really want to hear*, she thought. But then she began to tell him.

# Chapter 23

"Don't even think about it!" Patrick couldn't help yelling as he stood and stared at Kyra.

"I've been thinking about almost nothing else for a while, especially today." She was staring right back, with those beautiful dark eyes of hers glaring defiantly up at him as she remained seated.

"After all we've gone through over the past weeks to make sure you're protected so that the lousy SOB who's the Jewelry Slayer can't find you, let alone attack you—and now you want to tell him where you are so he can come and kill you?"

"Not kill me." Her tone remained calm, though he saw a shadow of fear cross her face that she immediately erased. "It'll be a setup. That's the point. We'll plan it well, and we'll finally catch him."

"Yeah, right." Patrick continued to protest what he was hearing—although he recognized what she was saying might in fact be the only way to finally bring Pete Coleman down. Identifying him and looking for him in his usual habitats and other likely places certainly hadn't worked.

But Patrick wouldn't do anything to put the woman he had been protecting—the woman he had come to love, even though he couldn't admit it to anyone else, let alone himself—in danger of losing her life.

"I understand what you're saying," she told him. "And if there was another way, I'm sure you, or others in the precinct, would have figured it out by now. But enough is enough. Look, I really want to talk to Colleen about it. Can we give her a call to make sure she's in her office, then go to the precinct? It doesn't need to be a long visit, so I can take Ajay, then come back here."

Patrick wanted to say no but felt certain Kyra wouldn't back down. "Okay, let's call Colleen," he said. Surely the precinct's captain, who seemed clearly more involved in bringing the Landmark Killer down at the moment, would talk Kyra out of her dangerous idea. And Kyra would have to listen to her even if she wouldn't listen to him.

Fortunately, Collen answered immediately. "Hi, Captain, this is Kyra Patel," Kyra said.

"I figured as much from your calling on your phone." Colleen's tone was dry. "What's up?"

"Kyra wants to come to the precinct to meet with you," Patrick said after making sure the phone was on speaker. And maybe it would be a good thing for them to go there so the captain could be the one to quash Kyra's ridiculous idea.

Although she hadn't told him yet if she actually had a plan about how to reach Coleman and what to tell him or where to lure him… No way. Patrick would make it clear to Colleen just how absurd the concept was.

Right now, Colleen seemed amenable to holding that meeting, even after Kyra said they wouldn't be able to stay long since she'd have her baby with her.

"That'll be fun," Colleen said. "I've looked forward to meeting him. Yeah, come on in. I'll make sure the patrols around your place follow and keep an eye on you."

Good, Patrick thought, just in case Kyra needed a reminder—and she definitely should have authorities looking out for her, not just him.

Kyra fed Ajay once more, then dressed the little guy in a cute outfit that Kyra called a footie—a piece of clothing that looked warm and snuggly with long sleeves and legs with built-in socks. It was light blue and appropriate for a little boy, and it seemed dressy enough for Ajay to wear to meet their coworkers.

As bad an idea as this whole outing seemed to be.

And it got worse.

First though, before they left Kyra's apartment and while she changed Ajay's diaper again, he received a text from Rory—one that appeared to have been sent to a lot of people, probably all those who had a particular interest in getting the Landmark Killer brought down. Had he shown up at the Rockefeller Center skating rink? Rory mentioned, for those who might not know it yet, that she had a new partner, Detective Isaac Donner, who had joined them and had gone undercover in an attempt to find the Landmark Killer. She ended the text with, *I finally get a new partner and he's off somewhere skating.*

She knew exactly where he was and why, and that he probably wasn't skating. Patrick knew Rory wasn't being flippant. She was a good detective, too no-nonsense for that. But she was surely reflecting the concerns in her department about what was going on, and how Donner was handling it.

They were undoubtedly all worried the new guy would end up in the morgue.

Patrick certainly hoped not, but he had other things to focus on now, like getting Kyra and Ajay to headquarters to present her ideas to Colleen, as much as he hated them.

They had no problems, at least, driving to the precinct, maybe partly due to the patrol cars that remained around them.

Once they arrived and parked, they walked inside with Kyra holding Ajay and received all kinds of loving remarks from people they saw, coworkers and visitors alike.

Colleen was apparently awaiting their arrival since when he called her from the lobby she told him to come right up with Kyra and her baby, which they did.

So what was Kyra going to say here? What was going to happen?

Patrick wasn't sure he wanted to find out. But here they were.

He wasn't surprised when the captain held out her arms, and Kyra immediately, and carefully, gave Ajay to her. Lots of coos resulted, and Colleen even held the baby up to her cheeks, allowing her blond hair to rub over him.

But soon they sat down, Colleen at her desk and Patrick and Kyra, with Ajay on her lap, on the chairs facing her. Colleen grabbed her phone and told whoever she'd called to come in. Patrick wasn't surprised when Wells quickly joined them.

He was a little surprised when Wells also made a fuss over Ajay. Or maybe that was a given. Patrick didn't know him well, but he'd heard the guy was raising his own nephew, who was only about a year old—with Patrick's cousin Sinead's help. But Wells soon sat down too.

"Okay," Colleen finally said. "Kyra, what's going on?"

Patrick thought about standing up and proposing his own plan—although nothing he'd thought of made a lot of sense yet. But anything he came up with wouldn't put Kyra in jeopardy.

He moved beside Kyra to attempt to take over, but she ignored him. "I've come up with an idea how to finally bring the Jewelry Slayer in. And I know Patrick's against it. But the guy is still out there, and the fact he knows he has been identified most likely won't keep him from stealing and killing again eventually, maybe soon. I think we'll all feel a lot better when he's in custody. Right?"

"Sure," Colleen said, "but what do you have in mind?"

Colleen's gaze focused for a moment on Patrick, then back to Kyra. She clearly was curious about what Kyra would say and would make up her own mind no matter what he thought or did.

Well, he recognized something needed to be done. And if Kyra did put herself in danger, as he anticipated, he would do his damnedest to still take care of her. At least by describing it here and getting Colleen to take charge of it, Kyra would most likely get a whole precinct team to back her up. He hoped.

Hugging her son on her lap, Kyra addressed Colleen.

"You were interviewed by a couple of TV reporters about the Jewelry Slayer and the murders he's committed, including the most recent."

"That's right," Colleen said.

"I assume you've still got their contact information. What about letting them know that some additional evidence may have been found at the site where he attacked me, and our team, including me, plans to return there to investigate it further—and encourage them to report it, including when. We can't be sure, of course, but if Pete Coleman is as angry with me as he seemed to be, he might show up there at that time both to figure out and hide whatever else we might have found—and to finally get rid of me... Even though he knows by now that others have seen him and could also probably ID him—maybe even suspects his picture is in the system, and he's been sought at his home and place of work. But if he's as angry and vengeful as I suspect he may be, he might want to kill me first. Only, we can have a team there to capture him and bring him in."

Even though he had expected something he would dislike, Patrick now felt shocked. Put herself out there publicly and goad the Jewelry Slayer into attacking her again? "Bad idea," he couldn't help asserting, looking straight at Colleen. "There's no guarantee we can keep Kyra safe under those circumstances."

"There's no guarantee the perp won't see through it and stay away either," Wells inserted. "But... Hey, I like the idea. We don't have anything else planned at the moment, so why not give it a try?"

Patrick saw Kyra glance at him with what appeared to be a smug expression on her pretty face. Wells obviously liked her idea, and Colleen hadn't spoken out against it.

Colleen finally said, "We'd have to be damned careful to protect you, Kyra. We especially wouldn't want little Ajay's mom to be injured—or worse." She looked toward Kyra's lap, where her baby was moving around and she was holding him snugly. "Plus, there are always a lot of other people in that area."

"As I said, it's a bad idea," Patrick began, but Colleen cut him off.

"And as I said, we'd have to be damned careful. But we could wind up saving lives in the future if we catch the guy now. Who knows what he might be planning? So, yes. Kyra, I appreciate your idea, and we're going to run with it."

*Good*, Kyra thought, keeping her gaze averted from Patrick. She hoped he would be on the team to be put together to carry out her proposal. He had been her protector all this time, after all.

But he might be mad enough at her to let her put herself into the hands of others, who would watch and make sure she remained okay despite what might happen at the revisited crime scene if Coleman did appear again.

They talked a bit more, and Colleen made a few calls to others in the precinct, apparently at least a couple who were in charge of several departments. Colleen seemed to be setting up a meeting for later, but she soon dismissed Patrick and her—a good thing, since Kyra wanted to take Ajay home.

"I'm going to get some other opinions about your idea," Colleen told her. "And if everyone's on board, as I am, we'll start setting things up. Not sure how long it may take, but I assume you'll go along with the schedule, whatever it turns out to be. But—" She looked tellingly toward Kyra's lap, where Ajay had fortunately settled down.

"I've been working things out so I should be able to leave Ajay with my parents for a while, but we'll of course have to determine when, and how long." Assuming she remained okay…

Worst case, she was sure her mom and dad would take over Ajay's care and feeding forever.

But she didn't even want to think about a worst-case scenario, in which she might lose her life. She would be fine.

And the Jewelry Slayer would finally be caught. That was how it had to be.

Time to go home then. That was fine with Kyra.

On their way out, they ran into Patrick's cousin Rory in the crowded precinct lobby. Patrick had mentioned he had gotten a text from her earlier but hadn't gone into details.

Now he stopped to talk to Rory and asked if she had heard from her new fellow detective Isaac, but she said she hadn't. Kyra got the impression Isaac had had some involvement with the text Patrick had mentioned but she heard no details.

Kyra wasn't surprised that petite but clearly professional Rory, dressed as a detective in her white shirt and dark pants, gushed a bit over Ajay. "What are you doing here?" she asked Kyra, staring with her pretty green eyes, as if she was surprised even a CSI might be at the precinct with her child.

"Just came in for a quick meeting with Captain Colleen," Kyra told her before Patrick could respond.

"Yeah, Kyra wanted to tell her about a zany plan she has to catch the Jewelry Slayer."

"Really?" Rory seemed interested.

"Well, I hope so," Kyra said.

"Tell me about it."

And so Kyra drew Rory off to the side of the lobby, with Patrick following, and quickly explained, with Ajay starting to fuss, what she had in mind to draw Pete Coleman to a location where they could capture him.

Rory seemed to ponder it for a minute, then said, "Sounds potentially dangerous, if the guy's as crazy as we think, but I'd like to participate if it goes forward. Let me know. And I sure hope there'll be a lot of other cops there to protect you."

She shot a glance toward her cousin, but Patrick just glared at her as he'd been doing at a lot of people as Kyra described her idea. "I hope there will be too," Kyra said. "And I'll be glad to keep you informed."

Finally, they left the lobby, with Patrick ahead of Kyra and Ajay, acting like his usual protective self. Which Kyra definitely appreciated. Even if he was furious with her.

He stayed with her that evening, and they didn't discuss the afternoon and her idea and how Colleen might, or might not, run with it.

The next day was quiet and sort of normal for them. Patrick left Kyra and Ajay in the morning, telling her he'd confirmed there were patrols around. Kyra called Colleen around eleven and was told plans were being put together, but nothing yet. The afternoon was about the same as usual too.

But when Patrick came home, he told her, "We need to watch the six o'clock news." He let her know which station, a local channel belonging to a major national network.

Really? Then something might appear on the news about what was going on—or what they wanted to happen? Things were actually progressing?

A short while after the news came on, Kyra, sitting with Patrick on the sofa with Ajay in her lap, was fascinated to see a well-known reporter for the local station inside Colleen's office, sitting near the captain's desk. Colleen held a microphone, and so did the reporter. Kyra had seen that reporter before. Her name was Wanda Shallman, and she was on the news a lot—including her earlier interview of Colleen.

"Captain Reeves," Wanda said into her microphone. "Is there any news about your finding the Jewelry Slayer?"

"No." Colleen appeared disgruntled—but was that an assumed expression under the circumstances?

"Well, word is out there that someone in the area where he last struck has pointed out where some evidence is that was previously missed, and your CSI team, including those who were there right after the homicide and apparently might have missed something, will be there tomorrow once more to check it out. Is that true?"

"I don't know what words you are listening to," Colleen retorted. "And we're certainly not about to confirm or deny anything like that."

Interesting. She didn't deny it. Which meant it could be real—or at least, hopefully, Pete Coleman would think so.

The camera focused on Wanda then, and she said, "We can't reveal our sources, of course, but we will bring further information to you as we receive it. Now, back to you in the studio."

And another reporter's face appeared on the screen.

# Chapter 24

Patrick was well aware of Kyra's turning toward him on the sofa. "Did that mean what I think it did?" she asked.

"Quite possibly," he told her. "Colleen asked me to stop in her office before I left. She said she had been in touch with some of the newspeople and conspired with them in a way she said shouldn't be done, but she worked things out so they'd get word out there to encourage Coleman to show up at the crime scene tomorrow. She said she didn't explain in any detail what we were planning, or at least hoping for, but in appreciation for their cooperation would work things out for them to be able to film anything they might consider useful—which they might have been able to do anyway. Of course, she indicated they'd be under protection at the site too, and might not get anything at all. But apparently they reached some kind of deal, since there was the story." He pointed toward the TV.

"I'm glad," Kyra said, although her voice cracked a little.

"Well, you'll need to be there, of course, but whatever protection the media gets will be just a fraction of what's planned for you."

"Right," she said. As if thanking him, she drew even closer and put little Ajay into his arms.

Patrick couldn't help himself. He kissed the baby.

Then he maneuvered a bit so he could kiss Kyra too, fairly gently. And they soon put Ajay in his crib after feeding and changing him.

Bedtime for the adults too. And their kisses, before settling in for the night, were long and hot and a lot more suggestive than made sense just then.

"I'll take care of you," he whispered against her mouth.

"And I'll do all I can to take care of you too."

That made him recall—as if he ever forgot—that he had recognized he might be in love with this incredible, brave woman.

Who might be in terrible danger tomorrow.

Patrick didn't sleep much that night. He wondered if Coleman had seen what was on TV, and figured the guy probably watched a lot of news, considering who he was and what he'd done.

Even if he'd seen it and believed the team would return to his crime scene, there was no guarantee he would show up. He wouldn't, if he was smart. But he'd seemed enough of a jerk to want to harm the woman who'd identified him, out of spite.

That didn't mean he would wait until tomorrow to try though. Patrick remained alert, as he so often did while trying to protect Kyra.

Before they had gone to bed, she called her parents

and asked if they could watch Ajay for a while the next day. Kyra didn't tell them why, which was also a good thing. Hopefully she would remain safe and their plans would be successful. But no need to worry her parents more than necessary.

Patrick held Kyra close for most of the night when he wasn't up checking things out. And morning arrived too fast.

When they awoke early, he helped Kyra rise and change Ajay, and even held a bottle with some of the formula Kyra now had.

They both showered, dressed, had breakfast—and gladly greeted Kyra's parents.

"Is everything okay?" Sam asked Kyra as Riya took charge of the baby. "I mean, you haven't been going into work much. Is that what you're up to today?"

"There's just some research going on that I need to participate in," she said. That was a good, neutral way to phrase it, Patrick thought.

They soon left, and he drove them in his car toward the crime scene site along First Avenue. Kyra had un-zipped the heavy jacket she'd worn on this cold day. Patrick had her call Colleen on her phone and put it on speaker.

"Is everything ready?" Kyra asked first, which was pretty much what he wanted to know.

"Our plans are underway," Colleen said. "We've no idea if the media attention will help draw the perp in, but nothing else has worked so far, so we'll see. Some stations besides the one where I was interviewed picked it up too. Lots of people are undercover, including some of our otherwise uniformed cops, some detectives and others—including a few reporters from the original station who've also been instructed to come in disguise if they want to hang out while whatever happens occurs."

"Sounds good," Kyra said.

Patrick agreed with her, then asked for some details, but he didn't feel entirely satisfied that all bases had been covered. At least it was a weekday, and any kids around would hopefully be in school and not in St. Edwina's Park. But who knew how many civilians might be in the area, going to and from work or the stores around there? And the media folks could be in danger too.

They finally reached the area. Patrick, wearing a black sweatshirt and warm pants, parked in a lot for one of the convenience stores close to the park and exited the car first. He looked around. Nothing seemed out of kilter there—yet. Sure, quite a few people were on the sidewalks near the streets. And almost immediately their fellow CSIs, also wearing warm clothing, joined them, clearly carrying gear to help them sift through the nearby sites again. Maybe they'd find something telling this time. Craig, Rosa and Mitch said hi and began talking to Kyra about what they'd look for that day that might be different from before, to actually bring the Jewelry Slayer down. Patrick stayed off to the side, not wanting to disappoint them. Yes, that was why they were here, though it wasn't likely they'd actually find more evidence. But Kyra's presence might make the difference if things went as planned by that brave, possibly foolish, CSI.

Noticing some cops he recognized from the precinct out of uniform and dressed in sweatshirts and jeans nearby, Patrick figured Kyra and he were under observation in case Coleman arrived. *When* Coleman arrived, or so he hoped.

As long as he was there and watching, and the killer was finally captured.

*Watching* was the key. Colleen had a lot of others primed to hang around unobtrusively and hopefully bring Pete Coleman down.

Patrick would only get involved if he had to.

But he would definitely be ready.

Kyra was thrilled to be with her team again—those who reported to Patrick and her. Having more CSIs here would definitely help to make her being here genuine, based on the lies Colleen had given to the reporter.

But it hadn't entirely been lies. Even if there hadn't been additional evidence found or sought at the moment, she was here.

Had Coleman heard the news reports? Would he come to try to find her?

With all the backup around, she definitely hoped so.

At the moment, she led Craig, Rosa and Mitch to the area along the curb where she'd picked up the evidence the Jewelry Slayer had left, weeks ago. They'd been here since and looked over the same area, but if Coleman was here somewhere watching, it would make sense for them to appear to go over old territory. Never mind that he'd grabbed everything she had found back then.

The air was chilly. The sidewalk and curb had lots of brown leaves on them that had blown off trees in the nearby park.

Evidence here that hadn't been located before? No way. But she still waved to the others to follow her toward the park.

Only before they got there, she saw a guy in a black hoodie and sweatpants, wearing boots, with the hood over his face, exit from a grove of trees and begin stalking in her direction. She froze.

The Jewelry Slayer? This felt much too similar to what had happened to her a few weeks ago.

But things were different now.

Except—where was Patrick? He'd disappeared after they arrived here. Knowing him, he'd tried to figure out a way to keep her safe, even if he didn't have to with all the undercover cops hanging out.

Kyra pretended not to notice the guy, even as she started shaking as she kept walking in that direction.

He drew closer, and she stopped. And waited. And hoped.

Sure enough, the guy was grabbed by two tall men wearing casual sweatshirts and knit hats, as she'd seen some of the undercover cops wearing when she'd checked before.

"Hey!" the guy screamed. "What the hell—"

She heard them demand his identification, which they pulled from his pocket when he didn't comply.

They hadn't pulled the hood off, but he had to be Coleman, since they yanked his hands behind his back and cuffed him, reciting his rights.

It was finally over! They'd caught him.

And a whole bunch of people clustered around them, other undercover cops and most likely reporters, and probably some nosy civilians as well.

But that was okay. At last, they had the Jewelry Slayer in custody.

Kyra couldn't help grinning. She started to approach her fellow CSIs who were also in the large group of onlookers observing as the perpetrator they had been after forever was finally taken into custody. Silly, but—

Hey! She was still a distance from them, and suddenly she was grabbed and pulled toward the street by another man wearing a hoodie. A man whose eyes looked too familiar.

She screamed and attempted to grab her gun from her pocket, but he was holding her too closely with both his arms wrapped around her. She struggled, attempting to get at least one hand loose to pull the covering off his face, even as he let go with one arm—and drew out a knife that he raised. "No!" she screamed as he started to thrust it down at her. She struggled more, even as her mind flashed to Ajay—and to Patrick. Could she survive this?

Was he about to stab and kill her?

He moved so quickly that she was sure it was all over—but his arm was stopped as another man grabbed it and pulled it away.

Someone else wearing a hoodie. Someone who was also familiar.

Patrick.

And he had a gun that he aimed directly at the attacker's head, after first using it to knock the guy's knife hand again so hard this time that the guy was the next one to scream as he fell to the ground.

"It's over, Coleman," Patrick growled, as the Jewelry Slayer was at last grabbed by the undercover cops.

He was so right, Kyra thought a few minutes later as Pete Coleman was handcuffed, read his rights and thrust into the back of a police cruiser.

The other guy who'd been initially taken into custody as the Jewelry Slayer remained under arrest too, and was put into another vehicle to be taken to the precinct. His crime though apparently wasn't robbery and murder and assaulting a law enforcement officer, but aiding and abetting a now-accused potential felon.

Coleman had apparently recruited the guy off the street and paid him to impersonate himself, indicating it was a joke.

Well, he undoubtedly knew now it was anything but.

"Thanks so much," Kyra told Patrick, standing on the curb and looking up into his wonderful hazel eyes that gazed down caringly at her as things finally wound down. "You finally achieved what you'd been trying to do for these last weeks. You captured the Jewelry Slayer."

"Yeah." He took her hand, and she let him, even with all the coworkers and superior officers around them. "But I still think this was one dumb plan."

Kyra couldn't help goading him a little. "Dumb? Yes. Successful? Oh, yeah." She hesitated. "But it only turned out successful because you—"

"I happened to assume the worst, as usual, and figured I'd believe the Jewelry Slayer had finally been brought into custody once he was identified by the evidence as such—fingerprints, DNA and all."

"And that wasn't the guy who first... Never mind." She paused. "Thank you."

"You are very welcome." He looked down at her as if he wanted to kiss her. Well, she really wanted to kiss him back.

But not here.

At her apartment?

But would he ever show up there again?

After all, he no longer had to protect her.

A lot went on during the rest of the day.

Yes, they returned to the precinct and everyone was questioned by some of the investigators. Individually, so once they were there Kyra didn't see Patrick. But they also received calls from some of their FBI superiors.

She returned home as soon as she could to take over her parents' care of Ajay.

"What happened today?" her dad asked as they all sat in the living room together. "You seem really stressed, but somehow relaxed too. Is everything okay?"

"Yes, and is Patrick coming here to watch over you tonight?" asked her mom.

She had to tell them. While she nursed Ajay, she explained what had happened that day.

"It's finally over," she finished. "I'm safe. Everyone with valuable jewelry that the Jewelry Slayer might otherwise have gone after is now safe, assuming he's tried and found guilty of all the crimes he committed, which should be the case."

"That's wonderful!" Her mom rose and gave her a hug, carefully not squeezing the nursing baby.

They brought in dinner, and Kyra had the sense they also wanted to give her some continued adult company.

She asked though if they would take care of Ajay again the next day, and even longer. She was delighted she would be able to go back to work at last.

And see Patrick there... No. There was nothing between them now. There couldn't be.

That was best.

Wasn't it?

She was delighted that she got a call from Patrick that night as she got ready for bed.

"How are you doing?" he asked.

"I'm doing great. I'm so glad I was involved in finally bringing down the Jewelry Slayer, and I really appreciate all you did too."

"It feels great being back at home," he said. "I'm so glad you're safe now."

"Me too." And she was.

But she also felt damned lonely without Patrick there with her.

Maybe she really had fallen in love with him.

If so, too bad. They'd be working together once more starting tomorrow.

And that was what was appropriate.

## Chapter 25

It was the next day. The old routine had resumed—sort of. Patrick was back in his office going through information on his computer, and it was certainly a busy day.

At least he got to see Kyra now and then, in his office and hers and Colleen's, for follow-up meetings. He had definitely missed being with her and her son the night before, but staying with them was now history.

Good history. The man who'd been threatening her was in custody. The man who'd been brought in last night thanks to their ploy had been officially identified as Pete Coleman. And there was enough evidence to confirm he was the man who had murdered three women and stolen their jewelry—and attacked Crime Scene Investigator Kyra Patel at the most recent crime scene.

There was enough, under these circumstances, to keep him in custody without bail.

They all were safe. Kyra was safe.

The day moved forward quickly. No crime scene visits, but he'd sent some of their subordinates out on a couple, and figured Kyra and he would start doing that again soon too—and not necessarily together.

Together. He missed that. But life was moving forward.

Except, as their workday drew to a close, Kyra popped into his office. "Can you come to my house for dinner tonight? I told my parents how things were finally resolved, thanks to your help all along, and they want to thank you."

All sorts of reasons not to do that bombarded Patrick's mind, mostly that he'd just been doing his job—and that the grand finale had occurred not because of his ideas, but hers.

Still… Well, he liked Kyra's parents. And especially her little son. So he accepted the invitation.

And he enjoyed all the attention the Patels lavished on him for helping to keep their daughter safe and preventing the horrible man who'd threatened her from ever being able to do so again.

He hugged them both and offered to help with cooking or setting the table, or taking care of Ajay, but everything was handled.

An enjoyable evening was the result. Very enjoyable. Patrick even felt a bit like part of this family, even though he had a generally caring family of his own.

In fact, he determined to contact some of the other Coltons soon to make sure he was included in any holiday plans. Surely at least one of his siblings, Ashlynn, Brennan or Cash, would be holding an event where he could participate. Or even his cousin Rory. He'd been seeing a lot of her at work lately, after all.

He'd have to check with them.

The Patels soon left, inviting Patrick to join them anytime, hopefully soon.

Then it was time to say good-night to Kyra, after she put Ajay down in his crib and returned to the living room.

"This was fun," he told her.

"Yes, it was." She drew close to him.

And yes, he kissed her. This would certainly be for the last time. After all, they'd returned to working together.

He considered staying longer but knew better. "Good night," he said and left.

He felt bereft as he drove home, especially while remembering that kiss over and over. And the sadness in Kyra's lovely dark eyes as she watched him go out the door.

Okay. Enough. He had been a lone wolf before, and now he was one again. That was fine. Who he was.

There wasn't much left of the rest of that night, and he soon went to bed. And tried hard to sleep despite thinking too much about Kyra. After all, he would see her at work again the next day.

Which he did. They even went on a precinct assignment together that the FBI approved, though their primary goal of finding serial killers meant they'd soon have to focus again on the Landmark Killer. This time, they sought evidence at an apartment building where a series of burglaries had occurred and no one had been hurt.

They were able to do their job just fine and collected evidence that pointed to one of the other tenants.

Their usual job. Their being together—at work. That was fine.

But it resulted in a night at home alone for Patrick. A lonely night at home.

Followed by several more, after additional similar workdays where he at least got to see and talk to Kyra. Ask about Ajay.

But he wanted more...

Damn. He recognized only too well what had happened. What he had suspected before was correct.

He had fallen in love with Kyra.

Work colleagues or not, he wanted her in his life in other ways. Together when they weren't working.

Nighttime.

Forever.

She was always sweet with him during the day and completely professional. But could he be reading something into the ways she looked at him so caringly at times? Was he just hopeful, or—

Okay. He had to find out.

And so, when the current workday finally ended, a Friday with a potentially lonely weekend facing him unless another investigation started to loom, he went into Kyra's office.

She sat at her desk, apparently getting things ready to leave.

"Oh, you're still here," he said, knowing she was. She'd gone home for a while earlier in the afternoon to spell her parents with Ajay, as she often did, but had returned.

"Yes, I'm on my way home now." Her brown hair framed her lovely face as usual.

He asked first, before mentioning the reason he was there, "How are your folks doing with watching Ajay?"

"They're doing great, and they're really happy about it. I mentioned trying to find a nanny, and they made it clear they'd take care of their grandson forever."

"That's good." He paused, then said, "Look, there are a couple of things I'd like to discuss with you and wondered if I could come to your place tonight. I can bring dinner." She looked even more inquisitive then, and he added, lying, "Work-related things."

She probably wondered why he didn't discuss them there, at work. But she simply said, "Sure. What time?"

Seven o'clock, they decided, and then she left.

Okay, could he do this? *Would* he do this?

Heck, yes.

And he determined what he would pick up for dinner.


Kyra was delighted that Patrick was coming over that evening. Wasn't she?

She pondered it even more after saying good-night to her parents, who, as always, had done a wonderful job caring for her baby.

They asked about Patrick, also as always. And, as always, she described, with no detail, some of the work they'd done together that day. She didn't mention that Patrick was joining her tonight. She knew they'd thought, hoped, that the two of them had begun a relationship, no matter how inappropriate.

A relationship? Of course not. But since Patrick had stopped hanging out with her at home to protect her, she had really missed him. Still, it was better this way.

Professional. The way it should be.

Now, she had put Ajay into his crib for a nap before his final feeding of the day and gone into the kitchen to set the table. She wasn't sure what Patrick was bringing for dinner, not that it mattered.

She'd changed into a frilly long-sleeved T-shirt and casual slacks. She wasn't surprised that, at exactly seven o'clock, the buzzer at her apartment door rang, which meant that someone had pressed the button downstairs to be let into the building.

Yes, Patrick had returned her extra keys when he no longer was coming here. She pushed the intercom button and said, "Yes?" in a tone that suggested she didn't know who it was.

But it was of course Patrick's deep voice that said, "Hi, Kyra. I'm here."

She buzzed him inside, and a couple of minutes later there was a knock on her door. She opened it, and Patrick stood there looking down at her. "Can I come in?"

She wanted to melt. She felt really glad to see the handsome man standing there, like her, dressed casually in blue jeans and a blue jacket and staring at her with hazel eyes that somehow looked so caring... No, she must have imagined that.

"Where's Ajay?" he asked.

"Sleeping in his crib," she told him.

She reached for the plastic bag he carried that had to contain their dinner. The label on the outside indicated it was from one of the most expensive restaurants in the area. Really? That didn't make sense. They'd brought in fast food sometimes when her parents hadn't brought stuff from the grocery store and she hadn't cooked, and that was fine.

Patrick followed as she took the food into the kitchen and laid the bag on the counter near the sink. When she turned back toward him, he was right behind her.

"So what did you bring for dinner?" she asked.

Without answering, Patrick said, "Can we go into your living room?"

There was something about his sweet tone that somehow made her insides warm. "Sure."

Soon they were there, but as Kyra started to sit on the sofa Patrick took her arm.

"Kyra, I came here tonight because—" He seemed to hesitate as he looked down at her with heat, and more, in his expression. Something caring…and—no. Never mind what she felt for him. He surely didn't love her, but—

"Because what?" her voice rasped.

He drew her into his arms and spoke softly against her ear. "Because I've missed you. Being alone with you, I mean, and not just seeing you at work. I want to know how you feel, because—" He hesitated, then said, pulling back to look into her eyes again, "Because I know for sure now that I love you, Kyra. I love Ajay too. I want us to be together, to become a family. I think it's too soon to propose marriage, but that's what I'm hoping will happen between us. But do you care for me that way too? Do you think we could be together, live together, forever?"

Kyra's heart raced as he smiled, and she drew even closer. "Oh, yes, Patrick," she said. "I love you, and want us, yes, to become a family. I'm sure Ajay thinks of you as his daddy, as much as he could at his age. And for us to stay together forever? Oh, yes!"

And as they kissed, Kyra realized she had never been happier.

A future together with Patrick, coworkers or not? She couldn't imagine anything more wonderful.

* * * * *

## #2259 COLTON'S YULETIDE MANHUNT
*The Coltons of New York* • by Kacy Cross

Detective Isaac Donner wants to catch the notorious Landmark Killer in the splashiest way possible—if only to prove to his father he has the goods to do it. But his by-the-books partner, Rory Colton, isn't ready to risk her life for a family feud. Her heart is another matter...

## #2260 DANGER ON THE RIVER
*Sierra's Web* • by Tara Taylor Quinn

Undercover cop Tommy Grainger stumbles upon a web of deceit when he rescues Kacey Ashland, bound and drowning, from the local wild rapids. Could the innocent-looking—yet oh-so tempting—elementary school teacher be tied to an illegal contraband cold case that involves Tommy's own father?

## #2261 A DETECTIVE'S DEADLY SECRETS
*Honor Bound* • by Anna J. Stewart

When Detective Lana Tate comes back into FBI special agent Eamon Quinn's life, he'll do anything for a second chance and to keep the woman he's always loved safe. Soon their investigation threatens not only their lives but also whatever future they might have together.

## #2262 WATCHERS OF THE NIGHT
*The Night Guardians* • by Charlene Parris

Forensics investigator Cynthia Cornwall is brilliant, introverted—and compromised. Her agreement to keep Detective Adam Solberg off his father's murder case has put her life in danger, job in jeopardy and heart in the charismatic, determined cop's crosshairs.

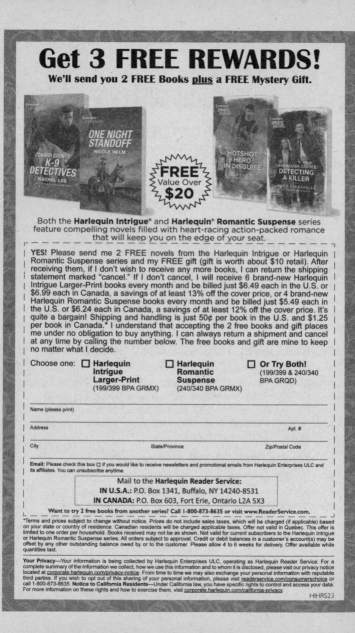

# Get 3 FREE REWARDS!

**We'll send you 2 FREE Books plus a FREE Mystery Gift.**

**FREE** Value Over **$20**

Both the **Harlequin Intrigue®** and **Harlequin® Romantic Suspense** series feature compelling novels filled with heart-racing action-packed romance that will keep you on the edge of your seat.

---

**YES!** Please send me 2 FREE novels from the Harlequin Intrigue or Harlequin Romantic Suspense series and my FREE gift (gift is worth about $10 retail). After receiving them, if I don't wish to receive any more books, I can return the shipping statement marked "cancel." If I don't cancel, I will receive 6 brand-new Harlequin Intrigue Larger-Print books every month and be billed just $6.49 each in the U.S. or $6.99 each in Canada, a savings of at least 13% off the cover price, or 4 brand-new Harlequin Romantic Suspense books every month and be billed just $5.49 each in the U.S. or $6.24 each in Canada, a savings of at least 12% off the cover price. It's quite a bargain! Shipping and handling is just 50¢ per book in the U.S. and $1.25 per book in Canada.* I understand that accepting the 2 free books and gift places me under no obligation to buy anything. I can always return a shipment and cancel at any time by calling the number below. The free books and gift are mine to keep no matter what I decide.

Choose one: ☐ **Harlequin Intrigue Larger-Print** (199/399 BPA GRMX)  ☐ **Harlequin Romantic Suspense** (240/340 BPA GRMX)  ☐ **Or Try Both!** (199/399 & 240/340 BPA GRQD)

Name (please print)

Address                                                                      Apt. #

City                              State/Province                        Zip/Postal Code

**Email:** Please check this box ☐ if you would like to receive newsletters and promotional emails from Harlequin Enterprises ULC and its affiliates. You can unsubscribe anytime.

Mail to the **Harlequin Reader Service:**
**IN U.S.A.:** P.O. Box 1341, Buffalo, NY 14240-8531
**IN CANADA:** P.O. Box 603, Fort Erie, Ontario L2A 5X3

**Want to try 2 free books from another series! Call 1-800-873-8635 or visit www.ReaderService.com.**

---

# HARLEQUIN
## PLUS

Try the best multimedia subscription service for romance readers like you!

---

## Read, Watch and Play.

Experience the easiest way to get the romance content you crave.

Start your **FREE TRIAL** at
<u>www.harlequinplus.com/freetrial</u>.